As a fae-vampire hybrid, scorned by all, Holden's life has never been easy. The one bright spot is his job testing blood at supernatural crime scenes. It's routine work, until the day he finds a victim he can't read.

When one murder becomes two, and then three, it's clear there's a serial killer on the loose—one with a penchant for collecting hearts. Finding the bad guy could cement Holden's career, but he's drawing a blank. And it doesn't help that the expert his boss calls in to assist him is the man Holden's been crushing on for years.

With lives hanging in the balance, Holden and Val must solve the case before the killer strikes again. But will they come out with their hearts still intact?

Blood Is Forever

Asta Idonea

A NineStar Press Publication

Published by NineStar Press
P.O. Box 91792,
Albuquerque, New Mexico, 87199 USA.
www.ninestarpress.com

Blood Is Forever

Printed in the USA
First Edition
June, 2019

Print ISBN: 978-1-950412-73-0

Also available in eBook, ISBN: 978-1-950412-72-3

Chapter One

"WHAT'S A FILTHY halfen doing here?"

Holden heard the comment. He could scarce avoid doing so, seeing as he possessed enhanced hearing and the speaker had made no attempt to lower his voice. The fae onlooker didn't know the half of it. Clearly he based his judgment of Holden's heritage solely on Holden's less-than-regal stature—a good few inches shorter than most fae—rather than having recognised him outright. That was a rare occurrence. Had he known the truth about Holden's lineage, the remark would have been all the more scathing.

Halfens—fae half-breeds—were considered the lowest of the low, ranked even below shifters in the supernatural community. Most halfens were fae-human hybrids. As a fae-vampire, Holden was as much of a social outcast as it was possible to be. The fae were notoriously snooty. For one of them to have had a liaison with a human was bad enough, but a vampire... It still amazed Holden that his father had committed such an act.

Cadeyrn was an important figure in the community—a leader in every sense of the word—and socially conscious in the extreme. Still, rumour had it Holden's mother had been a rare beauty. Holden couldn't confirm that. She'd died giving birth to him. Fae children were generally larger than vampire offspring, and her spine had snapped under the pressure of his delivery. With her passing, Cadeyrn had effectively shaken off the stigma attached to their brief encounter. The residue had stuck to Holden instead.

The fae who'd noted his presence spat on the ground near his feet as he passed, and a familiar icy fist closed around Holden's heart. Nevertheless, he acted as he always did in such situations: he made no response, pretending he hadn't heard anything, thankful for the dark sunglasses hiding his eyes. If he'd learned anything over the years, it was that he needed to maintain a thick skin, or at least the semblance of it. Such pretence wasn't his forte, however. So, keeping his gaze fixed on his destination, he forged as speedy a path as possible through the small crowd gathered around the gate and approached the house.

Upon reaching the front door, he nodded to the officer stationed by the entrance, whipped out his credentials, and waved the plastic ID card under the man's nose. The fae officer scanned them in silence, before raising the invisible strip of tape blocking the doorway, granting Holden access to the building.

From the outside, the Victorian terrace had no distinguishing features. A standard exemplar of its era, it sat in the middle of a long row of identical properties—former middle-class family homes long since converted into small inner-city apartments, for which young professionals had to pay top dollar. This particular example officially consisted of four flats. In truth, there were five.

Holden headed straight for the stairs and ascended to the third floor. To human eyes, this was the last living area, with only roof space above, but Holden could see the shimmer in the wall that indicated a hidden doorway. He passed through the gap, shaking off the tingle the magical barrier sent dancing over his skin, and mounted the small flight of steps to the fifth apartment. The door at the top stood open, and when Holden crossed the threshold, he entered a room bustling with activity.

Fae and witches hurried back and forth. Some wore full protective suits. Others were dressed normally, save for their softly scrunching shoe covers. Two photographers snapped away, their constant camera flashes blinding in their intensity. Meanwhile, several of their colleagues deposited a variety of items into plastic evidence bags, then whisked said bags away. Three witches were casting a spell to search surfaces for any latent fingerprints not belonging to the apartment's owner, while one of the fae glided behind them, retrieving and cataloguing those found. All in all, it was a pretty standard crime scene.

Holden removed his sunglasses and stowed them in his jacket pocket. Then he grabbed some shoe covers from the box near the door and tugged them over his worn trainers. Now suitably attired, he looked for his superior amidst the organised chaos. In the end, Owens spotted him first.

"Holden!"

Her bark cut through the noise, and everyone paused. They looked at Owens and then at Holden. Most swiftly returned to their respective tasks, but a few pairs of eyes lingered on him. He didn't recognise the faces attached to those keen gazes, but he could sense these strangers assessing him, judging him...and finding him wanting.

"Holden Fay, quit daydreaming and get your arse over here."

At the command, Holden squared his shoulders and marched across the room, pretending, as best he could, not to notice those who still observed him.

Owens pursed her dark-berry-coloured lips as he approached, hands planted firmly on her ample hips. "What the hell took you so fucking long? I summoned you forty minutes ago. We had to hold the scene for you."

"I'm sorry, Captain, but it's peak hour. You know London traffic." Actually, he'd had a pretty good run, all things considered, and after parking three streets down, he'd used a supernatural burst of speed to sprint the rest of the way—an action that always took a lot out of him.

"Oh yes. I'd forgotten about your...that you can't use portals." Owens had the decency to look momentarily abashed at having brought up one of Holden's numerous defects. "Anyway, you're here now." She chose to move swiftly past the elephant in the room, for which Holden was grateful, and he hastened to follow suit.

"What do we have?"

"Come see for yourself."

Holden trailed Owens through the lounge and into the bedroom. The sight that met his eyes there threatened to turn his stomach. However, he steeled himself and swallowed back the bile. This was his job, after all, and with his background and disadvantages, he was lucky to have any form of employment. He couldn't afford to lose his position with the Fellowship's Investigations Team because of a little blood. Not that the blood was the issue. He'd visited plenty of gory scenes, and being part vampire, spilled blood was liable to make him hungry rather than nauseated. No, it was the precision, the clear intent, which made this tableau so gruelling.

The body lay upon the bed, atop the sheets. Despite the look of terror permanently burned into his eyes, the victim otherwise projected a semblance of calm. There was minimal creasing to the sheets beneath him, suggesting there hadn't been a struggle. No one had forced him onto the bed. No one had thrown him there. It appeared as if he'd lain down of his own volition. His arms rested neat and straight by his sides, and there was no sign of any defensive action, which was strange, given the gaping hole in his chest.

"He's a witch?"

Holden waited for Owens's nod, but he didn't really need the clarification. What else could the victim be? His appearance ruled out him being fae, and a vampire would have turned to dust, or at least a pile of bones. That only left a human or a witch, and a human wouldn't know of this room's existence. They couldn't even detect the flow of the earth's energy through their own bodies, let alone recognise focused magic.

He moved closer and assessed the damage. The heart was gone. It was a clean job though. He was tempted to call it clinical. That, in itself, was unusual. When Owens called him to murder scenes, it tended to be a blood bath. He was used to that; it made sense. Maybe a newly turned vampire had lost control while feeding. Or someone had crossed paths with a shifter turned feral. Those deaths were understandable—a case of instinct outweighing control. A momentary madness. A mistake. This, on the other hand, had a worrisome aura of premeditation about it.

"Coven clash?" he postulated. It was an odd way for a witch to kill one of their fellow practitioners, but he could see no other obvious explanation.

Owens approached and studied the victim over Holden's shoulder. Although she seemed cool and collected on the outside, Holden could hear her elevated pulse. She, too, was on edge.

"Not as far as we can tell. I spoke on the phone to all nine coven leaders while I waited for you. None reported any particular tensions, aside from the normal intercoven rivalries. They certainly knew of nothing that would prompt anyone to commit murder." She stepped back. "Can you get anything from the blood? That's why we called you here, after all. We can do the standard detective work on our own."

Holden was glad he had his back to Owens, because he flinched at the slight.

Technically, he was only on the Fellowship's payroll as a subcontractor. There were no regular hours or weekly paycheques. They simply called him as and when they needed him. That was fine, but he yearned for more. He wanted to be a proper member of the team. He wanted to be a detective and see a case through from start to finish. Although he didn't possess the full abilities of either fae or vampire, there were things he could do, and given the opportunity, he'd work his arse off. However, he knew it was a pipe dream. With his genetic heritage, most people wanted nothing to do with him, and those who tolerated his presence only did so out of respect for his father. In all his thirty-four years, he'd known only two exceptions, and one of those was Owens.

Of all the members of the Investigations Team, Owens treated him the best. He would even go so far as to say she liked him. However, that only made her occasional, unintentional slips hurt all the more. He knew he wouldn't have been her first choice for this job, for example. Given the option, she'd have called Drake, Claude, or even Samuel, rather than him, considering the unexpected nature of the crime. But blood work was extremely time sensitive, and since the pure-blood vampires wouldn't rise for at least another three hours, she had to make do with him. So, he'd better get to work.

The blood had dripped down the man's sides and pooled beneath his torso. Holden reached out and dipped his index finger into it. It was already congealing, but he collected a good enough sample for his purposes and raised the reddened digit to his lips. At first contact, he screwed up his face. No vampire liked the taste of dead blood. It wasn't dangerous in small quantities like this, but it was far from pleasant. Nevertheless, Holden brushed aside his disgust and closed his eyes, focusing on his task.

Blood was a powerful tool in the right hands. It held memories—flashes of the life of the one in whose veins it had dwelt. Those memories faded after a time, though, once the heart stopped beating. Hence the need for a swift assessment. Holden rolled the blood on his tongue, seeking a connection. At this point, images usually bombarded him, coming so thick and fast it took concentration and practice to sort through them, separating ancient memories from recent events, picking out the important details from amidst the mundane. It was a skill, and he was adept. But on this occasion, there was nothing but blackness.

He opened his eyes and shook his head. "I'm sorry, Captain. There's nothing there. We're too late."

"But Philips estimated the time of death as two hours ago. Even with your delayed arrival, the blood should still be good."

"I don't know what to tell you." He shuffled, forcing himself to maintain eye contact despite his strong inclination to hang his head and look away. "The memories weren't even faint. They weren't there at all."

It was not the first time this had happened to him, and it wouldn't be the last. If the blood was too old, it was too old. There was nothing he could do about it. Nonetheless, Holden hated these failures. Neither Drake nor Claude could have extracted anything more from the sample, yet he had the greater need to prove himself. Lack of success clung more persistently to him than it did to them.

Owens swore loudly and virulently. "Very well. If you can't do anything to help, you may as well go. We'll wrap up the scene and head back to the office."

She turned and barked orders at the rest of her staff, completing the abrupt dismissal, and Holden finally allowed himself to sink into the slumped-shoulder posture that had been pressing down upon him for several minutes.

Although free to leave, and keen to extract himself from under the sea of condemning gazes, Holden hovered a moment longer and looked back down at the body. Aside from the lack of a struggle and the surgical precision of the cuts, there was something else odd about the scene. If he could just put his finger on it...

The body retrieval crew shoved past, and their jostling broke Holden's concentration. While they set about preparing the body for transportation, Holden spun on his heel and left. No one stopped his egress. No one called out a goodbye. He knew he was likely being paranoid, but he could have sworn he felt a wave of relief wash over the room when he rid the apartment of his presence.

Outside, the crowd from earlier had dispersed. Either they'd grown bored at the lack of action or members of the Investigations Team had moved them along, anxious to avoid drawing human attention. It was none of his concern either way.

The summer sunlight seemed at odds with the macabre scene he'd witnessed, and following the gloom indoors, its brightness hurt his sensitive eyes, so he whipped out his sunglasses. At the same time, he noticed he was still wearing the shoe covers. These he toed off, kicking them into the air and catching them. Not wanting to return indoors to dispose of them, he shoved them into the back pocket of his jeans.

A glance at his watch revealed that barely half an hour had passed since his arrival. Before Owens's call, he'd planned on enjoying a quiet night at home, curled up with a good book, but now he had other ideas. A drink was in order—preferably three or four. With his vampiric metabolism, it took at least that many to feel even the faintest buzz. Alcohol alone was never sufficient, however. There was something else he needed too.

Holden retrieved his phone and knocked out a text message as he mooched back to his car. It was still too early in the day to expect an answer, but he didn't doubt a favourable response when one finally came. Raoul had never once let him down. He would not be spending the night alone.

Chapter Two

FINGERS DUG INTO his biceps, the nails sharp enough they threatened to slice through his flesh. Holden groaned and writhed, but the pressure didn't let up. Moments later, his groan turned into a guttural moan as cold, hard flesh impaled him. He met each urgent thrust with abandon, and he sucked in a breath as a hand strayed to his shoulder, a long finger caressing his throat. He knew what was coming, yet still he hissed as the nail split his skin. The warm trickle of blood barely had time to commence its route toward his collarbone before lips fastened onto his neck, sucking hard at the wound.

Even with his eyes scrunched shut in ecstasy, Holden found his way to nuzzle his companion's throat. He could hear the blood drumming beneath the surface. He could smell it. He could almost taste it. A tingling in his gums preceded the descent of his fangs, and as soon as they emerged, he bit down, eliciting a muffled groan.

Time slowed, and the world melted away. All that remained were the sensations: the taste of the warm, fresh blood running down his throat (along with the flood of thoughts and feelings that accompanied it), the tug of his own life's blood as it left his veins, and the relentless, forceful pounding of flesh on flesh—the stretch and the pleasurable burn. It was complete and utter obliterating bliss.

His orgasm rocked through him, and he withdrew his fangs and cried out. The pull on his own neck disappeared an instant later as another shout joined his. Meanwhile, the cock buried deep inside him pulsed, its owner climaxing long and hard.

Holden took several gulps of air. "Fuck me!"

"I thought I just did…and from the sounds of it, most satisfactorily."

Holden opened his eyes and stared up, catching Raoul's smirk. Raoul's lower lip glistened with a smear of Holden's blood, and Holden surged up to lick it clean, before sinking back into the pillows. "Thanks. I needed that."

"I could tell." Raoul carefully withdrew and then flipped onto his back beside Holden. "I realise this is probably the wrong thing to say, but I do so love it when you have a bad day at work."

"Well, lucky for you, that's most days."

"How many insults this time?"

"Only one outright, but several implied, and stares aplenty."

"They simply don't know you as well as I do, my friend."

"I should think not!" Holden offered an expression of mock horror to accompany the retort.

Raoul chuckled. "So, you don't have any other lovers tucked away, even after all this time?"

"Who among our acquaintance—or, indeed, beyond—would touch me with a bargepole?"

Raoul propped himself on his elbow and studied Holden. "Perhaps I need to repeat my tales of your sexual prowess. I can, if you like."

"Please don't. It won't make a difference, and I'm not sure I'd want it to. The story served its purpose once. But even if the whole world believed you this time, all it would do is produce a queue of people eager to see what it's like to fuck a freak. Their opinion of me wouldn't change. It might even worsen when they discover I'm not the sexual acrobat you made me out to be."

"It didn't end badly for us. Quite the opposite, and on many glorious occasions."

Holden managed a smile. "That's only because you're such a kinky bastard."

"Why else would my brethren have dared me to bed you that first time? We both owe a great deal to my kink. Wouldn't you say?"

It was almost five years to the day since that fateful night. Holden had been heading home at the end of an especially vile day when a vampire blocked his path. Raoul had looked so handsome under the glow of the streetlight, but Holden's principal reaction had been one of annoyance. When Raoul had gone on to proposition him, Holden had been certain it was another mean prank. He'd brushed past and continued on his way. But Raoul had followed.

By the time they'd reached Holden's door, Holden had realised Raoul was serious. He'd dithered, but only for a moment. Curiosity and longing had swiftly won out. Society having shunned him all his life, he'd acknowledged this was likely to be his one and only chance to experience sex with anything other than his own palm, so he'd invited Raoul inside. Holden had figured he had nothing to lose. He couldn't become more of a social pariah than he already was, and if Raoul planned to kill him... Well, was that really so bad, given the way his life seemed to be heading? He could think of worse ways to go than at the hands of a handsome stranger, especially if they did end up making it into bed beforehand.

Raoul had been keen to get on with things, at first. However, he'd shown more restraint once he'd noted Holden's inexperience. Those initial hours together had proven enlightening and, frankly, awe-inspiring. Though he had remained convinced this event was part of an elaborate joke, Holden's spirit had soared to heights he'd never dreamed he'd attain. Knowing it was probably the sole time he'd experience such bliss, he'd tried to make the most of it and had given himself over to pleasure.

It was after their second round that Raoul had asked to taste his blood. At first, Holden had flinched at the request, but then he'd acquiesced. He'd known pure ecstasy; he could die happy. Only Raoul hadn't drained him. He'd taken only a couple of shallow swallows from Holden's wrist before pulling back and staring at him in wonder. The approaching dawn had forced them to conclude their revels, and Holden had assumed that would be the end of it. He'd been wrong. The next night, he'd found Raoul waiting at his front door.

Gradually, Holden had learned a number of things. One, Raoul's friends had dared him to sleep with Holden the first time—and he'd won a hefty cash prize for his success—but he'd returned of his own volition. Two, Holden's mixed-race blood, which had plagued him all his life, was apparently the most delicious Raoul had ever tasted. And three, the glimpses that blood had afforded Raoul of Holden's thoughts and memories had made him repent using Holden for his games.

They had begun to spend time together in the evenings. To explain his sudden fascination with a halfen,

Raoul had talked up Holden's bedroom skills, declaring him to be dynamite in the sack. It had been enough to make the others in Raoul's group of intimates grudgingly accept the growing friendship, to the point where they simply ignored it. Naturally, Raoul had made no mention of Holden's exquisite blood, since neither of them wanted Holden to become a target for hungry, curious vampires.

Over the last few years, they'd come to know each other well. Raoul was Holden's only friend, and they met regularly, with additional visits whenever Holden had had a particularly bad day and needed to let off some steam. Raoul maintained a hectic playboy lifestyle, but he always made time for Holden whenever he called.

"Earth to Holden. Come in, Hol."

"What?" For a moment, Holden had drifted into the past, and now he sat up and shook his head, trying to clear his thoughts.

"You really did have a nightmare day, didn't you! I said, I'd better get going."

"Already?"

"Hol, it's less than an hour till sunrise, and not all of us can weather those UV rays the way you do."

"Trust me when I say, that little trick is not enough to make it worth being me."

"Maybe not." Raoul reached over and brushed a lock of Holden's hair out of his eyes. "But that doesn't change the fact I'll become an unattractive pile of ash if I don't make tracks, and I don't think either of us wants that. Not to mention the terrible loss it would be to the world, to rob it of this." He gestured down his body.

"You could stay here for the day." It wasn't the first time Holden had made the offer, and he already knew the response.

"My friend, it's bad enough you insist on living in this dire part of town, making me cross the river to see you. But how's this for a compromise? When you finally get around to daylight-proofing this sad excuse for a flat, I'll gladly stay in your bed for twenty-four hours, or more, if work permits. Until then…"

Raoul stood, and Holden made the most of the opportunity to drink him in. His skin was so pale and smooth it was practically alabaster. In all respects, he was flawless. Holden watched as Raoul slid his long legs into a pair of skintight navy jeans, offering a final flash of a pert, rounded arse. Black shoes followed, and then a pale-grey T-shirt. A tailored, charcoal jacket completed the ensemble.

As always before departing, Raoul took a moment to fix his hair. Ever one to move with the times—unlike some vampires, who always seemed a century out of sync—he wore said hair short and choppy. That "just got out of bed" look worked well for him. It highlighted his well-defined jaw, and it was marvellously convenient, considering he spent most of his waking hours moving in and out of one bed or another. In fact, Holden had always wondered when he got any work done, though he seemed to fit it in somehow. Holden's money was on creative delegation. Raoul sat reasonably high up in the city's vampire pecking order. Therefore, he had lackeys.

Raoul checked his phone, then grinned at Holden. "Get some sleep. I'm sure you need it after the workout I just gave you."

Holden threw a pillow. However, even if he'd had excellent aim—which he didn't—such skill was no match for vampiric speed. Raoul was already out the door before the pillow struck the wall behind where he'd been standing.

With a sigh, Holden sank back onto the mattress. He *was* tired, but his mind was still too active to permit sleep. Then there was his stomach, which took its cue to rumble loudly. He'd not eaten before Raoul's arrival, and that small taste of blood had only served to sharpen his appetite.

Deciding he needed suitable fuel before attempting any deep thinking, Holden rose and pulled on his pyjamas. He padded into the next room, weaving around the random piles of books that littered the floor with a sure step borne of habit. Once in the kitchen, he opened the fridge. It was a meagre selection—he really ought to shop when his pay for today's work came through—but he managed to pull together enough scraps for an acceptable grazing platter. His meal assembled, he took the plate with him and settled on the sofa.

The stuffing-poor seat sank deeply and swiftly beneath him, until he could feel the chair's wooden frame pressing into the backs of his thighs. It was far from comfortable, but Holden did his best to ignore that, concentrating instead on filling his empty belly...and his mind.

His thoughts returned to that hidden garret apartment. Even now, something about the scene didn't make sense. He replayed it in his head, looking for the detail that would bring everything into focus. However, the answer remained elusive.

Why was he even bothering? He'd failed at his task assessing the blood for clues, and Owens made it perfectly clear she didn't believe he had anything else of value to offer. She and the rest of the team would track down the culprit soon enough, without his help. Besides, all he really had to go on was an unnameable hunch that something had been off, and that was probably a figment of his imagination. Had anything been wrong at the crime scene, one of the pure-blood fae would have noticed it. Details such as those were their specialty. Therefore, he would gain nothing from this replay of his failure. He ought to write it off as yet another bad day at the office and move on.

With his growling stomach appeased and his mind made up, Holden rinsed his plate and then shuffled back to bed. It was already dawn, but he decided he might as well try to get some shut-eye, however brief. He didn't bother setting his alarm. It wasn't as if he had any pressing social engagements for which to waken.

Chapter Three

TWO WEEKS PASSED. Holden's payment for the failed job came through—the callout fee stood, regardless of the results—but after settling his more urgent bills and doing a grocery run, there wasn't much left. Relief therefore mingled with anxiety when his phone rang and Owens's name flashed up on the screen. He accepted the call.

"Hey, Captain. How are—"

"No time for that. How soon can you make it to Clerkenwell?"

"I can leave now, but it will depend on the traffic."

"I'll text you the address. Hurry. There's been another one." With that, she hung up.

A few seconds later, the promised text came through. Holden glanced over the details, before tugging on his shoes, grabbing phone, wallet, sunglasses, and keys from the coffee table, and setting off.

He headed for his car, but then changed his mind. At this time of day, the Tube would be quicker. He covered the distance to the nearest station at a jog, and then made a mad dash for the train that stood at the platform, skidding into the car as the beep sounded, mere seconds before the doors slid shut. Most of the other passengers, used to such antics, ignored his undignified ingress, but the few looks cast his way reminded him that he'd forgotten to wear his hat.

Holden cast an anxious glance at his reflection in the window, relieved to note that his hair was successfully concealing his pointy-tipped ears. To allow for situations such as this was the main reason why he kept it long and always wore it down—a secondary form of protection, alongside the beanie he usually wore when spending an extended amount of time among humans. A glamour offered greater surety, but maintaining the mirage always drained him. Whereas a pure-blood fae had a never-ending supply of magical energy with which to work, his depleted with prolonged use, and he had to wait for it to replenish before he could do more. He would have to rely solely on his hair for cover on this occasion. He didn't want to start today's session at a disadvantage, not after his dismal effort last time.

When the train pulled into his stop, Holden shot through the opening door the second the gap was wide enough and then employed a subtle burst of supernatural speed to get ahead of the crowds. Out on the streets, he decelerated to a pace that, while fast, would neither draw undue attention nor use up too much of his energy reserves, and completed the journey on foot.

There were only a couple of intrigued bystanders this time, and they fled at Holden's arrival. Catching the eye of one of the pair as they passed, he saw they were only kids—young witches most likely, since they didn't smell like fae. The magic that hung in the air—an after-effect of the wards put in place to protect the crime scene—must have sparked their curiosity and drawn them in. A strong spell was always a powerful attractant to those who could sense it.

Owens opened the front door as he made his way up the path, and she beckoned him inside with a tilt of her head. Unlike the last residence he'd entered on official business, this place was a single-owner, two-storey dwelling. Typical of its period, it was narrow, though, and the grim atmosphere when Holden stepped into the living room only served to accentuate the spatial oppression. No one ever looked happy at a crime scene. That was a given, especially when the work involved witnessing grisly tableau after grisly tableau. Today, however, there was a distinct sense of unease, and Holden immediately saw why.

Although this victim sat upright on a sofa, there were clear similarities with the murder two weeks ago. Again, there was no sign of a struggle. Partially dried blood pooled in the victim's lap, but the cuts to remove the heart displayed the same precision as before. And the victim—a woman this time—bore an almost identical expression of pained shock.

Holden drew in a deep breath. The scent from the blood told him this was a mortal, yet he smelt no magic around the place, save for the Investigations Team's wards. That suggested a human, except the Fellowship wouldn't normally involve itself in deaths outside its jurisdiction.

He glanced at Owens. "She's not human, is she?"

"Witch."

Holden frowned at the unexpected news. "Same coven as before?"

"No."

"No?" That brought Holden up short. "But she lives in Clerkenwell."

"She only moved in about a week ago. Her boyfriend, who *is* in the Holborn-Clerkenwell coven, tells us it was to be closer to him. However, he says she had no intention of switching magical allegiances, so there's no reason for ill will amongst members of the Bloomsbury-Fitzrovia set. And before you ask, the boyfriend has a watertight alibi. He's been locked in a room with his coven members as part of an annual ritual for the last three days. They only let him come to the phone when I told them it was a murder investigation."

The victim's recent arrival explained why Holden hadn't immediately pegged her for a witch. The only way to tell humans from witches was by the residual traces of magic about their person or around their regular haunts. All witches warded their homes, but the spells required time and effort. The victim had clearly not had a suitable opportunity to start them yet. Indeed, it appeared she'd been so busy with the move, she'd not performed *any* magic for a few days at least.

The circumstances surrounding this new death also put pay, once and for all, to Holden's theory that the killings were some kind of extreme intercoven squabble. Sure, this second murder could have been undertaken in retaliation for the first, and conducted in the same vein, but Holden sensed a single hand here. The cuts were too alike to be the work of a mere copycat, and in any case, the Fellowship had released no images of the first murder to the public. So, a copycat couldn't possibly know sufficient details to replicate it.

Owens cleared her throat, and Holden remembered why he was here: the blood. He knelt beside the woman and collected a sample. Then he licked the blood from his finger and closed his eyes.

There was something this time, but it was vague. Random childhood recollections mingled with glimpses of what he assumed was the time of the murder. Through the confusion, he saw a dark shadow and the flash of a blade. The latter bore engravings, but Holden couldn't ascertain what they said before the vision vanished.

The pictures grew ever fainter. In the last, a head loomed toward him, and he scrunched his eyes tighter, concentrating his efforts on making out the features. For a second, he caught sight of lips pulled into a grimace. Then there was only darkness.

Holden opened his eyes and rose. "She saw her attacker, and I'm convinced she knew him, trusted him. I sensed initial calm in his presence. The spike of fear only came when she suddenly found she couldn't move—complete paralysis. That's why she didn't fight. She couldn't. I imagine the same is true of our previous victim."

Owens nodded. "Good work. See Campbell to put together a likeness of our suspect."

"I can't. I didn't see his face."

"It was definitely a man though? Did he wear a mask?"

"No, no mask. At least, I don't believe so. I think it was a man, but..." Holden tried to remember what he'd seen. "No, I can't be completely certain of that. Sorry. The blood was already heavily degraded." He paused, feeling the weight of a roomful of stares. "I did the best I could with it."

"Fucking hell! Degraded? Philips said she's only been dead for a couple of hours, same as the last vic. It's impossible."

"I got what I could, Captain."

What else was he supposed to say? He couldn't create memories where there were none. Anything else would be lying, and he would never mislead Owens, or risk the integrity of the investigation, simply to save face.

Peregrine Draper, a fae on the forensics team, who specialised in evidence collection, marched forward and waved his arm toward Holden. Despite the elegance of the movement, it brimmed with malice. "I don't know why you bother with this scum, Captain. What good is the half-breed? He's useless as a vampire, he's an insult to the fae, and he can't even do one simple job correctly."

"That's enough, Draper." Owens stepped between them. She stood up for Holden through her actions; however, her frown showed she was far from happy with him. "Holden, I think you need a break. Take some time off to recharge your batteries."

Holden's heart sank. "You're suspending me? For how long?"

"Why don't we call it an unscheduled vacation? We need you functioning at optimum capacity if you're to continue assisting us. I'm sure, with a little rest, you'll soon bounce back."

Bounce back? Aside from having experienced two crushing defeats in recent weeks, Holden wasn't aware he'd ever bounced off. He felt perfectly fine. Things were no different from usual. Then again, maybe Owens was right. He should have been able to glean *something* useful from blood that fresh. Was he sick without realizing it?

Whatever the problem, he hoped it wasn't permanent. He needed this work. No one else in the supernatural community would deign to hire him, and unless he found a job in which his employer would permit him to wear a beanie twenty-four seven, employment among the humans was equally impossible. He could maintain a decent glamour to conceal his appearance for two hours at a time, maybe three at a push. However, he'd never make it through an eight-hour shift without revealing himself—an act punishable by lengthy imprisonment if he got a testy judge.

He was so busy pondering these issues as he left, he didn't realise anyone had followed him until a shove sent him tumbling down the front steps. He landed heavily, and the impact knocked the air out of his lungs, leaving him gasping for breath.

"Halfen bastard." Draper sneered and ejected a globule of spittle that hit Holden square on the cheek. "Your mother was a filthy whore! She deserved everything she got, and more. If you've an ounce of sense and respect, you'll leave this city and never come back. No one wants you here."

Draper strode back inside, slamming the door behind him, and Holden let him go without a word. Retaliation was futile. Holden stood no chance against a pure-blood fae, even one as young and hot-headed as Draper. Enchantments would ensnare him before he'd so much as readied himself to strike a blow. He'd learned that vital lesson long ago.

He used his sleeve to wipe away the spit and got to his feet. His back twinged where he'd caught the edge of the bottom step, but it wouldn't smart for long. There was one advantage to his mixed heritage: his vampire blood would eliminate the bruises in a matter of minutes, with no need to perform any elaborate rituals or meditations. That talent had come in handy when he was younger too. Without enhanced healing capabilities, growing up in a community that despised and distrusted him would have seen him walking around with his skin mottled a permanent black and blue. Children could be more vicious than adults.

Today's treatment was nothing new, but that didn't make it any easier to bear, and as he headed home, he knew his plans for the evening: ice cream, alcohol, and a steamy session between the sheets, if Raoul was free. He would focus on that and try to set aside his worries until tomorrow, or, if he could find enough booze, maybe the day after.

Chapter Four

FOUR WEEKS LATER, Holden was still drowning his sorrows. Not that he'd been at the bottle constantly since attending the last crime scene—there'd been plenty of teetotal days too—but this was his third big drinking session, and as with the last two, Raoul joined him. He wasn't sure why it had hit him so badly this time. No, on reflection, he did. The jibes he could brush aside, or at least put behind him. What hurt most was Owens dismissing him. He'd heard nothing from her and had yet to pluck up the courage to call, despite Raoul having insisted he should do so at the end of his last bender. Without Raoul, Holden didn't like to think what might have become of him. Raoul was his rock, both emotionally and, at present, financially, since Holden had no income. The vodka he was currently consuming apace came courtesy of Raoul. They'd drunk Holden's own meagre stores dry the first night.

Tilting the bottle with partially inebriated precision, Holden poured them each another shot, and then made a wobbly return to the bed. He'd slipped back into his boxers after they'd finished their physical entrée, main course, and dessert, but Raoul remained gloriously bare, spread languidly atop the covers, at ease with his nudity in a manner Holden envied.

"To you, my friend." Raoul saluted him with his glass and downed the shot in a single gulp.

Holden did likewise, but with far less enthusiasm. "Don't see why I deserve a toast."

"And I don't see why not."

"Maybe because I'm a total failure and a freak?"

"You are neither."

"Am so!" Holden instantly regretted the burst of petulance. Raoul was only trying to help; there was no need to snap at him. "Sorry. It's just these murders, and the whole fucking mess surrounding them. They're what led to my suspension, and I know there was something off about both crime scenes. If only I could work out what it was... But I've revisited them in my mind so many times now, it's all beginning to blur."

He glanced toward the bottle of vodka set atop the chest of drawers. Why hadn't he brought it back to the bed with him, instead of leaving it irritatingly out of reach? He couldn't be bothered to stand and fetch it, yet he was aching for another drink.

"Would you like me to take a gander for you?"

Holden looked up sharply.

The blood he and Raoul exchanged during sex gifted them with insights into each other's minds. Nevertheless, over the years, they'd established unspoken boundaries as to how much they would glean from the other's thoughts—a level of privacy that suited them both. Given the confidential nature of Holden's work, that had always been one of the areas deemed off limits.

The offer hovered in the air like a tangible presence between them, and Raoul studiously avoided meeting Holden's gaze, staring into his empty glass instead. A part of Holden's brain miraculously still sober told him he should refuse. If the Fellowship learned he had shared details of an ongoing investigation, they would never take him back. However, the part of Holden that had already polished off two full bottles of premium vodka in as many hours said, *"Screw the Fellowship and its poncy rules."* They'd cast him out, and maybe the only way to return to the fold—something, deep down, beneath the ire, he desperately wanted—would be to walk through the door with a major breakthrough to present to them.

Of course, there was no guarantee that would happen, but Raoul would at least see things with a fresh perspective. With luck, he might spot something Holden had missed. Even a scrap of useful information, however slight, was better than the nothing he currently possessed.

"Do it." Holden thrust out his arm, nearly smacking Raoul in the face.

Raoul, who succumbed to alcohol even less readily than Holden, and who had superior reflexes to begin with, caught Holden's wrist before it struck his nose. "Are you certain?"

At Holden's nod, Raoul brought Holden's hand to his lips and nipped at the thumb. He slipped the digit into his mouth, closing his eyes as he drew forth several droplets of blood, letting them gather on his tongue.

It wasn't long before Raoul released Holden's hand and opened his eyes. His pupils were blown, but Holden could hardly blame him for that. The sight of blood sometimes brought about a similar reaction in him too. For a pure-blood vampire the effect was even stronger, and Raoul would have witnessed a lot of blood in Holden's recent memories.

"Both were precise jobs, not random attacks."

"I thought so too."

"The issue with the decayed blood is, indeed, strange. I can't explain it, but based on your memories, I doubt that I, or any other, could have done more than you did under the circumstances."

Although he'd thought as much himself, Raoul's confirmation did reassure Holden. It hadn't been his fault—not really.

"And, of course, you'll have noted the similarities with the Ripper murders."

"The what?" Holden straightened, sudden attention dispelling some of his half-drunken stupor. "You don't mean Jack the Ripper? I know you've lived long enough not to measure time in small units anymore, but come on, Raoul. That was over a century ago!"

"No, I mean the new ones."

"New ones?"

"You haven't heard? God, Hol, you really don't keep up with the human news at all, do you? Earlier this year there were three killings in Whitechapel—two women and a man. In each case, the killer removed organs. The first was sloppy workmanship, but he improved, somewhat, by the third. Surely you saw the headlines, if nothing else. They came out with nonsense such as 'Jack's Back.' The humans were in quite a panic for nearly three weeks, which was a hindrance for those of us trying to feed, I can tell you, but then the killings ceased."

"They caught the guy?"

"No, he simply stopped killing. At least, he left off killing humans. Looking at your bodies, my friend, I'd say he's upped his game."

"You're assuming it's a man."

"So are you."

It was true. He'd sensed a masculine edge to both murder scenes. Of course, Holden knew he shouldn't write off the idea that a woman had committed the crimes, not without real evidence to support the assertion. However, in his own mind, he was convinced that a male hand had wielded the blade.

Holden's thoughts ticked over. The mental exercise helped clear his vodka-addled brain, and he no longer spared a glance for either the half-full bottle, for which he'd longed but a moment ago, or the empty glass beside him. Instead, he reached over to the bedside table and retrieved his tablet. While it booted up, he drummed his fingers on his knee.

He became aware of movement in his peripheral vision and looked up, surprised to see Raoul dressing. "You're leaving? You don't have to go yet."

"I know what you're like when you start any kind of research. If I stay, you'll forget I'm even here within minutes, and I do so hate to be ignored."

"No, I would—" Raoul's quirked eyebrow of disbelief stopped Holden from finishing his sentence. "Okay. Maybe you're right."

"You *know* I'm right. Besides, the night's still young, my friend. It's far too early for me to waste a perfectly good evening watching you stare at a screen. Not when there's so much pleasure available elsewhere."

Holden couldn't suppress a grin. "Don't do anything I wouldn't do."

"Hol, if I agreed to that, life would be no fun whatsoever, and with eternity before me, that would be a curse indeed." He blew Holden a kiss, then departed.

With Raoul gone, Holden returned his attention to the tablet. A few quick searches soon led to plenty of information on the killings Raoul had mentioned— everything from serious journalism to sensationalist theories, with an abundance of public hysteria thrown in for good measure. Official photographs of the murder scenes were, understandably, limited, but from what Holden could glean, it looked as if Raoul was right. The timings worked out, and although the killer had taken multiple organs initially, the final victim had lost only her heart.

Holden reached for his phone, intending to call Owens. But then he hesitated. The fact that *he* lived in a bubble and had somehow escaped hearing about these killings didn't mean everyone else on the Investigations Team had been likewise oblivious. A few had human friends, so it seemed likely one of them would have put two and two together. If he called Owens at this time of night, with information she already had, he'd probably piss her off further. Then again, if she didn't know of it and he failed to tell her...

While he was prevaricating, his phone beeped. He checked the notifications and saw a message from Raoul. It was almost dawn. Raoul wouldn't contact him at this hour unless it was important. He opened the text.

> *One more thing, Hol. The calendar in the first room was wrong. Chin up, my friend. If they don't take you back on your own merit, I'm happy to open a few throats. :)*

Naturally, Raoul wouldn't really attack anyone at the Fellowship. Still, it was sweet of him to pretend, and the thought of it brought a smile to Holden's lips. Once he'd given a moment to the fantasy, he got back to business and reread the first part of Raoul's message, puzzling over the words.

He tried to remember the first murder, recreating the scene in his mind in as much detail as he could muster. He recalled the calendar. It had hung from a nail hammered at a jaunty angle into the side of one of the kitchen cupboards. He'd passed it on his way in and out of the bedroom. He'd barely spared it a glance, and he had to concentrate to bring it into focus now. He saw the English pastoral scene that topped the open page. The month view below had been divided into boxes, and each box had been crossed through up to the current date. Except...

Fates! Raoul was right again. The dates were wrong. The crosses had ended a good two weeks before the date he'd attended the scene. It could have been simple forgetfulness on the part of the victim, but Holden considered that unlikely. Anyone who marked off days in such a determined manner might miss a single day, but not two whole weeks.

Suddenly, the scrambled pieces spun into place. He knew now why he'd gotten nothing from the blood. It hadn't been hours old but weeks. His hand trembled as he pressed Owens's number. He wasn't sure if the shiver was one of exhilaration or terror.

Chapter Five

IT STILL FELT strange to enter the hallowed domain that was the Fellowship's headquarters. On this, his third day, the guard even managed not to look askance at Holden when he stood aside to grant him entry to the City-based office block masquerading as a financial investment firm.

Until this week, Holden had only set foot on these premises once before: on the day of his interview with the Investigations Team. His father, as the Council's current Minister for Justice, had engineered his entry into the workforce around the same time he'd gifted Holden his flat. Two final acts of parental attention before he'd cut all ties with Holden and left him to his own devices. They'd not crossed paths since, and in all honesty, Holden considered that no great hardship. Still, he supposed he owed his father some gratitude for helping him get his foot in the door with the Fellowship, and now, without Cadeyrn's help, he'd cemented his place within the organization.

He set a brisk pace down the hallway, passing marble columns, plaques, and statue-topped plinths aplenty. Everywhere, the Fellowship's motto stood proudly emblazoned: Preserve and Protect. Those had been the organization's twin aims since its inception. The Fellowship's role was to preserve the cultures of the three supernatural communities that fell under its umbrella, and to protect them from human discovery. It also ensured treaties between the groups remained intact and punished violations. Initially, treaty-related matters had been the limit of its purview, but as time passed, it had gradually assumed all judiciary functions, creating subbranches, such as the Investigations Team, to handle criminal matters.

Holden took the elevator to the third floor, which housed the Investigations Team's offices. He wasn't late. However, when he entered, he saw that he was the last to arrive. His colleagues stood around a large table set in the centre of the room, surveying various documents. Holden caught Owens's gaze, and she beckoned him over. The others made room for him, though some did so with obvious reluctance.

"We've run your theory past all nine covens now, Holden, and all agree it's possible. It goes far beyond the natural magic the fae employ. Therefore, the killer is most certainly a witch, and no novice in the magical arts. This person has training and skill. The spell required to seal each crime scene, preserving the body, wouldn't be an easy one. It would require a degree of power that worries the coven leaders."

"Can the covens track the perp?" This came from Philips.

"Not from the previous crime scenes. Not after we've 'muddied' them with our presence." Owens pulled a face. "But they think they might manage to do so with a fresher spell. They won't be able to say for certain until they try."

"Why would anyone do this, especially someone with that much power?" It seemed nonsensical to Holden. If the witch responsible was that powerful, surely he'd be able to get whatever he wanted without killing, even working within the limitations of the various interspecies treaties. What could have prompted such violence?

"That, Holden, is your job."

"My job?"

"Find me a motive. Your insight got us this far, and now I'm making you lead investigator."

"What? But he's totally unqualified for such responsibility." Draper's scowl could have frozen water.

"He's the only one who spotted the inconsistencies with the calendar. None of the fae here, you included, managed that much. He's earned this, Draper, and I expect you all," Owens added, glancing around the table, "to give him whatever assistance he requires. Now, back to work everyone." She turned to Holden. "You, my office."

The others wandered to their respective workstations, and Holden trailed Owens to her room, still in a daze. He had to have misheard. Surely she hadn't really assigned him the entire case.

Owens shut the door and muttered a spell which lowered all the internal blinds. "Sit down, Holden."

"Captain." Holden dropped heavily into the nearest chair, which gave an ominous creak of protest at the violent intrusion.

"You'll receive a weekly retainer for as long as you're working this case with us. You're in charge. I'm letting you run with it, but you still report everything directly to me. Understand? I want to hear about every new lead, no matter how fucking small. Got it?"

"Got it, Captain."

Owens leaned back in her chair and studied him. "I'm taking a big chance here, Holden. Don't let me down."

"I'll do my best. Only..."

"Spit it out."

"The others aren't going to follow me."

Holden's heart sank as he accepted the veracity of his own statement. The venture was doomed before it began. He'd experienced an initial thrill of excitement and expectation. For a second, he'd actually thought this could be the start of a new life—one in which he was judged by his deeds, not his parentage. However, that warm hope now shifted to cold dread. None of those working beyond that office door would listen to a single word he said. Well, maybe Philips, if he didn't bow to peer pressure, but certainly not Draper. Holden would have more luck talking to thin air. They wouldn't obey him. It was far more likely they'd seek to sabotage him the first chance they got, and this time there would be no coming back. A failure here, on such a high-profile case, would see his career with the Fellowship end. He didn't think the others would get him tossed out at the expense of the case—they all wanted to see this bastard behind bars—but if they found an opportunity that wouldn't jeopardise the investigation...

"They'll toe the line once you earn their respect."

Holden's incredulity at this assertion must have shown on his face, because Owens offered a tight smile and gave his hand a brief pat.

"I'm not saying it will be easy—prejudices are tough to shake—but you have to try. You think it was a walk in the park for *me* to reach my current position? I fought every fucking step of the way, and you can too. This is your chance to prove your worth."

Words could never hope to express the gratitude Holden felt toward Owens in that moment, so he decided not to try. She would know how much it meant to him, and the last thing he needed at a time when he wanted to come across as cool and professional was to choke up and sob like a baby. Better to focus on the job in hand, letting her know he was serious about solving these crimes.

"You think there'll be another murder?"

Owens followed his lead. "Yes, and soon."

Holden agreed. The killer's motives remained obscure, but the second murder had by no means felt like a grand coda. If anything, the crescendo was still building.

"What are your impressions at this stage?" Owens prompted. She leaned forward, resting her elbows on the desk and interlacing her fingers. "Talk me through them."

"The murders seem ritualistic."

"Good. And?"

"They're meticulously planned. Whoever this guy is, he's smart and he's careful. He won't rush into the next kill. He'll take his time and prepare well. It has to be perfect."

"So, what's your next move in the investigation?"

"I want to take a closer look at the victims. We need to see if there are any connections between them, however tentative. We have to find a pattern. If we know how and why he's choosing them, perhaps we can guess the identity of his next victim in time to foil his plans."

"Will you look at the three Ripper victims too?"

"No."

"Why not?"

Holden shook his head. "They were different. The killer was sloppy at first. They were opportunistic and emotional—the antithesis to these recent killings. It would be like comparing apples and pears. We'd be wasting our time."

"But do you think it's the same guy?"

Holden hesitated. Did he? Part of him wanted to say no. The vibe of those cases hadn't resonated with how he'd felt at the two scenes he'd attended. Then again, being on the spot was different from reading about it in a newspaper article. So, perhaps this wasn't the best time to rely on an uncorroborated gut instinct.

"I'm not certain. Though logic would suggest it's possible, even likely. The humans could have been practice runs. Maybe he wanted to perfect his technique before he started on his real work. That would explain why they feel different—it was just a series of trials to hone his method."

"Good. Your thoughts are identical to mine." Owens smacked her hands down on her chair's armrests. "So, get on with it, Holden. Keep me apprised of any new developments."

HOLDEN'S DESPONDENCY GREW as he reviewed his notes. He'd finished his comparison of the two victims, but he'd found nothing of use. They'd shared no close friends or interests. Victim one was a middle-aged male, whereas victim two was a young woman not long out of university. Victim one had been single, while victim two had been in a relationship. They'd come from different covens. Both were witches, but that sole similarity wasn't going to get him far. He'd been at this for three full days already, and soon he'd have to go to Owens with something, even if that something was his all-out failure to link the pair and discover a pattern.

He glanced up. The others were working busily, though on what he hadn't a clue. Owens seemed to be the only one who considered him in charge. The rest talked amongst themselves, but not to him. He'd seen the occasional huddle from whence they'd cast furtive looks his way, while discussing...the Fates only knew what. The case? Their lunch plans? Him? He felt certain the latter was the most likely topic, but he couldn't prove it.

The one time he'd approached to join in the conversation, his arrival had resulted in stony silence and downcast eyes. He'd not bothered to try a second time. Had the team made any progress without him? He doubted it, since no one had presented anything to Owens, but who could say for sure? Either way, his exclusion was apparently absolute. Most of the team was fae, and if the fae had one overwhelming trait as a species, it was pride. To them, dealing with him was akin to a human taking counsel with a pig.

Slipping his hand into his pocket, Holden toyed with his phone. The urge to text Raoul was strong; it had been all week. However, he'd resisted nobly thus far, and he forced his fingers away from the buttons yet again. Raoul was a good friend—the best—but as comforting as it would be to have Raoul pound his troubles into oblivion, Holden accepted that he was becoming far too dependent on him. Hot, mindless sex was a salve, but it was no cure. Owens was right. He needed to earn respect and learn to stand with his head held high. It was time to man up.

Holden rose and cleared his throat. "Everyone, I'd like to call a team meeting to see where we are on this."

Half a dozen pairs of eyes fixed on him, their gazes incredulous. Philips was so stunned he gaped. Draper merely afforded Holden one of his standard glowers. No one answered the summons with either movement or speech, and the tension in the room skyrocketed with every passing second. It was an impasse. Should he press on or retreat?

In the end, Owens's timely arrival spared Holden from making a decision. She charged into the office, already issuing orders before the door had closed behind her.

"Look smart, everyone. We have another victim. Same MO. We already have people securing the scene, and I've called in an expert to assist with the investigation. He'll meet us on-site. Well, what are you all fucking gawking at? Let's move! Do your prep, then get over there. Holden, with me."

Holden dashed to her side as she marched back out into the corridor and headed toward the elevator. "An expert?"

"Yes. We need someone with specialist know-how. You and he will work together."

Holden released a figurative breath. Owens wasn't replacing him. When she'd mentioned an expert, that's what he'd feared. But it was only a partner. She'd not pulled him from the case...yet. He tried to look at things positively. Perhaps another new perspective would bring enlightenment. It had worked with Raoul and that calendar.

"This guy," Owens said as she jabbed impatiently at the elevator buttons. "Well, he can be a bit...finickety, but I'm sure you'll do your best to get along with him."

Finickety? What was that supposed to mean? Who even said "finickety" anymore? Owens did, apparently, but Holden couldn't recall her ever having used the expression before. It seemed a galaxy away from her usual, curse-laden lexicon.

"I'll do my best, Captain," he promised when he noticed her looking at him expectantly. He always did—not that it ever helped. If the other party proved disinclined to act likewise, there was little he could do about it.

Chapter Six

THE SCENE THAT greeted Holden upon arrival was much the same as the former two, except the location had changed. This time, they'd proceeded to a residence in Marylebone. Another inner-city flat, this one was a little larger than his own and well furnished. The owner was clearly a collector of sorts, as items littered every available surface. Most looked benign—stuffed toys, holiday keepsakes, Royal Doulton figurines—but Holden glimpsed a few pieces here and there that screamed 'magic', so there seemed little doubt the victim was another witch, and one from a different coven yet again. Holden assumed so, anyway. He guessed Owens would confirm the victim's mystical affiliation shortly, once she'd spoken with the local coven leader.

As they moved from the open-plan kitchen–lounge toward the bedroom, Holden glanced around, looking for a calendar or any other telltale sign, but seeing nothing useful. Even if a calendar had been present, it didn't follow that this victim would also religiously cross off days. It was naive to think they'd be *that* lucky.

It was only as they reached the bedroom door that Holden noticed the odd atmosphere. Heavy anxiety hung in the air, and no one was speaking, each going about their work, making as little noise as possible. At first, he assumed it was due to his presence. Were they sending him to Coventry, advertising their displeasure at his leading role in the investigation outside the office, as well as in? But then he caught the furtive glances cast toward the closed bedroom door. He was being paranoid, as usual. Not everything was about him. Something in *there* had set the others on edge. Was this scene worse than the previous two? He mentally prepared for gore and dropped back to let Owens take the lead. However, she, too, was acting bizarrely.

Displaying uncharacteristic hesitation, Owens did not fling open the door and stride in, claiming authority over the scene. Instead, she halted before it and knocked, turning the handle only upon hearing a muffled yet imperious call of 'Come'.

The victim lay upon the bed. Another woman, Holden noted, and the scene was no more dire than the last, so there was nothing to account for the strange reactions in the other room. That was all he observed of the murder, though, as the living figure standing at the foot of the bed caught his attention. The man was gazing intently at the corpse, one hand tightly fastened on the wrought-iron bed frame. He was tall and imposing, and it wasn't only his proud, upright bearing that contributed to this impression. Even with only a back view, Holden could tell the fellow's suit had not come off a rack. It encased him in sleek lines, accentuating his fine figure in a way that screamed unadulterated style and sophistication. Raoul always looked good, but with him it was pure artifice—a clear intention of dressing to impress. This guy's style appeared effortless. His hair was trimmed short in a classy, timeless style, and as he started to turn, Holden caught sight of well-defined cheekbones.

There were more important things on which Holden ought to be concentrating—a dead woman, a murder investigation, keeping his job—yet he was desperate to see if this stranger was as gorgeous from the front as he was from the back. His desire coupled with shock a moment later, however, when the man faced him. For now Holden recognised him, and he understood the reason for the strange mood he'd sensed among the others.

Valerius Blackwood was the last person Holden would have expected to see in the midst of a murder investigation. Holden knew him—as would everyone in both the supernatural and human communities, in London and beyond. Nevertheless, that acquaintance came only from newsreels and gossip columns, since he and Blackwood moved in very different circles. Holden, as a halfen, barely clung to the bottom rung of the social ladder. Blackwood, as head of the Mayfair-Belgravia witches, London's most powerful and influential coven, was on top in more ways than one.

Although currently he held no official position within the Fellowship's upper echelons, rumour had it the Council often sought his guidance. The Blackwoods were one of the city's oldest witch families—a pure-blood line. Not only that, they also stood out in human affairs. Like his father before him, Blackwood was a well-known entrepreneur and philanthropist. He was in the papers every week, making donations here and cutting ribbons there. In both worlds, he was practically royalty. It took wealth, power, beauty, or breeding to open doors in this life, and Valerius Blackwood possessed all four in abundance.

While Holden was still trying to process Blackwood's presence, Blackwood's gaze flittered over him before settling on Owens.

"Captain Owens." He elegantly inclined his head. "You were right to call me. I sense strong magic use here. Someone definitely sealed this room. Tracking the magic to its source may prove possible, but it will be a protracted and complicated process. If you expected me to point to the culprit this instant, I'm afraid I must disappoint you. Have your team gather some samples for me once you're through here. I will need hair, nail clippings, and some of the victim's personal items from within this room. Send them to my house. I'll see what I can do and will be in touch."

He stepped forward, clearly intending to leave, and Holden automatically shuffled to the side to allow him to pass.

When a man like Valerius Blackwood strode forward, no one dared stand in the way. Deference to his "betters" was something Holden's father, and many others, had instilled in him from a young age. Apparently, though, Owens had missed that lesson, for she moved to block the doorway.

"Before you depart, Mr Blackwood, allow me to introduce Holden Fay. Holden is leading this investigation in my name, and I would like the two of you to work closely on this. Please involve him every step of the way, and communicate with him directly when you have any information to share."

Blackwood turned slowly and studied Holden, and Holden stared into eyes of such a rich brown they appeared to be pools of melted chocolate. Photographs were nothing compared with seeing them in person. They drew Holden in, deeper and deeper, until he feared he might end up living the cliché and drowning in them.

His earlier glance in Holden's direction must have been cursory indeed, as now Blackwood's brow furrowed. For a moment, he seemed confused. Then confusion turned to outrage.

"You aren't serious?" He broke the connection with Holden and spun back to face Owens. "You can't honestly expect me to work with...*that*? I came here to help you with an investigation. One which, so far, has demonstrated nothing but your team's gross incompetence. I am under no obligation, yet you would repay my generous assistance with such an insult? Excuse me. There are many important matters requiring my attention."

This time, Owens didn't prevent his egress, and Blackwood stormed from the room. Through the open doorway, Holden observed the seas part before him, everyone fleeing from his path, and then Valerius Blackwood was gone, taking his pitch-black suit and even darker attitude with him.

HOLDEN DIDN'T RETURN to the office that day. He wasn't certain he ever would. So much for earning his team's respect. There was fat chance of that now they'd witnessed a man of Valerius Blackwood's standing snub him so forcefully and loudly. If Holden were lucky, they'd continue ignoring him. However, he suspected that Blackwood's public display of intolerance would incline a few of the more obnoxious fae—Draper came to mind—to ramp up the verbal abuse once more. Blast the ignorant son of a bitch. He could have at least kept his voice down.

He couldn't deny that some of the hurt stemmed from genuine disappointment. He'd always rather hero-worshipped Valerius Blackwood. Yes, the man came across as proud and aloof, but with his heritage and talents, who wouldn't be? Setting that aside, he'd seemed a decent guy. At least, that's how the media presented him, and reporters usually gloried in dishing out dirt rather than praise. It was tough to discover your idol was just as prejudiced and small-minded as everyone else.

After Blackwood's abrupt departure, Owens hadn't said a word. She'd turned back to the scene, and Holden had followed suit. He'd sampled the blood, for the sake of being thorough, but as expected, he'd gotten nothing of use from it. Sticking around had seemed pointless, and Owens had not protested when he slunk out.

Since then, he'd been at home, wallowing. Luckily, he was still out of alcohol, so he'd escaped the lure of another binge, but he had consumed an entire tub of chocolate chip ice cream—waistline be damned—while watching repeats of some old 60s sitcoms. Once dusk had fallen, he'd called Raoul. They'd spoken for several minutes, but Raoul couldn't come over as he had to attend a meeting—vampire business. He'd commiserated with Holden. However, he'd also expressed surprise. Raoul knew Blackwood. They weren't intimates, but their paths crossed on occasion. Raoul accepted that Blackwood could be overbearing but added that he usually showed more restraint. Apparently, Blackwood was a smooth talker, quite the diplomat, and Raoul had never known him to be publically rude to anyone, regardless of his personal opinion.

When Raoul ended the call to get ready for his meeting, Holden once more retreated to his sofa, taking with him a second tub of ice cream. As he ate, he considered what to do. He couldn't hide out forever. Nor could he continue to rely on Raoul for emotional and financial support. Maybe the time had come to move on. He'd tried to forge a life for himself here, but clearly he'd failed. If not for meeting Raoul, he doubted he'd have stayed in London this long. Too many people knew him here. What he needed was a fresh start, in a place where no one knew his name, and where he could live in relative isolation.

He could sell the flat and find somewhere in the country, he decided suddenly. Sure, he'd still need an income stream, but there had to be something he could do. For a start, he'd research online jobs. If he worked from home, he wouldn't have to worry about maintaining a glamour or dealing with hostility. He'd purchase his new home outright—proceeds from the sale of a central-London flat should more than cover the cost of a tiny cottage in the back of beyond—so he'd only need to earn enough for utilities and food.

His thoughts skittered back to the three murders. The case had gotten under his skin, and it felt wrong not to see it through, but it was probably better this way. The team had a powerful witch assisting now, and the others would be happier without him around. Once Holden was out of their way, doubtless they'd catch the guy in no time. So, that was it. Tomorrow he would hand in his resignation, effective immediately, and call a few real estate agents to get the ball rolling.

The sudden ringing of his phone startled Holden. He grabbed it from the coffee table and glanced at the display. It was a private number. Who the hell would be calling him at this time of night? He considered ignoring it, but after two more rings, he changed his mind and answered.

"Yep?"

"Is this Mr Holden Fay?" asked an unfamiliar voice in clipped tones.

"Yeah. Who's this?"

"Mr Blackwood wishes to speak with you."

Holden felt his jaw drop. It took him a moment to force it closed and then respond. "Oh...uh...yeah...sure. Put him on."

"He would like to speak face-to-face."

"Oh. All right. Tomorrow?"

"He hoped you could come now."

"Now? It's gone ten."

"Shall I tell him it's too late?"

Holden didn't miss the note of admonishment. Although part of him screamed that, after what Blackwood had done to him, he had every right to make the bastard wait, years of social grovelling were not something he could easily brush aside, and he answered, "No, no. Now's fine."

"Excellent. You know the address, I trust?"

Holden nodded, before remembering the guy couldn't see him. "Yeah, I know it." Who didn't? You'd have to have been living under an iceberg at the North Pole not to know the Blackwood mansion.

"We'll expect you shortly, then."

Before Holden could respond, his interlocutor hung up.

For several long seconds, Holden stared at his phone. He wasn't entirely convinced he hadn't fallen into an ice cream–induced stupor and dreamed the whole exchange. Except, never in his wildest imaginings would he have supposed Valerius Blackwood would wish to speak with him. Therefore, the conversation had to have been real, and that meant...

Shit! He had to get going. One didn't keep someone like Blackwood waiting. Holden glanced down at his worn, baggy sweatpants and stained T-shirt. Although, on reflection, maybe taking five minutes to change before departure would be time well spent.

Chapter Seven

THE BLACKWOOD MANSION had always struck Holden as equal parts intimidating and elegant. Its white façade was bright and alluring, set against the plainer brown-bricked properties on either side, while its two noble Doric columns framed the doorway in the manner of a grand museum entrance. Even now, glimpsed only in the harsh glow of the streetlights, the sight was impressive.

Grosvenor Square wasn't in an area of town Holden often frequented. Nevertheless, whenever he did pass by, the mansion always drew his gaze. He'd often wondered what it was like within those walls. Now he was on the verge of finding out, he wasn't certain he wanted to know.

Holden slowly mounted the three spotless steps to the black front door, which looked even darker and more daunting than it had from the street. He glanced behind him, still half expecting to discover the phone call had been a vicious trick, and someone was about to jump out and laugh at him. Yet, the square remained still and quiet. There were no passers-by, and he didn't spot so much as a twitching curtain in response to his presence.

Unable to conjure any further reasons for delay, Holden resolutely rang the bell, which produced a melodious chime. Footsteps sounded, and the door opened to reveal an older man dressed in black. His suit was plain, except for the colourful Blackwood crest embroidered into the lapel, but his shoes shone with the gleam of a thousand polishes.

"Mr Fay, I presume?"

The man's expression remained neutral, but Holden thought he detected a hint of distaste in his tone. He recognised the voice, in any case. This was the man with whom he'd spoken on the phone. Therefore, the call had been genuine, which was a relief in some ways, if not in others.

"Yes." He shuffled on the spot, wondering what else to say. "I got here as soon as I could."

"I'm sure. Follow me, please. Mr Blackwood awaits you in the library."

Holden stepped into the entrance hall. He fought to keep his expression as impassive as that of his companion, but that was no easy feat when faced with such a view.

The interior of Blackwood's home was stunning. Holden felt as if he'd stumbled onto the set of a period drama, or entered a National Trust property. The house was every bit as stylish and elegant as its owner. Period details vied for Holden's attention everywhere he looked, and though he was no expert, he suspected every piece on display was a bona fide antique. He couldn't see the Blackwood family accepting reproductions or fakes. Not when they could afford the real thing with money to spare. The foyer's centrepiece was a beautiful staircase that curved to either side as it reached the first floor, and Holden took an involuntary step toward it, craning his neck to view the paintings hanging from the walls above him.

The butler—Holden assumed the man's role—cleared his throat, and Holden guiltily snapped back to attention. For a moment, the splendour of his surroundings had made him forget why he was here. Reminded of the purpose of his visit, he hastened after the butler, keeping his eyes firmly fixed on the man's slightly stooping back and balding pate.

They passed to the left of the staircase and reached a closed door. The butler gave two soft knocks, awaited a muffled response, and then opened the door and gestured Holden inside.

"Mr Fay, sir."

"Thank you, James." The voice came from somewhere to the right. "That will be all."

James briefly caught Holden's gaze, his expression hard to read. Then he departed, shutting the door behind him, trapping Holden in the room.

Still, as Holden glanced about, he had to admit there were far worse places in which to be confined, and, indeed, he could think of few better. Floor-to-ceiling bookcases lined every wall, each shelf brimming with tomes. There were a few paperbacks in evidence here and there; however, the bulk of the collection comprised hardback editions. Some were clearly ancient, their spines cracked and their lettering faded. Others had been privately bound, the spines embossed with the Blackwood crest.

Holden sucked in a deep breath, relishing the pervading musky scent of old paper and leather. He could imagine spending hours here, perusing the titles, letting the rest of the world go by. Such a library would keep him occupied for years. He'd never want to leave the house. Enamoured, he reached toward the nearest shelf.

"You're a book lover, I see."

The voice jolted Holden, and he snatched back his arm, realizing, yet again, he'd allowed his surroundings to rob him of all reason. He cringed as he met Blackwood's eyes, and then swiftly lowered his gaze to the rich burgundy carpet.

"I'm sorry, sir. I didn't mean to—"

"No matter." Blackwood waved away the apology and rose smoothly from the leather armchair in which he'd been seated. "Never apologise for appreciating books. They are one of life's pleasures—one of the few means of escape we have, and an opportunity to expand our minds."

"That's true," Holden readily agreed, still not sure what to make of Blackwood's easy, open manner, coming, as it did, after their prior exchange.

"What do you like to read?"

"Spec fic mostly. Fantasy. Paranormal." Holden blushed at the admission. "I know that's cheesy, considering the world in which we live, but I enjoy the humans' varied takes on us. I also like the classics," he added swiftly. He doubted there was a single speculative fiction text on these shelves, and he was desperate not to look too uncultured. "Especially old adventure stories."

"Ah. So, I imagine you enjoy the works of Dumas?"

"Yes! *The Count of Monte Cristo* is one of my favourites."

"And mine. Although, I can't help but think that, were I in Edmond Dantès's shoes, I would have acted differently. I'd have taken the money and my new identity and headed in the opposite direction from my past." He smiled faintly, but he wasn't looking at Holden, seemingly lost in his own thoughts. "What is revenge compared to the chance to make a fresh start?"

Holden mulled over the idea. "Huh. I've never thought about it that way."

At Holden's words, Blackwood abruptly turned and crossed the room. He lifted the lid on a large antique globe, revealing a collection of bottles. "Drink?" he asked, his manner polite but more distant than a moment ago.

"Oh. Sure." The comfortable literary discussion apparently over, Holden's unease returned. A few hours ago, Blackwood had referred to him as 'that'. Now he wanted them to drink together? Conflicting emotions rooted Holden in place. He had no idea if he ought to be insulted or appeased. Did he even dare be insulted?

Blackwood came forward carrying two glasses. He held one out, and Holden automatically took it. When Blackwood sipped his drink, Holden did likewise.

Fuck! If that wasn't the smoothest whisky he'd ever tasted. How old was it? Moreover, how much did it cost? It occurred to him that, in this pour alone, he was probably consuming an entire day's salary. He hesitated, but then he downed the rest in a single swallow. It wasn't like he had to pay for it. At least, he hoped not.

Without a word, Blackwood took Holden's empty glass and set it down alongside his own. When he turned back, he leisurely looked Holden up and down, his expression contemplative.

"I owe you an apology, Mr Fay."

Holden stilled. This was...unexpected. The drink was one thing—customary courtesy to a guest—but he never would have dreamed he'd been summoned here to accept an apology. Aside from Raoul, no one had ever apologised to him before, and he was at a loss as to what to say or do in response. Part of him wanted to take the moral high ground. After all, Blackwood did owe him this. However, it was the well-trained little boy and not the self-assured man who came to the fore, as usual.

"No, you don't, sir. It's fine. Really."

A strange look crossed Blackwood's face, but it was so fleeting it was gone before Holden could name it. "It's not fine. I was unbelievably rude. The murder scene must have affected me more than I thought it would. I spoke without thinking."

Only without thinking, Holden noted. So, Blackwood wasn't necessarily saying he didn't believe what he'd uttered. Then again, Holden would have been a fool to assume otherwise. Pure bloodlines were as prized among the witches as they were among the fae. Even the vampires gave preference to those created genetically, rather than those infected with the vampiric virus later in life. By anyone's standards, Holden was an object worthy of derision, and as such, any kind of apology, however carefully couched, was a novelty. He decided he might as well be gracious in turn.

"Apology accepted."

Blackwood nodded. There was a finality to the gesture that suggested he now considered a box ticked and the matter closed. He confirmed this hypothesis a moment later with another abrupt change of subject.

"Your captain shared with me your comments on these murders. Your deductions regarding the time delay were insightful."

"Oh. Thanks." Holden cleared his throat. Despite the liquid gold he'd just consumed, it still felt dry and tight. "Think you'll be able to tell who cast the spell?"

"Perhaps."

An awkward silence fell in which Blackwood studied Holden while Holden tried not to squirm under his piercing gaze. Holden was used to finding himself the subject of intense observation. Sometimes those gazes were merely curious. More often than not they were openly hostile. Blackwood's regard, however, felt different. Holden got the uncomfortable impression Blackwood was not cataloguing his external appearance but rather staring directly into his soul. He shivered, and Blackwood glanced away.

"Well, it's late. Your captain sent the items I requested, so I have a long night ahead of me."

"You won't leave it till morning?"

"Considering there have been three murders in my community already, I assumed I should carry out the task with a degree of urgency." The tone was sharp and carried a hint of sarcasm, but Holden thought he also caught the shadow of a grimace. More likely he'd only imagined the expression, though, because now Blackwood looked neutrally stern, staring at him pointedly.

"Oh. Right. Of course. I'll go, sir." Holden turned, only to pause. Was he supposed to wander out on his own? Should he await an escort? What was the correct protocol? They'd doubtless covered it in one of the long, tedious lessons he'd sat through in his youth, but he'd not had to worry about those for years, and the answer had slipped his mind.

He half twisted back toward Blackwood, in time to see his host tug on a tapestry-clad bell pull. James must have been close by, because the library door opened almost at once.

"Show Mr Fay out, thank you, James. No. Wait." Blackwood focused on Holden. "I will attend you at your office at nine sharp tomorrow morning. I trust you'll be in by then?"

"You're coming to the office?" The words came out with more of an attached squeak than Holden would have wished, but Blackwood had, once again, taken him by surprise.

"Would you rather I didn't share anything I learn overnight?"

Holden struggled to form a response. What was wrong with him? He couldn't even string together a simple sentence. Did Blackwood have to gaze at him so keenly? It was discomforting and distracting. "No. Yes. I mean—"

"Look." Blackwood shook his head, finally breaking eye contact. "Your captain wants us to liaise on this, so we may as well make the best of it, however awkward it is. I trust nine will suit?"

"Yeah." Had that sounded rude? He decided he'd better try again. "Uh...yes, sir."

Should he bow? Maybe he should. Or was that too much? He dipped into a basic fae courtly genuflection—nothing too elaborate. But apparently it had been overkill, because Blackwood rolled his eyes.

"Oh, by the powers, you're more servile than my servants! I prefer respect to grovelling, especially during a collaboration—even an enforced one. I will call you Mr Fay, and you will address me as Mr Blackwood. Yes?"

The commanding tone sent an unexpected tremor through Holden. "Yes, sir."

Blackwood grimaced.

Holden tried again. "Yes, Mr Blackwood." The syllables felt foreign and heavy on Holden's tongue, but he willed them out.

"Better. Very well then. I will see you in the morning. Goodnight, Mr Fay." With that, Blackwood turned his back and strolled toward his desk.

James coughed softly and gestured to the door, and Holden fled the room. His pulse was racing, and he had no idea why. He'd had worse meetings. In light of some of them, this one could almost be termed a success. There'd been no open insults, and he'd scraped by on his responses, for the most part. Why, then, was he so tense? And why was he sweating?

The cool night air worked like a slap to the face, and he stood on the front steps for a moment, letting it wash over him, calming his frantically beating heart. An hour ago he'd been all set to up sticks and, essentially, run away. Now it looked as if he would be staying, at least in the short term. Blackwood expected to see him tomorrow. He guessed that meant he would be returning to work after all.

Chapter Eight

HOLDEN ARRIVED AT the office early. He was waiting outside when security unlocked the doors. The guard looked at him askance but said nothing, and Holden proceeded upstairs. It was strange to find the room so empty and silent, instead of the cacophony and general bustle that usually greeted him. Today, however, he'd wanted to be in place before anyone else. Normally, crossing the floor to his desk in the far corner was akin to running a gauntlet, and that was the last thing he needed when Blackwood's imminent appearance on the scene was already sending his tension levels through the roof. He hoped, by being in situ when the others walked in, he would avoid any unpleasantness. If he kept his head down and addressed no one, he trusted they would leave him alone.

His plan worked.

Owens was the first to enter. He sensed her looking his way and feared she might approach, but she seemed to think better of it and veered left into her office instead. The rest of the team cast cursory glances in his direction and then ignored him, and that peace lasted until nine a.m.

Blackwood arrived as the hour struck. Such precision seemed magical, and given that Blackwood was a powerful witch, it possibly was. Or else it was a matter of simple, old-fashioned punctuality. Before the final chime sounded from the office clock, in he strode, bringing sudden silence in his wake. Holden's breath hitched. Blackwood wore one of his customary, perfectly fitted suits, and the sight was, quite literally, breathtaking. Some men looked as good in suits as others looked naked—and Blackwood was most definitely a member of that hallowed group. It was enough to make blood rush to Holden's face and groin.

Immediately, he cursed himself for a fool. Blackwood already looked down his nose at him. The last thing Holden needed was to make matters worse by revealing a ridiculous sexual attraction. Not that he thought Blackwood would be in the least bit surprised. After all, the entire world was in lust with Valerius Blackwood. Anyone who'd ever seen him, whether in the flesh or merely in a photograph or on TV, succumbed. But this was work; this was serious, and Holden needed to remember that. No matter if he'd been awake half the night, unable to tear Blackwood from his thoughts. He was here to solve a murder, not sigh over a man who never in a million years would view him in the same way, who had already made clear his revulsion.

Seemingly oblivious to the stares, and the mood shift within the room, Blackwood focused on Holden and proceeded toward him at a brisk, determined pace.

"Good morning, Mr Fay. Where can we speak?"

"Oh...uh." *By the Fates, get it together, you moron.* "The interview room?" Holden gestured to the door on his right.

"Good."

Blackwood headed in that direction, and Holden grabbed a notepad and pen from his desk and scrambled to follow.

"Shut the door, if you please."

Holden obeyed and then stood there at a loss. Blackwood had not taken a seat; he strode to the window and now looked out over the city. One hand was in his pocket, the other hanging loosely at his side. His back was straight. However, Holden thought he detected a hint of tension in his shoulders. It was a pose at once both relaxed and yet poised for action. Was he awaiting an invitation to be seated? Did he prefer to conduct the conversation standing? Did that imply Holden shouldn't sit either? Under these circumstances, would it be considered an insult if he took a seat while Blackwood stood? He reminded himself that Blackwood was neither a king nor a god...but he may as well have been.

Blackwood turned, and for a moment, Holden was caught in another of those unfathomable stares, but then Blackwood motioned to the table and chairs. "Shall we?"

He waited until Holden sat. Then he popped open the button on his suit jacket and pulled out the other chair, which he proceeded to slide into with far more grace than Holden believed the action warranted.

"I thought it best for us to speak in private. Constant stares and whispers from every direction are so distracting."

"I didn't think you noticed them."

The words were out before Holden could stop himself. He feared he'd committed a major faux pas, but instead of a frown, Blackwood offered a wry smile. The twist of his lips softened his face, making him appear less imposing.

"Of course I notice them. I simply do my best to ignore them. When faced with the same reactions day in and day out, there's little else to do but feign indifference.

It becomes second nature. But it's never fully effective. Shields are only as strong as you make them."

Hearing Blackwood's explanation, Holden began to wonder how much of Blackwood's supposed hauteur was actually due to that mask of indifference. He supposed, in some ways, he and Blackwood were in similar positions, though for very different reasons. One might even say Holden had it easier. Unlike Blackwood, he only had to worry about everyday interactions. He didn't also have the press (both human and supernatural) dogging his steps.

Holden nodded. "Yeah. I know what you mean."

"Yes, Mr Fay, I rather imagine you do."

A contemplative expression crossed Blackwood's face. Their eyes met, and for the first time since Blackwood's abrupt exit from the crime scene, Holden didn't feel the need to flinch at the contact. That was a mixed blessing, however, as it then took extreme effort to wrench his gaze away from those perfect dark lashes and deep chocolate-coloured irises. When he finally managed it, he focused instead on Blackwood's tie—charcoal silk decorated with hypnotic crimson swirls. The silver tiepin holding it in place bore the familiar Blackwood crest.

"So, did you find out anything useful last night?" Fates! That had sounded too abrupt and rude, hadn't it? "I mean...I hope you weren't kept up too late."

"Yes and no." Blackwood relaxed in his seat. He propped his elbows on the armrests and steepled his long, slender fingers. "I can tell you which spell they used to seal the rooms—a very beautiful, archaic bit of magic that holds matter in a form of stasis until disturbed—but I cannot yet identify who worked the charm. A witch, as you doubtless know, channels all their power from the world around them, drawing what they need for each magical act. Therefore, little of the caster's essence exists in the spell to act as a marker."

Holden slumped. "So, it's hopeless." Maybe he would still be leaving town after all. If this was another dead end, he didn't see how the investigation could possibly progress.

"Not entirely. Now that I've established which spell was used, I can devise a way to check for more of them. That will alert you to any as yet undiscovered victims—although, I certainly hope there are none. In addition, it may be worthwhile interviewing those London witches who possess sufficient power to perform such magic. I can provide a list of names and set up meetings. It's an advanced bit of spellcraft, so while there will be a few candidates, the list will not be excessively long."

Holden's spirits rose. He couldn't go to Owens with a definite suspect, but this still constituted a significant step forward in the investigation. If Blackwood could help them narrow the field, perhaps there was hope of nabbing this guy before he struck again.

"That would be awesome. I mean, thank you, si—Mr Blackwood."

Although it seemed marginally inappropriate, Holden grinned, enthused by this progress, and to his surprise, Blackwood returned the smile. But only for an instant. His lips had barely tugged upward before a cloud passed behind his eyes and his mask of neutrality returned. For a fleeting moment, they'd shared something. But now it was gone.

Blackwood rose sleekly, rebuttoning his suit jacket with a practiced hand. Holden, meanwhile, stumbled up and out of his own chair. He rushed to get the door, holding it open for Blackwood, who passed through with a terse nod of thanks. Outside the interview room, Holden was uncertain once again. Should he show Blackwood out, or would walking him to the lifts be too much? Luckily, Blackwood freed him from this dilemma by halting abruptly in the middle of the office and spinning to face him.

"Come to my house tomorrow, Mr Fay. I should have something for you by midday, so shall we say twelve thirty? My cook will prepare luncheon."

Blackwood made no attempt to keep his words low, and they carried through the almost-silent room. Immediately, Holden sensed all eyes not already looking their way turn upon them, and he flushed. Blackwood maintained his usual cool exterior, betraying no sign that he was even aware of the scrutiny. Holden wondered how he did it. It was a trick he would dearly love to learn.

Clearly Blackwood required no response to his invitation—order?—because without waiting for one, he departed, leaving Holden to stare at the still-swinging door for several seconds before he finally pulled himself together and headed into Owens's office to share the latest developments.

The news they would soon be able to detect other instances of the same magic was momentous, and Holden knew that should have been his primary concern. However, he couldn't help his thoughts constantly straying, instead, to the fact he would be eating lunch with Valerius Blackwood tomorrow.

Chapter Nine

WHEN THE NEXT day dawned, Holden ensured he arrived punctually for his lunchtime appointment. He'd dug out his smartest shirt and tie for the occasion. In fact, it was his only tie, so it would have to do. The accompanying black suit was off the rack and nearly nine years old. Holden could count on one hand the number of times he'd worn it, the answer being once: to his job interview at the Fellowship. It sort of still fit. As long as he left the jacket undone and didn't flex his shoulders too much, it should be okay. Considering he was joining Blackwood for a meal, it hadn't seemed right to arrive in his customary jeans and T-shirt. He didn't suppose Blackwood gave two figs about what he was wearing. Yet, as always, his sense of protocol prevailed. If that meant two or three hours of minor personal discomfort, so be it. Not everyone could afford to fill a wardrobe with bespoke suits and silk ties, and Holden had done the best he could under the circumstances.

James opened the front door, and Holden followed him into the house. This time, instead of heading for the library, James took him to a room on the other side of the staircase. He knocked, as before, but upon receiving a command to enter, he merely nodded brusquely at Holden, then departed. Left alone, Holden reached for the ornate brass handle and pushed the door open.

The room into which he stepped was like none he'd ever seen. Benches lined one wall, while shelves and drawered units occupied every other side of the square space. In the centre of the room stood a vast workbench, half wood and half steel, its surface littered with bottles and flasks. A flame burned below one beaker, in which brown contents bubbled. A human would think this a rich eccentric's pet science project, but Holden could feel the power in the air. Like a dense transparent cloud, it tickled against his skin. Meanwhile, the strong scent of mingled herbs, spices, and flowers, though not strictly unpleasant, was cloying. When he breathed in, it caught at the back of his throat.

Blackwood stood at the workbench. Even in here, thus employed, he was meticulously dressed, the only concession a linen apron to protect his suit from splashes. An ancient-looking tome lay open before him. Its pages were rough and uneven, the ink frequently blotched. Holden recognised a few words of Latin before Blackwood flipped the leather cover closed.

"Mr Fay, you arrive in good time. I am just completing the spell to find any further instances of that sealing magic. It needs about half an hour to simmer, so let's eat while we wait."

He stripped off his apron, then led the way back to the entrance hall, before proceeding into one of the front two chambers. The dining room—for such it was—was a picture of Georgian elegance, from its decoration to its furnishings. Two places were set at the table, and the sideboard brimmed with dishes and platters. So much food! Even Holden, with his oft-giant appetite, knew that the two of them would never clear it all, no matter how hungry they were.

"Please help yourself." Blackwood swept his arm toward the feast. "I realised after I left your office yesterday I had omitted to ask what you liked. Therefore, I took the liberty of ordering a little of everything, much to my cook's delight, since she and the rest of the staff will get the leftovers." Suddenly he froze, a look of horror passing over his face. "By the powers, you do eat, don't you? Forgive me. I should have thought to check. I never considered the fact that you might, well...require a liquid diet."

"No, no. It's fine," Holden hastened to assure him, discomforted by Blackwood's embarrassment. "I can survive on blood if I have to, but I prefer proper food."

"Ah. Good," Blackwood said in a curt manner Holden interpreted as relief. "Shall we, then?"

Blackwood still made no move to partake of the feast, so Holden guessed it was a "guests first" kind of etiquette. He picked up his plate and approached the buffet. He was starving, and everything looked delicious, but he only selected a slice of bread and some cold meats and cheeses. Having already dealt with the blood versus solids debate, he didn't now want to come across as a glutton. After he stepped back, Blackwood made his selections, and together they repaired to the table.

For a while, they ate in silence. However, once Holden finished his relatively meagre repast, his gaze drifted back to the sideboard, inextricably drawn to the collection of cakes he'd studiously ignored until now.

"You're welcome to more. No need to stand on ceremony."

Blackwood's tone was politely neutral, and Holden cringed inwardly. Nevertheless, he managed a tight smile. "Thanks. Maybe a little."

He forced himself to stay true to his word and only selected two small cake slices. Blackwood didn't rise for seconds, but he did reach for the silver teapot set between them and poured them each a full cup.

The cakes were sublime. It took all Holden's restraint to eat them carefully with a cake fork, rather than wolfing them down. Nonetheless, he still got cream all over his lips and had to lick away the vestiges when he was done. He could have eaten more, but present company excluded such uncouth behaviour. His throat was dry now, though, so he gulped his first cup of tea and poured himself another. Even the damned tea was somehow fuller and more flavoursome than the store-brand teabags he bought in bulk from the supermarket. Suddenly fearful of having made another social misstep with his vigorous slurping, Holden briefly glanced up to judge his host's reaction to his dining-table manners.

Blackwood wasn't looking Holden's way, however; he was occupied with his own beverage. He held his tea cup just so, the little finger not quite extended, but almost. Then he raised the delicate bone china to take a sip. Holden followed the movement—the parting of Blackwood's lips, the bob of his Adam's apple as he swallowed. Their eyes met as Blackwood lowered the cup, and Holden immediately looked away.

"So, Mr Fay. If we are to break bread together, I suppose we should observe a few social niceties. Tell me about yourself."

"Holden," Holden said impulsively. Hearing himself addressed as Mr Fay felt...wrong.

Blackwood blinked. "I beg your pardon?"

"No one ever calls me Mr Fay. Everyone just says Holden." *Or halfen scum, filth, half-breed...*

"Holden." Blackwood rolled the word around on his tongue. The timbre of his smooth baritone made Holden shiver, but in a pleasant way. "And Cadeyrn is your father, is he not?"

Holden swallowed, and all remnants of the relaxed contentment he'd experienced a moment ago, however briefly, vanished in a figurative puff of smoke. "Yes."

He stiffened, preparing himself for whatever was coming next. Were they really going to open this can of worms over tea and cake? Small talk was bad enough in generic terms. Did Blackwood have to bring up his parentage?

"Hmm. A good fellow, on the whole. Though rather...intransient at times."

"I'd have gone with pig-headed."

Holden regretted the words as soon as they left his mouth. He'd not been brought up to disparage his parents, period, and certainly not in public. Yet, he couldn't deny saying what he really felt for a change had felt good. Better than good—freeing, a release. Blackwood's faint smile could have expressed approval or polite condemnation; Holden didn't know him well enough to judge.

"I remember your mother too," Blackwood continued, choosing not to respond to Holden's comment. "I was only about five when I met her, but it's hard to forget such beauty. She left a lasting impression, even on one so young. I see something of my memory of her in your eyes."

Holden shuffled in his seat. In many ways, talking of his mother was worse than speaking about his father. "I'll have to take your word for it. I never met her."

"Of course not." A brief pause. "Forgive me. That was thoughtless."

Silence fell as both reached for their tea cups. Holden's was empty, but he raised it to his lips anyway and pretended to drink. The charade of doing so was preferable to having to find something to say, or to decide where to fix his gaze.

Finally, Blackwood set down his cup and glanced at his watch. "Well, that spell should have finished brewing by now. Shall we go?"

Holden nodded, relieved to escape the increasingly awkward nonconversation and embarrassed tension.

Back in the workroom, he stood by while Blackwood turned off the Bunsen burner and hummed and hawed over the beaker, stirring the mixture within. There was something beautiful about the way he worked. The subtle tilt of his head and the soft furrowing of his brow lent him an academic, studious air. Meanwhile, it was a joy to follow each deft movement of his hands, to see those slender, agile fingers caress the side of the glass beaker or gently grip the stirring rod. Holden could have silently observed him for hours and never grown bored. It was like glimpsing a living work of art.

"Yes, this should work," Blackwood said suddenly, jolting Holden from his contemplations. He waved toward a rolled document lying atop one of the nearby benches. "Bring me that city map, would you?"

Holden passed Blackwood the A3 print, and Blackwood spread it across the steel part of the workbench, pinning down the corners with whatever items of scientific paraphernalia came to hand. He lifted the beaker containing the mixture, only to pause and glance at Holden.

"This is a variant of fire magic. I don't expect any major reactions, but you may want to take a step back." He flashed a brief smile. "Just in case, mind. I don't want to singe you."

Holden moved a good two paces from the table. "How does it work?"

"Hopefully the liquid will simply soak the map. That means there are no more sealing spells in existence at present. If there *is* another, a flame will mark the spot."

Holden took a third step back—just in case, as Blackwood had said—and Blackwood tilted the beaker. The potion splashed onto the paper, and a second later there followed a bright, red-orange flash that forced Holden to shield his eyes. When he looked back, a pinpoint flame rose from the map. It was both burning and not burning, for though he could clearly see the fire, the paper didn't smoulder or char. Holden's knowledge of witchcraft was sufficient to tell that this was a neat piece of magic. Then again, Blackwood was a coven head, and you didn't reach a position of authority like that without being the best of the best.

After a few moments, the flame winked out, and Holden approached the table and leaned over the map. The paper was bone dry, as if never doused in liquid, and there was a tidy, petite black dot where the flame had been, marking a midway point along a street in the middle of Westminster.

He glanced up at Blackwood. "Does that mean what I think it means?"

Blackwood's expression was grim. "We need to go at once. It's highly likely another murder scene awaits us." He turned sharply and strode toward the door, his posture stiff.

"Shouldn't we phone Owens?" Holden called, scurrying after him.

"Do it on the way. We won't be able to pinpoint the exact house until we get to the street anyway."

Chapter Ten

WHEN THEY ARRIVED at the place the flame had indicated, Holden was confused. The road seemed even longer than he recollected from looking at the map. Had the flame's position in the middle of the road been simple chance, or neatness, or was it really the middle house they were after, and if the latter, did that mean they had to count them and hope there was an odd number?

Blackwood evidenced none of Holden's hesitation. He led the way down the street with a purposeful stride, before stopping abruptly in front of one of the entrances within the uniform row of red-brick, terraced apartments.

"Here."

Holden turned to face Blackwood, more than a little in awe. "How do you know?"

"Can't you feel it?"

Holden squinted at the doorway. As he focused, he realised that, yes, he *could* sense some form of magic within, but he never would have noticed it if Blackwood hadn't highlighted the place. "It's faint."

"That's intentional. It truly is a clever piece of spellcraft. Only an adept witch would notice it, or an older fae. Although, I imagine most of the fae would likely just ignore it, deeming it beneath their attention."

Blackwood started toward the door.

"Where are you going?" Holden called after him, momentarily forgetting politeness in his surprise. He quickly corrected his manner. "What I mean is, shouldn't we wait for Owens and the others? They'll be here soon."

Blackwood sighed and turned back. "I very much doubt the killer is still present, if that's what concerns you. That would be sloppy, and he's been anything but careless so far. If there proves to be a body inside, what harm can the corpse do us?" He glanced over his shoulder, toward the door. "In any case, it would be most useful if I could assess the spell at the moment it's broken, before too many others traipse through the scene, muddying the waters, so to speak."

In the back of his mind, Holden registered the terminology. It must have been Blackwood who'd upset Owens earlier with a similarly phrased comment. In other circumstances, he might have smiled, but he had weightier matters to ponder at present.

In truth, he was torn. Protocol dictated they should hold back. Nonetheless, Blackwood's need to see an uncontaminated crime scene made perfect sense. Owens had called upon Blackwood for this very purpose, so it seemed wrong to hinder him on that front. Then there was the added fact that Blackwood's high standing in the supernatural community rendered his word almost law. Under these circumstances and considerations, a compromise seemed in order.

"Very well, Mr Blackwood. We'll go in. But I should lead the way...just in case."

In case of what, he wasn't certain. All he knew was that, as far as the Fellowship was concerned, he was in charge of this situation. Therefore, it seemed only right that he should enter an unknown environment ahead of any civilians, no matter how powerful and important said civilians might be. The last thing he wanted was an argument, though, so he was relieved when Blackwood stepped aside without complaint, saying, "After you, then, Holden."

They approached the front door, and Holden rested his fingertips against the lock, seeking to grasp the mechanism with strands of energy. It took longer than he would have liked, considering his audience, but finally the tongue clicked back and the door opened.

Inside, there was no sign of life. That was to be expected, however, since it was the middle of the day and most of the residents were probably civil servants or other office workers. With the building's brick walls no longer acting as a barrier, the scent of magic was stronger, now noticeable to the vampire in Holden as well as the fae. He followed his nose to a nearby doorway and glanced back at Blackwood for confirmation.

"Here?"

"Indeed."

"Ready?"

Blackwood gave a curt nod.

This lock was, thankfully, simpler than the one on the street entrance, and it only took Holden a few seconds to work it undone. The lounge room visible beyond the now-open door was neat, yet homely, its owner most likely a man, based on the choice of furnishings and the collection of magazines Holden saw lying atop the coffee table. There was no sign of a body yet. However, there were other rooms still to explore. Holden called out a greeting but received no answer. Hearing nothing stir within, he took a step forward, crossing the threshold.

Something whizzed through the air, heading straight for him. Instinctively, he hunched over and raised his arms to shield his face, squeezing his eyes shut. Behind him, Blackwood yelled. It was a single word, but Holden couldn't make it out above the sudden pounding of blood in his ears.

Impact should have been imminent, but when nothing struck him, Holden inched his arms away from his face and forced his eyes open. He leaped back with a yelp at the sight of a sizeable iron dart, whose sharp point was mere centimetres from his head. It took him a couple of seconds to process that it was stationary and posed no threat.

"By the Fates!"

"An unexpected defence mechanism." Blackwood eased around Holden, his arm extended, palm outward. It was his magic holding the weapon in place. "It must have been set to go off if someone other than the owner opened the door." He murmured a few words of Latin, then slowly lowered his arm. The dart remained suspended. "Installing a lethal security measure such as this contravenes several Fellowship laws pertaining to the use of magic as a weapon. If this witch *isn't* already dead, he'll be in serious trouble." He turned his earnest gaze upon Holden. "Are you all right?"

"You saved me." Holden stared at Blackwood, the enormity of what had happened finally sinking in. "That means I owe you a blood debt."

The fae took blood debts most seriously; Blackwood would know that. In speaking the words, Holden was effectively binding himself to Blackwood until the debt was paid. It was no small thing, yet he couldn't ignore it and hope to keep his honour. Not that making good on this particular debt would be a hardship. Of all the people to whom he could have been so bound, he was glad it was Blackwood. Their first meeting may have been fraught, but since then things had changed between them in a way Holden never would have expected and still struggled to believe.

He knelt and offered Blackwood his hand, palm up, in the traditional manner. However, rather than performing his part in the ceremony, Blackwood shook his head.

"I'm the one who insisted we enter without waiting for your team. I exposed you to danger. Therefore, there is no debt." He paused. "I'm assuming it wouldn't have killed you, anyway, given your vampire blood, even though it's iron?" He waited for Holden's nod. "So I thought. Although, I guess you're lucky my reflexes are so keen."

He flashed a warm smile—the most natural Holden had seen from him. It opened up his face, lightening his brow like a burst of sunlight through the clouds. Holden returned it, even as his legs threatened to turn to jelly.

Blackwood reached down, grasped Holden's forearm, and tugged him back to his feet. They stood only inches apart, looking into each other's eyes. The air between them was so charged Holden could have sworn he felt it sizzle against his skin.

"Holden, I—" Blackwood said, at the same time as Holden began, "Mr Blackwood, you—"

"Just what the fuck is going on here?"

Owens marched toward them, her expression stormy, and her sudden arrival saved Holden from having to think of a suitable response to Blackwood's actions. Aside from saving his eye, Blackwood had released him from a serious debt as if it were nothing. Holden should have felt gratitude—he *was* grateful—but he also experienced niggling uncertainty. Had Blackwood cancelled the debt because he believed Holden had nothing useful to offer? But what, then, had that smile meant? And what was it that had just passed between them? He was aware that Owens was still staring at him, waiting, and knew he needed to supply a suitable response, but all he could do was gape.

"We have dismantled a rather vicious booby trap, Captain Owens," Blackwood said, taking the lead, drawing Owens's attention. He gestured to the dart that still hovered in the air. "Would you happen to have an evidence bag for this, so I can let it go? I would suggest this is the work of the occupant, not the killer, since he's never employed such methods before. However, I assume you'll want to check and would prefer if I didn't just drop it onto the floor."

With the projectile bagged and logged, they proceeded into the apartment. No further unexpected assaults took place, and it wasn't long before they located the body in the adjacent kitchen. However, this time, things were different.

Today's victim lay crumpled against the kitchen cabinets, the blood splatter around him severe. A broken mug, its contents spilled over the counter, and a smashed cupboard door indicated a fight. Meanwhile, the chest wound lacked the neat incisions they'd seen on other victims. The knife had slipped off course several times, no doubt as a result of the victim's struggles.

It made an interesting comparison with the earlier scenes. In those, Holden had considered the killer cool and detached. It was tempting to view this one as an escalation to something more passion-driven, but Holden didn't think that was right. He saw no anger or excitement in the mess here. Instead, he saw desperation, even despair. What did that mean? Was the killer weary of his work? Would he now cease? Or would whatever had happened here spur him on?

After a collective drawn breath as everyone took in the scene, the team members immediately set about their respective tasks, including Holden, who sampled the blood. He got nothing from it, but by now neither he nor Owens were surprised about that.

Blackwood had paced from room to room amidst the bustle, but now he approached. Holden thought he looked pale, but he supposed anyone would if they were unused to such grisly sights. This scene was certainly bloodier than the last, and Blackwood had confessed that even the first experience had upset him.

"I assume Mr Fay has apprised you of the events that led us here?" he said, addressing Owens, who rose from her crouch beside the body.

"He has."

"Excellent. Unfortunately, I have nothing new to add." He gave an elegant, apologetic shrug. "I had hoped to obtain a better trace on the spell's caster by being the first to enter, but this witch remains elusive. I will continue to look into the matter, liaising with the other London covens. However, I doubt my presence at these crime scenes will be of any further value, and to be honest, I would prefer not to see them if we derive no benefit from the viewing."

Holden noted that he'd been right about the bloody scene upsetting Blackwood. He was impressed, though, that Blackwood was man enough to admit as much and bow out, rather than putting on a brave face in an attempt to appear macho.

"Of course. I quite understand, Mr Blackwood," Owens responded. "We're grateful for all your help." She offered her hand, which Blackwood shook. "May we contact you if we have any further questions?"

"Naturally. I'm always happy to assist the Fellowship in any way I can, especially as it concerns the well-being of my people." He turned to Holden and extended his hand, raising his voice as he said, "Goodbye, Mr Fay. Were it not for the difficult circumstances of our meeting, I would say it has been a pleasure. My regards to your father."

Blackwood's grip was firm and his palm achingly warm. Witches tended to run a little hotter than humans, and vampires colder, so the discrepancy was not unusual. However, Holden didn't think that was the sole reason for the shudder that passed through him. For an instant, he met Blackwood's gaze and thought he glimpsed a flash of...something behind Blackwood's eyes, but then it was gone, and Blackwood's hand along with it.

Once Blackwood departed, Owens pulled Holden aside. On the pretence of a cigarette break, she led him out onto the street, away from the others.

"I never would have believed it had I not seen it with my own two eyes, but you must have done something to impress Valerius Blackwood, because he just did you a solid favour."

"I know. If he'd not acted so swiftly, that dart would've gone right through my eye. I'd have been half-blind for weeks, if not months." Vampire blood gave Holden many medical advantages, including immunity from the iron allergy that affected all fae, but supernatural healing of major wounds could still take a long time and used up a lot of energy.

"Really? In that case, it looks like you owe him twice over."

"Twice?"

"Blackwood just publically acknowledged you. He shook your hand and addressed you in respectful, friendly terms."

"So?" Holden squirmed.

Fates! Had Owens noticed his reaction to that simple handshake? Had the others? Was she making fun of his infatuation? It was laughable, given how untenable the idea of him and Blackwood was. That didn't mean he appreciated anyone rubbing it in.

"So? What a thing to say! Blackwood is an influencer, Holden. Or have you been living under a stone? What he says goes, and he treated you with respect. In practical terms, you just took a step up the social ladder. You know, perhaps better than anyone, appearances matter. They always have and they always will. And Blackwood has marked you as worthy of attention." She took a single, long drag on her cigarette, then stubbed it out. "Now, get back in there and help me solve these fucking murders before the Council wails on our arses."

Chapter Eleven

TO HOLDEN'S SURPRISE, Owens was right. The sun had barely set that evening before Raoul called.

"Did Blackwood really shake your hand?"

"Hello to you too. Yeah, he did. But how'd you know that?"

"It's all anyone's talking about. I woke to find my social media feeds full of it."

"It's on social media?" Holden's voice came out as a squawk, and he coughed to clear his throat.

"Oh, only in some key private groups." Raoul's laugh seemed forced, and he quickly pressed on. "But tell me... What did you have to do in exchange?"

"What do you mean?"

"Blackwood isn't known for handing out free favours. He's his father's son, and with that family, it's always a case of quid pro quo. He must have asked you for something."

"Nothing." Holden bristled. "In fact, as well as the handshake, he rescued me from potential eyeball impalement and declined the blood debt when I acknowledged it."

Raoul sucked in a breath. "Well, be careful, Hol. He may contact you with a demand. He is something of a collector."

"Of artworks? First editions? Antiques? I don't own any of those sorts of things." He was being deliberately obtuse; he knew what Raoul meant. Nevertheless, the tone of the conversation was starting to irk him.

"You know that's not what I meant. He has a reputation."

"And you don't? Honestly, Raoul, I would almost think you were jealous."

There was a sharp pause. Then Raoul chuckled, and this time it sounded natural.

"Maybe I am, at that. I'm not used to having to share you."

"It was one handshake. It's not like we announced our engagement. Besides, Blackwood's preference is for gathering individuals with raw talent around him. His little clique only includes the best of the best, and I'm as untalented as they come." He knew he should stop there, but he couldn't resist stirring the pot a little. It was a novel situation to have someone express jealousy over him. He wanted to revel in it, if only for a moment. "That said, if he asked me out, I wouldn't turn him down."

He spoke the words as if they were a joke, but of course, they were true, and he experienced a twinge of guilt, wishing he'd never brought it up. Luckily, Raoul didn't notice anything amiss in his tone and appeared to take his comments in good humour.

"Stop! Stop! I can't stand any more. I feel the need to go caveman and reassert my prior claim. How would you feel about having some company tonight? If you can tear yourself away from work, Mr Lead Investigator."

Holden could hear the grin in Raoul's voice and mirrored it. "Well, we must remember that old 'all work and no play' adage. I reckon I can spare you an hour or two from my busy schedule, and I'm due a dinner break. I always do my best thinking when suitably stuffed."

THE PROPOSED TWO hours morphed into four. But they were well spent, and by the time Raoul departed, Holden was wide awake despite how late it was. Too hyped even to contemplate heading to bed in the sleeping sense, he logged onto the Fellowship's secure server and reviewed the photos and reports from the crime scene.

Most of the information matched closely with that of the previous murders. However, those few differences plagued him. Owens was doubtless correct in her initial, on-scene assessment that the position of the body was because this victim had fought back. But why this guy and not the others? Holden was certain there was more to it than that. The scene had looked sloppier than the older ones, as if the killer had been uncertain of what he was doing.

The reason why hit him in a flash: because they weren't older scenes. Westminster wasn't the last of the quartet but the first. The victim had put up more resistance than the killer had anticipated. In future endeavours, he'd eliminated that issue by subduing them effectively ahead of completing his work.

First kills were important in so many ways. Technically, this killer's firsts were possibly those he'd enacted among the humans in Whitechapel, but Holden still wasn't certain on that point. And even if they were by the same hand, he doubted the murderer would view them in the same light as the witch killings. Of all the victims so far, this one was the most likely to have had a personal link to his attacker. It was always easier to start something on home turf, familiarity breeding composure. They needed to do a full background check on this victim's life, and question everyone close to him. Their killer could very well be within that pool. Maybe they could cross-check against the list Blackwood would be sending.

Holden was reaching for his mobile, intending to call Owens, when something else in the crime scene photograph caught his attention. He set aside the phone and zoomed in on the image, bringing the item into focus centre-screen.

There, beneath the kitchen cupboard door, close to the body, was a tiny carving. Almost invisible, he'd not have spotted it if the splattered blood hadn't seeped into the knife marks. It was some kind of symbol or glyph—that much was obvious—but not one he recognised. Then again, always conscious of his meagre magical skills, Holden had dropped out of such studies at an early age, and his father, ashamed of his son's incompetence, had allowed it.

Owens might know more, as might—Fates forbid—someone like Draper. Holden's thoughts strayed to Valerius Blackwood. *He* would certainly recognise the sign, and he had agreed the Fellowship could contact him with any further questions. The memory of the warmth of Blackwood's hand grasping his overcame Holden for a moment, but then he rallied his common sense and brushed it aside. Any contact with Blackwood would be strictly business. Blackwood may have saved his sight and given him a social boost, but the former had been an instinctive reaction in the face of danger, with the latter representing either an unconscious action or, at best, Blackwood's charitable deed for the week. Holden knew the difference between reality and a fairy tale. They might dwell in a supernatural world, but it was still beyond the possibilities of magic for a guy like Blackwood to end up with a guy like him. Not even illegal love potions were *that* strong.

Forcing his mind back to the matter at hand, Holden glanced at the time stamp on his phone screen. It was far later—or rather earlier—than he'd thought, making it impossible to call anyone at present. Owens had a twenty-four seven rationale when it came to work, yet he didn't think she'd appreciate a wake-up call at this hour for anything less than a full-scale emergency, and while his news was important, a short delay wasn't likely to make any difference to the case. He considered trying to get a little shut-eye himself. However, he decided it was pointless. By the time he nodded off, he'd have to rise again. Sleep was overrated anyway.

A new thought occurred to him, and he clicked out of the current album and into that of the previous crime scene. He scoured the photos taken of and around the body. At first he thought his theory disproven, but then he found it.

There, carved low down on one of the bedposts, almost invisible, was another sigil. Only one photo had caught that section of post in frame, and the angle was awkward, but the glyph was just discernible. Hopefully they could get further access to the bed and acquire additional shots.

Spurred on by this new discovery, Holden reviewed the remaining two files. One he found straightaway; the other required perseverance and some epic swearing before he glimpsed it carved into the leg of a coffee table. He scrawled all four symbols onto the back of that night's takeaway receipt and studied what he'd found. The carvings were different from one another, yet they shared a distinct style that suggested they belonged together.

Holden was both elated and perplexed. As if there weren't already sufficient unanswered questions about these cases, he'd now added an additional layer of intrigue. Or maybe not. Perhaps this was the final breakthrough that would help them catch the bastard. If they could work out what these symbols meant, it might open up a whole new line of inquiry.

A glance at the clock revealed that the hour was now a suitable one at which to call, so Holden retrieved his phone and hovered his thumb over the number pad. Once again, Blackwood shimmered through his thoughts, but in the end, it was Owens's line he dialled. He ought to make this official with his captain first. If they needed help deciphering the symbols, they could always call on Blackwood later. He told himself it didn't matter either way, but deep down, he hoped they would require such assistance. Apparently, he had a masochistic streak.

Chapter Twelve

OWENS HAD BEEN both delighted and concerned at Holden's discovery, the symbols adding a definitive ritualistic dimension to the case that set her on edge. She didn't recognise the shapes, but when they shared them with the rest of the team, Draper did.

Although annoyed it had to be Peregrine Draper, of all people, who shed light on the mysterious markings, upon learning their origin, Holden wasn't surprised at Draper's insight. Demon sigils were not something widely studied, due to their dark nature. They'd certainly never been on Holden's curriculum. While they were not exactly forbidden, it was well known that the Fellowship frowned upon any communication with demons, preferring to pretend that such things did not exist. That was probably why it had taken Draper a full twenty-four hours to decide to share his knowledge. Doubtless he'd spent the night considering which would hurt his career most: not sharing intelligence that might help catch the killer or revealing he knew anything about such ominous markings.

As it turned out, his dabbling with demon runes had been cursory at best. A misogynistic bully in adulthood, Draper had likely run with one street gang or another in his teens. Nearly all the younger fae who, like him, had adopted a surname and partially integrated into a human lifestyle had done so at one point or another. Holden could picture Draper and his friends acquiring books on demonology in an effort to look cool and tough. Being cowards at heart, like most bullies, however, Holden imagined they'd never gone so far as to actually attempt any of the rituals. That would explain why Draper knew the markings' provenance but not their exact meaning.

All the renowned scholars of demonology—every one of them a witch—had died years ago, long before Holden's birth. No one openly studied demons now, except from a historical perspective, so the Investigations Team's sole source of information would have to come from old treatises. They'd approached the Council for access to such tomes, only to find themselves stonewalled. According to the Council's head librarian, the Fellowship archives did not hold 'that sort of thing', save for a few highly restricted texts that could not be released—not even for the purposes of a criminal investigation. That left private collections. Thus, Holden found himself once more knocking upon Blackwood's door.

Every coven maintained its own small library of magical knowledge, and enquiries among the nine coven leaders had led them to a handful of extant texts. Holden suspected there were more, but given the almost-illicit nature of the topic, he wasn't surprised that many witches would be reticent about coming forward with any documents. Blackwood had proven the exception to the rule. Although official commentary would have it otherwise, everyone knew his collection rivalled that of the Fellowship in terms of its scope and value, and he'd professed himself happy to throw open his doors and allow them full access, stating that he had several volumes he believed could help them understand the meaning of the glyphs.

Owens had made an appointment with Blackwood for this morning, intending to accompany Holden. However, much to Holden's secret (and guilty) delight, an urgent matter pertaining to one of her other cases had demanded her attention at the last moment, so Holden had set off alone. Well, semi-alone. It depended on whether you counted the kaleidoscope of butterflies merrily aflutter in the pit of his stomach.

The weather had turned miserable of late, a lingering summer finally giving way to a soggy autumn, and Holden hunched his shoulders and raised his jacket collar to keep the rain off his neck as he cut across the square to Blackwood's house.

"Morning, James," he said when the door opened. "I believe Mr Blackwood is expecting me." He was impressed at his even tone, which revealed none of his inner excitement and anxiety at the thought of seeing Blackwood again.

"Indeed, Mr Fay." James glanced down at Holden's muddy trainers and grimaced. "If you'd be so kind as to wipe your feet, sir?"

Holden did as instructed and then trailed James to the library door. He looked behind him a couple of times along the way, relieved when he saw no obvious signs of having left an embarrassing dirt trail in his wake.

Within the library, a fire blazed, the cosy ambience welcome after his gloomy, wet journey. He shivered at the sudden change in temperature. He preferred to blame the tremors on that, rather than the sight of Blackwood, in rolled-up shirt sleeves, bent over a book, his hair sleek and shiny in the firelight and his bare forearms highlighting each move of his beautiful, pianist's fingers.

Blackwood raised his head at Holden's approach.

"Ah, Holden." He flashed a brief smile, before glancing behind Holden to the empty doorway. "Captain Owens is not joining us?"

"She got called away. She sends her apologies. I hope it's no hassle that I'm alone." He was babbling, but he couldn't stop. "I mean, I'm sure you'd rather have Owens. My input—"

"Will be perfectly fine." Blackwood cast a critical eye over him. "You need to have more confidence in yourself, Holden. You are smart, insightful. You have a lot to offer. But others won't see or accept that if you don't project it. Self-confidence is almost more important than ability. Even the illusion helps. Make others believe you can do anything, even if you doubt it inwardly."

"I..."

"Come." Blackwood waved him closer. "I have selected several texts I hope will be of use. All are old and fragile, so I would appreciate you wearing archival gloves to turn the pages. Pull up a chair and we'll get to work. I'm sure we'll manage well enough, just you and me." He suddenly frowned, making Holden halt. "By the powers! What was James thinking, leaving you in that wet coat?" He leaped out of his seat and moved toward the bell pull.

The thought of James coming in to wait on him, as if he were someone of import, was mortifying, and Holden threw out a hand. "Oh, don't worry him. Please. I'll dry out soon enough."

"Take the sopping thing off, at least, before you catch a chill."

Holden turned aside to hide his smile as he shrugged out of his jacket. Blackwood's manners were clearly deeply engrained. Had he paused to think about it, he would have realised Holden's lineage made any such illness impossible. Vampires were not prone to catching chills, or any other infection, whether viral or bacterial.

As he faced front again, Holden felt oddly self-conscious. He remained fully clothed, but the loss of his jacket left him with a strange sense of naked vulnerability. Naturally, he couldn't put it back on—chills aside, he didn't want to drip on any priceless manuscripts—but what should he do with it?

"Here." Blackwood whipped the jacket out of his hands and hung it over the back of the chair closest to the fire. There was an energy about him today Holden hadn't seen before. Or maybe he was imagining it. Blackwood's presence did tend to set his nerves on edge.

"Now, come." Blackwood guided Holden to one of the leather armchairs set close to the desk. His fingertips were like spots of fire where they pressed into Holden's shoulder. "See if you recognise any of these from your crime scenes." He stepped back, taking his burning touch with him.

It took a few seconds to regain his concentration, but once Holden pulled on the pair of white archival gloves Blackwood passed to him and began to turn the pages, he found that the images therein *were* familiar.

"Two of them are here."

"Show me." Blackwood leaned over Holden's chair. His breath tickled the pointy tip of Holden's ear. "Hmm. Turn to the next page, and tell me if you see any others."

Holden did as instructed and immediately spotted the two remaining symbols. "This pair." He hovered his fingers over them, trying not to touch the delicate parchment more than necessary.

"Oh!"

The exclamation, uttered on an exhale, was not spoken in the kind of tone Holden wanted to hear. From Blackwood, in particular, that note of quiet alarm seemed out of place; he was always so self-assured.

"What's wrong? Can you translate the glyphs, Mr Blackwood?"

"Yes. Although, not in the way you mean when you say 'translate'. Each doesn't equal a single word. Rather, their component parts—every line and curve—have meaning. Taken alone, the precise definition of each mark is inconsequential. Together, on the other hand..." Blackwood straightened and strode to the pile of books at the far end of the table. He sorted through them and then returned to Holden's side bearing a leather-bound volume. "What do you know of summonings?"

"I know they're forbidden."

The study of demonology and general communication with demons might be grey areas, legally speaking, but the summoning of a demon into this plane was not. In fact, it was one of only two acts that still carried a potential death sentence—the other being murder. Not that anyone had faced such charges in Holden's lifetime. It was simply one of those archaic laws that no one had bothered to change. The city of London still operated under many rules and regulations that no longer held any value, save as interesting talking points, and the Fellowship's Codex—the rulebook for England's supernatural lcommunity—was no different. What would actually happen to someone found guilty of conducting a summoning in this day and age was anyone's guess.

"Well, apparently its illegality doesn't worry your killer. Look here." Blackwood opened the book to the centre spread and slid the volume in front of Holden. "All four of your symbols feature in this ancient summoning spell."

Blackwood was correct: there they were. Holden made a swift count of the rest.

"Nine in total. Fates!" He glanced up at Blackwood. "Does that mean five more murders?"

"Yes. If my assumptions are correct. Don't take my word as fact, mind. At this stage, it is mere speculation. For all we know, the killer may have stumbled across a book of demon sigils and is carving them for his own amusement, rather than with any purpose. A summoning is a definite possibility, but not yet an irrefutable probability."

"But if it *is* a summoning, what would be the reason for it? Why would anyone want to call a demon?"

Blackwood perched elegantly on the edge of the desk. His thigh brushed Holden's arm for an instant, until Holden drew back. "I would hesitate to hazard a guess. It could be any number of things. However, the old tales generally say that demons have the ability to bestow great power on the one who brings them into this plane."

"You said the person doing this was already a powerful witch. What more power could they need?"

The ghost of a smile crossed Blackwood's face, but it was not an expression of gaiety. "Consider your own position, Holden. Thanks to me, your standing has improved of late. Can you honestly tell me you're satisfied, and you don't want to climb higher?"

Holden considered the question and accepted that Blackwood was right. It wasn't enough. Having gotten a foot in the door, he *did* dream of further advancement, of reaching a stage where no one mocked him for his birth, where they admired him, or at least treated him with true respect. Maybe he could even get to a point where someone like Blackwood would deign to give him a second glance.

He transferred his gaze to the carpet to avoid meeting Blackwood's eyes. "I do want more."

"Of course you do. It's in the nature of every being at our level. The drive for something more than mere survival is what distinguishes us from animals. It is both a gift and a curse." He brushed Holden's sleeve, and when Holden looked up, he caught and held his gaze. "Such desire has the potential to make madmen of us all."

Blackwood's fingers lingered on Holden's arm, and there was something unfathomable in his eyes. The room felt suddenly close. The warmth from the fire, which Holden had welcomed upon arrival, now stifled him. He couldn't breathe. He needed air.

Holden rose so fast he nearly toppled his chair and had to grab the arm to steady it. "I should report back. Can I take that book with me? Owens will want to see it."

Blackwood rose gracefully. "No. I'm afraid I cannot permit the removal of any volumes from this collection. However, we have all the texts here digitally archived—a little project I started a few years ago—so I can email you copies of the relevant pages. Will that suffice?"

"Thanks. Yeah. That would be great."

Holden lunged for his jacket. As he slid his arm into the second sleeve, he twisted and found himself chest to chest with Blackwood, who had approached from behind.

"May I offer you some unsolicited advice?" Blackwood didn't wait for a response before continuing. "Be careful, Holden. In my experience, power is a harsh mistress, as fickle as Lady Luck. Pursuing it can rob us of our better judgment, as these recent killings prove. It's a dangerous, slippery thing, no sooner won than lost again."

"Not for someone like you." The words came out sounding bitterer than Holden had intended, so he tried to temper them. "I just mean you've never had to fight for it."

"You'd be surprised. True, I had power handed to me at a young age, along with my wealth, but I've still had to fight all my life. Imagine an existence in which someone is always watching, admonishing you never to fail, not to sully the family name. The constant pressure of familial obligation is what made me the man I am today." He grimaced but pressed on before Holden could interject. "To maintain power in this world, you have to be as hard as a diamond, and as showy. But there's always a cost. After a time, you realise the sparkle is only skin deep, and what's below the surface has warped beyond recognition." He reached out and brushed Holden's hair back, trailing his fingers over the pointed tip of Holden's ear in a gentle, reverent caress. "Try not to let the thirst for power and position ruin your inner beauty, Holden Fay. You are perfect as you are."

Before Holden realised what was happening, Blackwood leaned in and pressed his lips to Holden's. The chaste, soft kiss lasted barely a second or two. By the time Holden's brain acknowledged it, Blackwood was already moving away, heading to the bell pull.

The door opened and James entered, but Holden remained rooted to the spot.

Valerius Blackwood had just kissed him—sort of. Or had he? Perhaps Holden had taken a micro nap and dreamed the entire scene. He glanced toward the desk. Blackwood had resumed the same pose in which Holden had found him upon his arrival: seated and gazing down at his paperwork. He appeared unruffled and at ease.

Either Holden *had* conjured the moment in his mind or Blackwood was pretending it had never happened. For want of any other suitable response, Holden assumed he ought to do likewise.

He stiffly inclined his head. "Thank you for your time, Mr Blackwood."

Blackwood didn't look up. "Goodbye for the present, Mr Fay. I will have copies of those pages to you within the hour. My kindest regards to your captain."

Chapter Thirteen

OVER THE NEXT couple of weeks, Holden experienced a sense of frustrated impotence that made his past complaints seem like pointless grumbles about nothing. He'd thought that knowing he had to live out his life in a society that would never accept him was as bad as it could get. Turns out, far worse was knowing someone would soon be murdered but being powerless to stop it.

They'd gleaned a lot from the scans Blackwood had emailed. Although Owens accepted there was no way to prove Blackwood's posited theory, she'd made the call to take it as fact for the time being, stating that it was best to prepare for the worst-case scenario. The supernatural community would hardly view the Fellowship in a positive light if they discovered the organization had known there could be a further five attacks but had failed to act.

So, Holden and the others had pieced together what they could about the summoning ritual. According to the text, a full moon was a prerequisite, since it helped focus the magic, and this information had allowed them to establish a timeline for the previous murders, as well as predicting a date for the next: the fifth of October. Knowing that did them little good, however, considering they still had no idea how the killer was selecting his victims.

Holden's recently formed hypothesis answered one aspect of that. The killer needed nine hearts, and there were nine major London covens. The initial four victims had all been members of different groups. Therefore, it made sense that the killer was taking one from each coven. They'd issued formal warnings to those groups as yet unaffected, telling them to take extra care at the next full moon, but other than that, their hands were tied.

The Investigations Team couldn't muster sufficient manpower to guard everyone individually, and the covens had baulked at the suggestion they gather their members in a central location for the night—a venue which the Fellowship would then patrol. They claimed they had no wish to see their members put under surveillance by the vampires and fae, and all arguments that it was only for their protection fell on deaf ears. When a few of the more outspoken witches began spouting conspiracy theories about a planned purge of the city's witch population by the other factions, the Fellowship gave up on the idea and took a significant step back. Things were bad enough as it was; they didn't want to start an interspecies war.

Too soon the dreaded night of the fifth of October arrived, and Holden was spending the evening at home. He finished his meal and rinsed his plate, leaving it in the sink with the rest of the dirty dishes he was trying to ignore. Then he settled on the sofa, where he powered up his tablet and logged into the secure site. At seven p.m. a live broadcast commenced. It screened via the Fellowship's server, from whence it filtered through several secret social media groups. The scene opened on a stage, empty save for a lectern bearing the sigil of the Mayfair-Belgravia coven. A moment later, Valerius Blackwood strode into frame. He positioned himself behind the lectern and began his speech.

Blackwood elaborated on the great work the Fellowship was doing in these dangerous times. He then urged his fellow witches to exercise caution and, wherever possible, not to spend the night alone. The bulletin ended with a reiteration of the number for the Fellowship's emergency hotline.

As always, Blackwood exuded a quiet confidence, and Holden felt reassured. Immediately, he wondered if that was such a good thing. Wouldn't it be better for the witches to maintain a modicum of concern? If they were too relaxed and unfazed, they might lower their guard and not take sufficient precautions. Perhaps, on reflection, Blackwood should have stressed the danger, rather than focusing on the Fellowship's awesomeness, as politically astute and diplomatic as that had been.

Blackwood surrendered centre stage to Owens, and Holden logged out. He didn't need to hear Owens's speech. He'd already experienced it in the office earlier in the day, when she'd used the team as guinea pigs to see how it would come across. Mostly, she would be reiterating Blackwood's key points, but with a stronger focus on individual action and personal responsibility.

With the lull of Blackwood's honey-like baritone gone, Holden's sense of uselessness returned. A killer could be prowling the streets tonight, and here he was sitting at home, doing nothing to stop him. The rational part of Holden's mind accepted there was little he *could* do at this stage. He was on call, in case anything happened, but unless the killer made a move, any presumptive action on the Fellowship's part would be a waste of time and resources—the proverbial stab in the dark.

The knock on his door took Holden by surprise. He hurried to open it, thinking it had to be work-related, but it was Raoul who stood in the doorway, brandishing four bottles of whisky and a broad grin.

"Thought you could probably do with some company tonight."

Holden stepped aside and gestured Raoul in. "Sure." He eyed the liquor. "I'm on call, though, so I can't go on a bender."

"*I'm* not, and who said I brought any of this for you? Surely one would be okay. You won't even notice one little dram."

"Okay. But just one."

Raoul was already opening Holden's kitchen cupboard and fishing out two glasses. His pours, in Holden's estimation, were probably double doubles, but Holden decided to let it go. He'd eaten a decent meal, and with his metabolism, one drink, even though it was four in disguise, wouldn't impair him should he need to drive somewhere.

Holden settled back in his preferred spot on the sofa, and Raoul joined him, handing him the brimming glass.

"I take it you watched your boyfriend just now?"

This new way of referencing Blackwood was currently Raoul's favourite joke, and Holden suspected his embarrassed reactions were only perpetuating the soubriquet. He was thankful he'd chosen *not* to tell Raoul about that kiss. It would only have added fuel to the fire. In any case, he'd been trying to dwell on it as little as possible. Blackwood had been in a strange, hyper mood that day. It couldn't have meant anything. Besides, the way Blackwood had dismissed him without a glance immediately afterward suggested he'd come to his senses the second he'd stepped away. Remembering the exquisite press of Blackwood's lips against his— something he was certain he'd never experience again— only served to make Holden tense, with an unhealthy dose of bitter yearning thrown in for good measure.

"He's not my boyfriend. I've only met him a handful of times. You've seen more of him than I have."

Raoul raised an eyebrow and assumed an expression of mock shock. "Not true! Tall, dark, and proud isn't my type. You should know that. Besides, Blackwood is such a walking cliché."

Holden bristled. "No, he's not. There's more to him than you see on the TV and in tabloid photos."

Raoul chuckled. "Now you're really making me jealous." He pouted prettily. "Still, we are friends, first and foremost, so if you wish to do any lovesick ranting, extolling Mr Blackwood's many virtues, as you see them, I'm all ears."

"There's nothing to say, Raoul. Can't we talk about something else?"

To Raoul's credit, he always knew when he'd taken a jest far enough. He paused to down his drink, poured himself another overly generous glassful, and set off on a new tangent.

"Are you really expecting another attack tonight?"

"Yes, it does seem likely. Of course, we hope all these preventative measures will be enough to foil it."

"What makes you so sure the killer will strike again, and on this particular day?"

The potential demon summoning was not an aspect of the case the Fellowship had wanted made public knowledge, and Owens and Blackwood had both agreed it was better that way. The last thing they needed was to spark panic or inspire any vigilantes. Had it been a personal matter, Holden would have had no compunction about trusting Raoul, but this wasn't his call. He still held some residual feelings of guilt over that one time when he *had* made Raoul privy to confidential information.

"I can't tell you. Sorry."

"Oh, one of those times, is it? I understand. Maybe when it's over."

"When it's over," Holden echoed, already contemplating that tantalizing possibility.

From what they could tell about the ritual, if the killer failed in his task tonight, it would indeed be over. With the chain broken, if he wanted to continue, he would have to start again from scratch. Not that that was necessarily a comforting thought. Anyone willing to kill nine people in cold blood seemed the sort of person committed enough to his cause to do just that, unless the Fellowship caught up with him first and put him out of action permanently.

Raoul tactfully changed the subject again, and they spent the next few hours in pleasant conversation, Raoul getting ever so slightly tipsy, and Holden making do with orange juice. Although, now and then, Holden's thoughts strayed to what might be going on in the world beyond his flat, Raoul's presence provided a welcome distraction, and he accepted it was lucky Raoul had had the foresight to make his unexpected appearance. He was indeed a good friend. Without him, Holden would likely have been a nervous wreck by now, staring at his phone, waiting for it to ring.

But no calls came through. And as the minutes ticked by, Holden began to hope they'd succeeded in thwarting the killer's aims. He started to believe it, until another knock sounded on his door.

Holden scrambled to answer the summons, ready to greet Owens, or whomever she'd sent to collect him, steeling himself to hear the worst. However, it wasn't Owens. Nor was it anyone else from the team. Instead, it was the last person in the world he ever would have expected to find on his doorstep.

"Ah. Good. You're still up. I thought you might be. I'd hoped."

Without waiting for an invitation, Blackwood brushed past. However, he didn't accomplish this entrance with his usual calm authority. He seemed agitated, and Holden noticed that his hands were shaking. His gaze moved around Holden's apartment in a frantic manner that suggested he wasn't really taking in anything he was seeing. That changed, though, the moment he spotted Raoul.

Blackwood tensed. He kept his eyes fixed on Raoul as he addressed Holden. "I didn't expect you to have company."

Raoul rose with as much hauteur as one could muster after emptying four full bottles of whisky almost singlehanded. He offered Blackwood a tight nod. "Blackwood. What a surprise."

"Dubois."

The two stared at each other without saying another word. Holden let it continue for a good thirty seconds, but at that point, he decided he'd had as much testosterone measuring as he could handle for one night.

He addressed Blackwood. "Did you need to talk to me?"

The question seemed to rob Blackwood of all his remaining vigour. His shoulders slumped, and he reached out to grip the back of the sofa. "I'd hoped you'd be alone."

Something was clearly very wrong. Blackwood's heart was racing. Holden could hear its frantic rhythm. He could only assume it was connected to the case, and that Blackwood was reluctant to elaborate in front of an audience. He shot Raoul an apologetic look, and Raoul got the message.

"I was just leaving anyway."

Holden followed him to the door. As he departed, Raoul quirked his eyebrow in a silent question. Holden answered with a shrug. Blackwood's arrival was an anomaly to him too. He only hoped that whatever news Blackwood carried wasn't too dire. Yet, if there'd been another murder, surely Owens would have called. Unless he was off the case and they'd rung one of the pure-blood vampires instead. Would Owens do something like that without telling him first? Maybe—if the Fellowship had demanded it.

With a million questions making mincemeat of his brain, Holden closed the door behind his first guest and turned to face the second.

Chapter Fourteen

BLACKWOOD STOOD WHERE Holden had left him: slumped against the sofa. Creases lined his normally pristine suit. He looked almost dishevelled. Whatever had gone on this evening, it had clearly taken its toll. He made no move to turn at Holden's approach, not reacting until Holden lightly tapped his shoulder. When their gazes met, Blackwood's eyes looked haunted.

"We're alone now, Mr Blackwood," Holden ventured. "What's wrong?"

"Val."

"What?"

"My friends call me Val. There's no need to call me Mr Blackwood anymore."

"Oh. Okay...Val."

The single syllable lingered on Holden's tongue and in his ears. *Val.* A frisson of joyful excitement pulsed through him at this sudden change. If only Blackwood's friends called him Val, did that mean he now counted Holden among them? At the same time, Blackwood's demeanour was so different from usual that everything about this scene felt wrong.

When Blackwood continued to stare, without further comment, Holden pressed on. "Has something happened? Another murder?"

Blackwood glanced away. "Yes."

"Fates! Then we should get going. Right? Is the team still at the scene? Just let me get my coat."

Blackwood shot out a hand and grabbed Holden's arm, halting him. The grip was so strong it bordered on painful. "No. They don't need you there. Not yet. But you should know that it's over. Tonight will be the last attack."

"They caught the guy?"

"They'll have him come morning."

That should have been good news. It *was* good news. However, confusion robbed Holden of the elation he would otherwise have felt at these tidings. Owens had made him lead investigator. Shouldn't he be there with them at the crime scene? Wouldn't Owens at least have called to let him know what was happening? Then again, Blackwood was here doing just that, wasn't he? Owens must have sent him. Although, that didn't explain why they'd deemed Holden's presence unnecessary.

"Am I off the case?"

Blackwood frowned. "No. Why?"

"You said they don't want me there."

"You're not off the case. There's simply no need for you to go over there yet."

"Owens will call me later?"

"Yes. Of that I'm certain."

Blackwood still hadn't released his arm, and Holden wondered if he should pull free. Would that be rude? The pressure of Blackwood's fingers was making his flesh ache, and this exchange was becoming increasingly more bizarre with every passing second. He almost wished that Raoul hadn't left. Yet, he was unsure why. Sure, Blackwood's behaviour was peculiar, but he was likely overwrought that they'd failed to prevent this fifth attack on his people. Holden could understand that. The case had gotten under his skin, too, and he didn't have so personal a connection to it.

He cleared his throat. "Well, thanks for coming over to fill me in."

"That's not why I'm here."

"Oh. Then wha—"

Blackwood yanked Holden forward and kissed him fiercely. At first, Holden froze, shock overriding all other sensations, but then he melted against Blackwood. He could taste the desperate hunger in the kiss and wondered what to make of it. Was Blackwood drunk? It seemed an obvious explanation, yet Holden got neither whiff nor tang of alcohol. How else to account for the fact Blackwood was clinging to him in this manner? Unless...

As much as his body urged the opposite, Holden's rational mind took charge, and he eased away, breaking the kiss. Raoul's words were echoing in his head, and before this went any further, he needed to know one thing.

"Are you trying to collect me?"

Blackwood's look was blank.

"I know you have an interest in rare objects and people with unusual talents. Is this"—he waved between them—"simply to satisfy your curiosity about me?"

Blackwood cast a glare toward the closed front door. "Was it Dubois who gave you that idea?"

"Does it matter?"

"Are you sleeping with him?"

Holden began to wish he'd gone with the flow, regardless of where it led and why. A minute ago, he'd been kissing Valerius Blackwood, living one of his greatest dreams. Now, he couldn't be certain if he was the interrogator or the interrogatee in this flurry of unanswered questions.

He fixed his gaze on Blackwood's finely chiselled chin, a flush heating his cheeks, and shrugged. "Sometimes. But it's not serious. Mostly we're just good friends."

For a long moment, silence reigned. Then Blackwood sighed.

"I'm not trying to 'collect you', as you so eloquently put it. I want you. I'm attracted to you, and I thought... Well, I thought you felt the same. Clearly I was wrong." He rubbed his temples, his expression pained. "I don't know why I came here. It was a mistake. I'll go." He started to turn.

"Wait!" Holden grasped his sleeve. "You don't have to go." He strengthened his voice. "I don't want you to go." He hesitated for a second, then went on. "You weren't wrong. It's just... I'm not used to this. No one but Raoul has ever shown the slightest interest in me. It's hard to believe that you, that someone like you, would ever..." Words failed him. He was gabbling like an idiot. *Oh, screw it.*

Holden surged onto tiptoes to kiss Blackwood. It wasn't elegant at first—all clashing teeth and some unfortunate drooling—but then Blackwood resumed control, and the embrace became more fluid and sensual.

They stumbled against the sofa, the unyielding obstacle serving to press their bodies closer. The hard line of Blackwood's erection dug into Holden's stomach. As impossible as it seemed, Blackwood clearly *did* desire him. How had this happened? Why? The questions flittered through his mind, but he forced them aside. Who the fuck cared about the whys and wherefores during a moment like this? If he called another stop to ponder it at this juncture, he was certifiably insane.

He was fully hard now, his cock painfully yet deliciously restricted within his jeans. Desperate for more friction, he rubbed against Blackwood's thigh.

Blackwood broke the kiss with a soft growl. "Bedroom?"

Holden indicated over Blackwood's shoulder with a sharp nod. "Through there."

They tumbled across the room in a shambles of flailing limbs and falling clothing. By the time they reached the bed, both were shirtless and Blackwood's Oxfords were gone. Holden ran his fingers over Blackwood's bicep, tracing the toned muscle. He could have spent days pouring over every inch of Blackwood's skin, cataloguing it, worshipping it, but that would have to wait, because Blackwood was already guiding him onto the bed, his fingers working at Holden's belt buckle.

Holden raised his hips so Blackwood could tug off his jeans. He then sat up and dealt with the fastenings on Blackwood's trousers. They slid down his legs to reveal a tantalizing bulge. Holden couldn't help himself. He leaned forward to lap at it through the soft cotton.

Blackwood flung his head back with a moan, sinking his fingers into Holden's hair and giving the strands a gentle, teasing tug. "Damn, Holden. Do you have—"

"Top drawer."

While Blackwood collected supplies, Holden wriggled out of his briefs and tossed them aside. He rolled onto his knees, and when Blackwood returned, he pulled him close and trailed kisses along his jaw and down his neck. He paused over the jugular. Blood pulsed just below the surface, its steady flow an inviting call. But when Holden dragged his tongue over the sweet spot, Blackwood tensed and jerked away.

"No blood." He held Holden back with one hand, clenching his other fist, avoiding Holden's gaze. "Promise me."

"No blood. Sure."

Although he yearned to have that additional intimacy, to know Blackwood fully through his blood, Holden accepted that such bedroom games weren't for everyone. Raoul might glory in them, but Blackwood was a witch, and they generally held dim views about blood exchanges, and vampires in general. Just being here with Blackwood was enough. If that meant holding some instincts at bay, so be it.

Blackwood looked up, and their eyes met. Holden could feel the weight of that gaze. Blackwood was deciding if he could trust Holden's word. Whatever he saw must have satisfied him, because he gave a fleeting smile, stripped out of his remaining clothing, and joined Holden on the bed.

"You are beautiful, Holden Fay."

He stretched over Holden, propped on one elbow, and trailed his hand down Holden's chest in an exploratory caress. Holden tried hard not to react, desperate not to ruin the moment, but as Blackwood reached his hip, he couldn't suppress a sharp gasp.

Blackwood halted. "What's wrong?"

He looked so concerned and serious that Holden couldn't help but chuckle. "It's your ring. The metal's cool, and it tickles."

Blackwood laughed, and for the first time since his arrival on Holden's doorstep, some of his anxiety melted away, revealing the man Holden was more used to seeing. He sat up and removed the ring. Once it was off his finger, he flung it over his shoulder. There followed a series of *clunks* as it bounced along the hardwood floor. Then Blackwood's hands were back on Holden's body, and all other thoughts vanished.

HOLDEN REFUSED TO admit he was awake. Burrowed beneath the covers, he grinned as he relived the previous night, moment for moment, touch for touch. If he focused hard on the memories, he could still feel Blackwood inside him, taking him in strokes that had begun deep and languid, only to gain momentum until all Holden knew was the tremor of each thrust and the sound of their panting and mumbled words.

He fought to suppress an undignified giggle. By the Fates, it had been spectacular. He could scarce accept it hadn't been a dream. But he knew it wasn't. Valerius Blackwood had spent the night in his bed, and it was no exaggeration to say it had been the best night of his life.

Sudden remembrance struck him. The sensation was akin to being dowsed with ice-cold water. Someone had died last night. Fates! Here he was getting high on the recollection of a sexual romp when some poor witch lay slaughtered. Blackwood's touch, his kisses, had blocked all thoughts of the murder from Holden's mind for several blissful hours, but now he needed to get up and get to the office. He was still lead investigator—as far as he knew— and he had a job to do. There were too many unanswered questions: Who had died? What had the scene revealed? Had they caught the perpetrator as Blackwood had said they would?

"Val?" Holden stretched out his arm.

Then he sat bolt upright.

He blinked and rubbed the sleep from his eyes. It didn't help. The other side of the bed was just as empty as it had felt. Blackwood was gone.

"Val?" Holden called louder. Maybe he was in the bathroom, or the kitchen.

When nothing but silence greeted him, Holden leaped out of bed. A second later, he cursed as his foot came down on something angular and hard. He hopped for a moment, rubbing his bruised sole. Then he bent to retrieve the offending item. It was Blackwood's ring. At least that proved he hadn't dreamed it all.

Holden checked the other rooms, but Blackwood was definitely gone. The clock read a few minutes to six, so wherever he was, he'd left early. Holden wasn't sure what to make of that. Was it bad: a sign that he either regretted what they'd done or had been severely underwhelmed by Holden's skills in the sack? Or was Holden taking his absence too personally?

Just then, he spotted a scrap of paper on the kitchen counter. When he went to investigate, he saw it was the receipt from his last lot of groceries, with a note scrawled on the back.

> *Dear Holden,*
>
> *Sorry for leaving you like this, but there's something I have to do, and I must do it now, alone.*
>
> *I hope one day you can find it in your heart to forgive me.*
>
> *Val*

It was Blackwood's copperplate script, but it was messier than usual, the message obviously scribbled in a rush. The text seemed a little overdramatic, but Blackwood had been in a hurry, and perhaps he already knew Holden well enough to guess that he'd leap to the wrong conclusion and panic and was, therefore, trying to reassure him.

At least there was no cause for concern. He now knew for certain Blackwood had only left without a word because he had something important to do. Not because he regretted what had passed between them.

Speaking of things to do...

With Blackwood's disappearance solved, it was high time he checked in with Owens, to see what was happening and where they needed him. Apparently, the old adage that great minds thought alike was true, because as he reached for his phone, a call came through, and Owens's name flashed across the screen.

Holden snatched up the mobile and answered after only a single ring. "Captain, what's happening? What went down last night? Did you catch the bastard?"

"We have him."

She didn't sound thrilled. Shouldn't she be happy about the news? Then it struck him: she was angry they hadn't nabbed the guy *before* he struck. Getting him prior to the fifth murder would have been the greater victory.

"Mr Blackwood said you weren't in time to save the victim. You could have called. I would have—"

"You saw Valerius Blackwood last night?" Holden heard the strain in her voice.

"Well, yeah. He came by to update me."

Holden flushed at the thought of what had happened after that. Memories of it made a certain part of his anatomy wake, and it was then he realised he was still walking around naked. Thank the Fates Owens hadn't decided to make it a video call.

He waited a moment, but there was only silence from the other end of the line. "Uh, Captain? Are you still there?"

"You need to come into the office right now, Holden." The note of tension he'd detected earlier in the call had ramped up a notch; each word thrummed with it.

"Of course. Are you all right?"

"Just fucking get here."

Chapter Fifteen

FROM THE MOMENT Holden reached the office, he could tell something extraordinary had happened. The place was in a frenzy, with people darting in every direction and voices rising ever louder as everyone competed to be heard over the din. Only one or two colleagues noticed his arrival, and they were quick to look away. Holden's enhanced hearing made the racket in the room even worse for him, causing a ringing in his ears, so he did his best to block it all out, while making a dash for Owens's door.

He knocked and immediately entered, for once not waiting for a reply. Closing the door behind him eliminated the worst of the noise. However, when he turned and observed Owens's expression, he wondered if he might not have been better off staying at his desk.

Owens looked drawn. Her eyes were bloodshot, the lids drooping, and deep furrows creased her brow as she pressed her lips into a thin, grim line.

"Sit, Holden. I need to ask you some questions."

Holden sank into the empty seat opposite her and gripped the armrests. "By the Fates, Captain, what's going on out there? What went down last night?"

Owens held up her hand. "Sorry, but we have to do this by the book." She set her phone upon the table and launched the sound recorder app. "It's gotta be on record."

"On record?"

"I'm afraid you're now a person of interest in this investigation."

"What?"

Holden stared. He must have heard wrong, or else Owens was joking with him. She didn't crack a smile though. If anything, she looked like she might throw up at any second. A shiver ran down his spine. Nonetheless, he swallowed and gave a sharp nod for her to continue. Better to get this over with. He had nothing to fear; he'd done nothing wrong. This was clearly a misunderstanding. Unless they'd discovered that he'd shared details of the case with Raoul. Fates! That could get him a bollocking. Though surely it wasn't so dire as to warrant this treatment.

"Holden, do you understand what I'm saying? I need to ask you several questions. Do you wish to have a lawyer present? We can postpone until someone arrives if so."

"A lawyer?" Holden's head was spinning so fast it was making him dizzy. Why would he need a bloody lawyer? "No. Ask your questions, Captain. I've nothing to hide." If this *was* about Raoul, he'd confess and take whatever punishment they saw fit to deal out.

"Let's get this over with, then." Owens pressed the Record button and kept her gaze fixed on the mobile as she said, "Initial interview with Holden Fay, conducted by Captain Gloria Owens. The time is six forty-nine a.m." She looked up and met Holden's eyes. "Please tell me where you were yesterday evening."

"At home."

"All night?"

"Yes. I had my phone with me, expecting a call from you. I didn't want to go out and risk not being ready when you needed me. I didn't feel like doing much under the circumstances, anyway."

Owens nodded, and scribbled something on her pad. Holden tried to read the words upside down, but her generally indecipherable handwriting was all the more impossible to make out from his present angle.

"Were you alone?"

"Only until about seven. I had company after that."

"Blackwood?" Owens seemed to struggle over the name.

"Not at first. He arrived later. Raoul was with me before that. Raoul Dubois," he added helpfully, before she prompted him for the surname.

She looked up sharply. "The vampire?"

"Yes. He's a friend."

Owens added to her unreadable notes. "How long did he stay?"

"Until Blackwood arrived. I think..." Holden shrugged and shook his head. "Honestly, I didn't look at the clock. I guess it was around eleven or so. Maybe a little later."

"And when did Blackwood depart?"

"I don't know. I fell asleep. When I woke, a few minutes before your call, he was gone. He'd left a note apologizing, saying he had something to do." He shifted in his seat and cradled his hands in his lap, interlacing his fingers and squeezing tight. "Look, Captain, what is this about?"

"Just a few more questions, Holden. And we're gonna need that note." She scribbled a couple more words on her pad, then cleared her throat. "What did Blackwood say while he was with you?"

"Say?" Holden frowned. Where was this heading? Why was Owens so obsessed with what he'd been doing last night? Of what, exactly, did they suspect him? His frustration was steadily mounting, but he did his best to consider the question calmly. "He didn't have a lot to tell me. I mean, he confirmed there'd been another murder. I assumed he'd come to fetch me to the crime scene, but he said you didn't need me there yet. He also told me you'd have the guy by morning." He met her gaze. "You do, don't you? We've really got him?"

"Yes." Owens tapped her pen on the desk. "That was all?"

"Yeah. We didn't do much talking." Holden clamped his mouth shut when he realised how that had sounded. The fact that it actually *had* gone exactly as it sounded didn't help matters. He could feel the flush heating his cheeks, and clearly it was visible, because Owens's eyes widened.

"And after you'd...spent this time together, you fell asleep and woke to find him gone? Is that what you're telling me?"

"Yes."

Holden awaited another question, but after a brief pause, Owens set down her pen and pushed aside the notepad.

"Interview terminated at seven-o-six."

She turned off the recorder, ran a hand through her hair in a jerky motion, and then leaned back in her seat. She looked exhausted. Holden guessed she'd been up all night.

"Well, I sure as fucking hell am glad you weren't involved in this. For a moment there..." She sighed. "Look, I think it best we try to keep your testimony to a minimum. There are some who'd take great delight in tying you to this simply because of who you are, including a few in this department, I'm sorry to say. I can't shield you entirely, however. There will be more questions, and you'll likely be called to the stand during the trial."

"The trial? So you caught him alive?" A queasy feeling settled in the pit of Holden's stomach. Suddenly, he didn't want to know who was behind the murders. He didn't think he was going to like the answer.

"We didn't 'catch' anyone. The murderer turned himself in a few hours ago."

"He confessed? Why now?"

"A representative from the Council is taking his formal statement as we speak. We should know more soon."

"Why aren't you in there? It's your case."

"It's become...complicated. Actually, it's more accurate to say it's a fucking diplomatic nightmare. Therefore, the Council has assumed full control of proceedings."

A dreadful suspicion had clawed its way into Holden's mind during the conversation, and everything that Owens uttered only seemed to confirm it. Nevertheless, he needed to know for certain.

"Who is it, Captain?"

Owens studied him intently, no doubt ready to observe his reaction to the news. "Valerius Blackwood."

Whatever his expression as the name crossed her lips, his attitude must have confirmed his innocence in her mind, because her posture softened, and she looked at him with such pity he had to glance away. He'd thought hearing it spoken aloud would help him accept the truth. He'd been wrong. Rather than bow to the facts, his consciousness rebelled, refusing to believe it was possible.

He rose and began to pace, channelling his emotions into the movement, trying to keep his head clear. "But Blackwood was with me last night. He couldn't have done it."

"Holden, you said yourself he didn't arrive until late. Preliminary analysis places the time of death between eight and ten. That gives him ample time to clean up and travel to your house."

Holden thought back to Blackwood's unexpected appearance on his doorstep. He had looked dishevelled and anxious. That made sense if he'd come straight from committing a grisly murder, and yet…

"He was helping us. We'd not have known to expect another murder last night if not for his insights."

"What better way to deflect attention than to work alongside us? Plus, it gave him an opportunity to keep tabs on the investigation, allowing him to stay one step ahead. He was toying with us, Holden." She paused. "You more than most, it seems, and I'm sorry for the part I played in that. I'm the one who pushed you together. He must have seen you as an easy mark."

Holden shook his head. Once he'd started, he couldn't stop. "No. No. No. There's been a mistake. I know it. This has to be a mistake. Val wouldn't—"

"Not another word!"

The authoritative demand came from behind him, and Holden spun so fast he nearly toppled. "Father!"

"Is that how I raised you to greet an elder of the Unseelie court?"

Holden collapsed into a deep, formal obeisance. He fought to maintain his balance in the awkward position, only now noticing how badly he was trembling.

Cadeyrn stormed into the room and slammed the door behind him, rattling the glass pane. The force of his gaze, heightened by the pure power behind it, made Holden's skin break out in goosebumps.

"You will say nothing else regarding these murders or your...relations with Valerius Blackwood until the trial, when you will speak only the truth and not a word more than is necessary. Do I make myself clear? I only hope you're innocent of any complicity and are not about to drag my good name further through the mud."

A little voice in the back of Holden's head shrieked that his father had ruined that 'good name' himself, by bringing Holden into the world to begin with, but prudence made him bite down on his rebellious tongue. "Yes, Father."

"Enough of that. You're no son of mine."

That blazing gaze moved away, and Holden risked glancing up to watch as Cadeyrn addressed Owens.

"Captain, the prisoner has made a full and free confession. I will have a transcript of his testimony for you shortly. However, your department has nothing to celebrate in closing this case. Without Blackwood's sudden attack of conscience, you would have failed in stopping a brutal murderer. Worse, you included said murderer in your team and shared with him classified information, and not once did you suspect the truth. You and your lackeys are a disgrace to the Fellowship. How Blackwood must have laughed at you."

Holden's gaze shot back to the floor as his father looked his way once more. Blood pounded in his ears, and it was hard not to wobble.

"Get up."

"Yes, Fath—Cadeyrn." Holden staggered to his feet, swaying slightly before finding his balance. He caught his father's expression of disgust and did his best to stand straight and tall once he was finally upright.

"Come."

Cadeyrn was already out the door while the instruction still hung in the air. Holden scrambled to follow, keeping his eyes fixed on his father's back, trying to ignore the many stares boring into his. Only when the lift doors had closed and the car began its descent did his father condescend to address him again.

"Go home and stay there. You're not to set foot outside until the trial. The press will be on this in no time, so hold your tongue if they contact you. I used to think it impossible for you to be any more of a disappointment to me than you already were, but apparently even the wisest can err from time to time."

Luckily, at this pronouncement, the lift reached the ground floor and a *ping* preceded the opening of the doors. In the lobby, Holden made a final leg to his father, then shot away. He had no recollection of the journey back to his flat, but he made it there somehow, and once within the familiar four walls of home, he collapsed onto the sofa.

He must have slept, because when he came to, several hours had passed. It had clearly been an unquiet rest, however, for he felt exhausted rather than refreshed. When he checked his phone, he found over fifty messages from reporters, all clamouring for his exclusive story. He deleted them without responding. It was barely noon, but he knocked out a quick text to Raoul. After that, he switched off the mobile and tossed it onto the coffee table. If the Fellowship wanted him, they knew where to find him.

Holden's thoughts were in disarray, images from the murder scenes alternating with flashbacks of last night. What had that been—more misdirection? Had Blackwood only slept with him to keep him off balance? That was what most people were bound to think when they heard about the incident, as doubtless they would come the trial. Yet, it didn't ring true. It hadn't felt like a dispassionate fuck. Holden might not have a wealth of sexual experience, but he trusted his instincts that much. Then there was Blackwood's comment about them catching the killer in the morning. He'd said it with conviction, suggesting that he'd already decided to turn himself in. Thus, sleeping with Holden served no strategic purpose. There'd been no need for him to call on Holden at all.

But he had to remember that Valerius Blackwood was a cold-blooded murderer.

That much was now fact, whichever way he looked at it. The hands that had caressed Holden had wielded a blade and shed innocent blood mere hours before. Perhaps if Holden had been paying more attention he'd have smelled lingering traces of the foreign blood alongside Blackwood's own. But what did that matter now? It wouldn't bring back the dead.

Holden knew he should be thinking of himself at this juncture. Any credibility he'd gained in recent weeks was lost. Moreover, Owens was right in saying there were plenty of people who would try to link him to the killings, through his recent association with Blackwood. He should be planning a defence, working out how to combat any questions they might ask. However, to his mind, there was only one question worth answering at present: Why would Valerius Blackwood, the most powerful witch in London, if not the entire country, want to summon a demon?

Chapter Sixteen

TWO WEEKS DRAGGED by, each second seeming a minute and each minute an hour. Though accustomed to spending the majority of his time alone, Holden experienced every year-long day as if it were his own personal circle of hell. Trapped with nothing but his increasingly sombre thoughts for company, the only break in the monotony was the weekly visit from one of his father's assistants, bringing him groceries. He supposed he ought to be grateful his father hadn't left him to starve after issuing his 'stay at home' edict.

Holden stuck to that directive. He hadn't wanted to face the retribution that would follow had he failed to do so, but in truth, remaining sequestered suited his mood too. There was no one he wanted to see, no one with whom he wished to speak. Save one—and that was impossible. His phone mostly remained off, and he'd soon discovered his father had called in a witch to ward the house when a glance out the window revealed a gaggle of reporters unable to pass the front gate. Unfortunately, it also prevented Raoul's ingress when he'd tried to visit. Although, maybe that was for the best.

With Raoul unable to enter that first night, they'd spoken on the phone instead, but the conversation had not lasted long. When Holden picked up, Raoul launched into a long stream of I-told-you-so. Holden could have brushed that off, but Raoul went on to speak of Blackwood in such vile terms that he'd awakened Holden's ire. Harsh words followed on both sides, and they'd not communicated since. To be fair, Holden hadn't turned on his phone for several days, so he had no idea if Raoul had tried to call, but he'd made no move of his own toward reconciliation.

The trouble was, deep down, he knew Raoul was probably right. What was more likely—that Blackwood had truly felt something for him or that he'd spun a web of deceit, trapping Holden like a hapless fly? He'd lied to everyone else every step of the way. Why not to Holden too? Blackwood was a callous, murderous bastard who cared only for himself. So why did Holden still care about *him*?

He fingered the ring in his trouser pocket. In a sense, it was evidence, and he ought to have handed it in along with Blackwood's note. Instead, he'd kept it close, touching it so often the metal rarely had time to fully cool. He'd traced the Blackwood crest so frequently with the pad of his thumb, he believed he could draw it in his sleep. If the Fellowship wanted to take this from him, they'd have to pry it from his cold, dead fingers.

The knock on the door made him jump, despite the fact he'd long expected it.

He rose and crossed the room, and when he opened the door, his father looked him over with a critical eye, taking in his ill-fitting suit. It was the one he'd last worn to Blackwood's house—a recollection that brought further unease. Apparently, his appearance was good enough, or at least no worse than expected, for Cadeyrn nodded and set off back the way he'd come, taking for granted that Holden would follow.

Trial day had come at last, both sooner and later than Holden would have wished.

THE ROOM IN which Holden sat contained a chair, a table, a jug of water, and a single glass. There was no clock, and he'd neglected to wear his watch, but he judged that several hours had passed since his father had deposited him in the lower levels of the Fellowship building just before sunset. With not so much as a magazine to help him while away the time, Holden's mind drifted. He wondered what was happening in the courtroom. How badly were things going for Blackwood?

He shook his head. Fates! What sort of man was he? He shouldn't be concerned about Valerius Blackwood. He should be eager to obtain justice for the dead. That was his job. However, try as he might, he couldn't pretend he'd never cared for Blackwood, or that he didn't continue to hold strong feelings for him.

The lock clicked back and the door opened. An officious-looking witch poked his head through the gap. "Holden Fay. Follow me."

One corridor led into another in what seemed like a never-ending labyrinth. The stark white walls of the hitherto unseen basement pressed in on Holden, and there was something distinctly ominous about the length of the walk. Neither he nor his companion spoke, so the only sound was that of their echoing footsteps.

The courtroom, when they reached it, proved no better. Here, the fluorescent lights were too bright, hurting his unshielded eyes. Holden blinked against the glare as his companion guided him to the witness stand. A gavel thumped somewhere to his right, silencing the murmur that had grown louder at his arrival, and Holden forced open his eyes and looked toward the bench.

One of the vampire leaders—Jackson Banks—was presiding. To his left sat the jury. As at all Fellowship trials, there were nine of them: three witches, three fae, and three vampires. Only community leaders could perform the role, and a ballot at the start of each trial selected who among the limited pool would sit in each session. Holden flinched when he saw that Raoul was one of today's jurors. Raoul had no love for Blackwood. Holden knew which way his vote would swing. When Raoul attempted to catch his eye, he looked away. This new line of gaze proved no better, however, for now he stared directly at the accused.

Valerius Blackwood did not present a good picture. His hair was a mess, and he was unshaven. Creases and stains marred his suit. It looked suspiciously like the outfit he'd worn to Holden's flat, and unlike Holden, he possessed more than one. Holden therefore deduced no one had allowed him to change his attire or do much in the way of personal grooming since his arrest. Surely that had to be against one rule or another? Confession or not, Blackwood ought to have *some* rights. He looked gaunt, too, although he stood as straight and tall as always. Dark circles shadowed his eyes, and as he turned his head, he revealed an ugly bruise purpling his cheek.

Holden ground his teeth. Blackwood had given himself up. There'd been no violent takedown. So who had struck him? *That* was definitely against the rules. No matter how bad the crime, the prisoner was not supposed to suffer mistreatment. How could the jury sit there and ignore this? Someone had to say something. *He* intended to say something. If Cadeyrn didn't like it, he could go to hell. Holden started to open his mouth to speak, but, as if he'd read Holden's mind, Blackwood met his gaze and gave a barely perceptible shake of his head. To others, it may have looked like the brief flex of a stiff neck, but Holden recognised it for the message it was.

"Holden Fay."

At this summons to attention, Holden tore his eyes from Blackwood and looked up at Jackson Banks.

"Do you swear that your testimony here today will be the truth?"

As Banks spoke, one of the attendant witches puffed a handful of fine sand into Holden's face, and the magic settled around him. Asking someone to tell the truth was a moot point; the spell clouding his visage would turn from pale grey to black if he lied. Nevertheless, he gave the expected answer.

"I do."

Banks turned to the prosecutor—a female fae whose expression suggested she'd recently been sucking on a ton of lemons. "Your witness."

Holden could not have said how long he stood there. The two lawyers fired question after question at him. Some were frankly ridiculous, others embarrassingly personal. He struggled to meet the prosecutor's eyes when she demanded a blow by blow account of the night before Blackwood's arrest. Even so, he did his best to answer, and the dust cloud surrounding him never darkened. Little in his testimony would work in Blackwood's favour, yet neither did he believe there was anything in his responses that would make things worse for him. Where possible, within the confines of the questioning, he tried to emphasise the assistance Blackwood had given them. He also dwelt for as long as he dared on the time

Blackwood had saved him from the dart. However, the prosecution twisted that to its own purposes, proposing that Blackwood had probably set the trap to begin with. Saving Holden had merely been another way to garner trust.

By the time the court dismissed him and moved on to the next witness, Holden was fatigued and numb. With his part in the trial over, the same witch who'd brought him to the stand led him to a common room with tea and coffee facilities. It was so mundane it seemed unreal. Holden would have preferred a return to his former solitary confinement. The witnesses who'd gone before him mostly ignored his entrance. The few who didn't peered at him as if he were a leprous sore. He imagined they were all there as witnesses for the prosecution and, as such, would have found his testimony too light on accusations. And they would have heard every word of it, because, in here, a speaker system broadcast proceedings. It wasn't blaring out, but if you chose to listen, you could hear what was being said.

With nothing better to do, Holden *did* tune out the muffled conversations taking place around him and zeroed in on the courtroom narrative. The witness who'd succeeded him turned out to be the last, and he listened as the defence and prosecution made their closing statements. Unsurprisingly, the prosecution pushed for the death sentence, calling Blackwood a cold-hearted killer without whom society would be better off. The defence didn't ask outright for clemency, but they highlighted the fact that Blackwood had repented of his actions and turned himself in, also citing his years of charity work and service to the supernatural and human communities.

To Holden's surprise, neither party mentioned the reason for the killings. The word 'summoning' never passed anyone's lips. Nor had it done his, he realised suddenly. None of the questions the lawyers had posed had provided him with an opportunity to go into the details of the case. That seemed strange. Then again, he'd never been to a real trial before. Maybe what you saw on TV didn't reflect reality.

The jury members made up their minds without delay, returning to the courtroom in less than twenty minutes. The room fell silent as Holden and the other witnesses listened to the verdict. Several people standing behind Holden cheered when the jury declared Blackwood guilty, only to quiet once more, waiting to hear the sentence.

The judge loudly cleared his throat, then spoke.

This time, indignant cries filled the room, but Holden slumped in his chair, relief flooding through him. The judge had eschewed the death penalty, in light of Blackwood's previously clean record. The sentence was one of lifelong imprisonment, here in the Fellowship dungeons.

Holden waited while the others departed, blocking out their mutterings. He gripped Blackwood's ring so tightly that, when he finally withdrew his hand from his pocket, the seal had left an imprint on his palm. He'd hoped that by letting the crowd leave first he would avoid any undue attention as he made his exit. However, the press was waiting for him.

Cameras and microphones swamped him the moment he stepped into the lobby. He brushed them aside as best he could, but the reporters crowded around, calling out questions, most of which focused on his 'night of passion with a convicted killer'. A burst of speed and strength would have seen him break free, but he was loath to add fuel to the fire. All he needed was for one of them to fall and twist their ankle, or damage their camera, and they'd be crying assault at the top of their voices. His hesitation to act proved fatal, however.

After a few steps, they'd created such a solid wall of bodies he couldn't move at all. The flashing cameras all but blinded him, and the storm of questions became a deafening roar. His stomach somersaulted as a wave of panic swept through him. He was trapped. There was no way out. Then, something forced the mob out of the way.

A hand encircled Holden's wrist, and someone tugged him forward at high speed. They escaped the crowd, passing through the doors, onto the street, and around the corner in a matter of seconds. When they came to a halt in a dark, sheltered alleyway, Raoul backed Holden against the wall and grasped his shoulders.

"They'll be waiting at your flat too. I swear, reporters are worse than the Parisian sans culottes on execution day. You'd better stay at my place until they tire of the story." He paused. "If you want to, that is."

Holden nodded his acquiescence. There was no point maintaining his anger toward Raoul. The trial was over, the outcome better than he'd dared hope. He needed his friend more than he needed to make a statement. With a verdict passed, he could do nothing more for Blackwood. It was time to mend a bridge or two and decide what to do next.

Chapter Seventeen

HOLDEN SPRAWLED OVER Raoul's leather sofa, nursing his third double brandy. A faint buzz, centred in his temples, told him the alcohol was finally taking effect. Another eight or nine and he might be able to pass out. Raoul sat beside him. They'd exchanged little in the way of conversation since Raoul had rescued him from the camera-wielding horde, but a subtle shift in Raoul's posture suggested that was about to change.

"Sorry about the other week."

Holden waved away the apology. "Forget it. For what it's worth, I'm sorry too."

There was a pregnant pause. Raoul clearly had more to say, so Holden waited, taking another gulp from his glass to fill the void.

"He defended you, you know."

Holden nearly choked. "My father?"

Raoul made a sound somewhere between a cough and a laugh. "The day *he* has a kind word for anyone, hell will freeze over. No, I mean Blackwood. Before you took the stand, the prosecution was trying to put you forward as an accomplice. He'd been pretty subdued up till then, barely reacting to anything, keeping his answers to a simple yes or no. However, at that suggestion, he came to life. He demanded to speak and made a loud and vehement declaration of your innocence. The prosecution had no choice but to back down. He may be a bastard, but I'll allow he has some marks of honour."

"Why did he do it? Did he say?" As he spoke, Holden realised the question was ambiguous; however, he trusted that Raoul would understand his meaning, and he did.

"Power, apparently. He wanted to maintain his position as the city's greatest witch. Although, I can't see how murdering a few low-level witches would help him achieve that." Raoul shook his head. "Honestly, Hol, the court didn't seem to care about the whys and wherefores. The prosecution was only interested in revealing all the gory details of each murder, pushing for a swift conviction. Even his defence counsel made no attempt to provide a detailed motive or offer any extenuating circumstances. In fact, there was a distinct haste to the proceedings as a whole that I didn't much care for. That, coupled with the way he protected you, is what made me change my vote."

Holden blinked, confused. "You said he was innocent?"

"Oh no. He was guilty as sin. We all knew that; he'd confessed as much. But we can put forward a recommendation regarding the sentencing. Under other circumstances, I'd have been in favour of the death penalty on this one. As it happened, my vote tipped the balance toward imprisonment."

"Thank you!" Holden flung his arms around Raoul. The action sloshed brandy over the couch, and Raoul broke free of Holden's grasp and leaped to his feet.

"Damn! Watch the leather!" He shot across the room to grab a tea towel, and then began to mop up.

"Sorry," Holden said, patting at a damp spot with his sleeve. "I was just relieved."

Raoul paused in his cleaning and studied Holden. "He really got under your skin, didn't he?" He set the tea towel on the coffee table, dropped to one knee, and clasped Holden's hands. "Look, Hol. Please don't take this the wrong way—I don't want us to fight again—but you do realise it's over. Right? Whatever you felt for him, you have to quash it. Blackwood will rot in a cell for the rest of his days. You'll never see him again. Promise me you're not going to spend your life pining for something you can't have."

"I won't."

As hard as the words were, Holden meant them. Raoul was correct. He couldn't mope over Blackwood forever. That was the definition of futility. Nonetheless, neither did he wish to stay here. Knowing Blackwood resided in the earth beneath his feet, having to pass over that spot as he moved about the city, was more than he was willing to bear.

"I'm leaving London, Raoul. As soon as possible."

Raoul settled back on the couch beside him. He didn't look surprised by the news. "You're resigning from the Investigations Team?"

"I doubt that's necessary. After everything that's gone down, even my father would be hard-pressed to persuade them to keep me on, and that's supposing he deigned to try. It would be in Owens's best interest to wash her hands of me at this point too."

"Where will you go?"

"To the country. Vague, I know, but I've not given it much thought yet. I'll sell the flat and buy a little cottage somewhere."

"I'll miss you, Hol."

"I'll miss you, too, but you can always come and visit."

"You'd better not delve too deep into the wilderness, then. You know I can't stand to be far from civilization."

"Be adventurous for once."

"I *am* adventurous, in all the ways that matter: in the bedroom and in a bar. At least make sure there's indoor plumbing."

Holden managed a smile. "That much I *can* guarantee."

THE DAYS THAT followed proved busy—Holden ensured it was so. The more he had to do, the less time he had to think. Raoul knew a guy who knew a guy, and Holden was able to sell his flat quickly and efficiently, without the bother of agents and open days. With a transfer date only a week away, the bulk of Holden's time had disappeared down the rabbit hole of online house listings as he sought his dream cottage. Raoul had said there was no rush, that Holden could stay with him for as long as he needed, but he was in no mood to linger.

On the morning after the trial, Owens had called to confirm what he'd already suspected: his services were no longer required. She'd sounded apologetic, but it was an awkward conversation for them both, so Holden hadn't maintained it any longer than necessary. Thankfully, he'd left no personal belongings at the office, thus evading the walk of shame. Even if he had left anything there, he'd probably have chosen to abandon it rather than have to fill a cardboard box while Draper and the others ogled and gossiped.

In the end, it was on Halloween that Holden finally came across the perfect property. The one-bedroom cottage in the Cotswolds was well within budget and available immediately. So anxious was he to leave London behind that he phoned the agent and offered the asking price sight unseen. It was a risk. But from the photos, the place looked to be in reasonable condition, and if it wasn't, he would still have enough money remaining to effect repairs. The agent emailed the contract, and Holden signed and sent it back. An hour later, he received confirmation that the cottage was his.

His relief was palpable. For the first time since that dreadful day of revelation, he felt as if he could breathe freely again. His thoughts strayed to Blackwood. How was *he* faring, locked away? Holden had never seen the dungeons, but he'd heard the tales. Were the stories even half-true, the medieval vaults were not somewhere anyone would wish to be confined. Still, it had to be better than death. Or was it? Would Blackwood have preferred a swift end to a lifetime trapped deep underground?

Holden trampled the idea before it could take hold. What good was such conjecture? Dwelling on the point wasn't going to change anything. It would only serve to drive him mad. As heartless as it seemed, the best thing he could do would be to try to forget Valerius Blackwood. Tomorrow he would leave London. This was his chance for a fresh start, and he needed to embrace that wholeheartedly. Otherwise, he might as well stay here, for all the good the move would do him.

Chapter Eighteen

HOLDEN LOVED HIS new home. The night prior to his departure from London, Raoul had helped him pack, and early the next morning, just before Raoul went to bed, he'd set off. The drive had gone smoothly—in commencing at sparrow's fart, he'd beaten the worst of the motorway traffic—and he'd arrived to find the cottage exactly as pictured. Sure, he'd had to replace a couple of washers on leaky taps, and the pipes did make quite the percussive symphony when you turned on the faucets, but that added to the character of the place. Perhaps Raoul would disagree on that point when he came to visit. However, Raoul could be a snob at times, and his opinion wasn't the only one that mattered. Holden liked the house's creaks and quirks.

It hadn't taken long to unpack; Holden didn't own that much stuff. Even so, there was already a homely feel about the place, especially when he got the wood fire going in the evenings, drawing on his limited magical abilities to create the necessary spark to ignite the tinder.

Aside from taking long, brisk walks in the bracing autumnal air, and a couple of quick trips to the closest town for supplies, he'd spent most of the time since his arrival looking into work options. That was one thing he'd not been able to settle prior to departure. He had enough cash left from the sale of his flat to see him through the first few months—maybe six if he was frugal—but he couldn't afford to be complacent. Eventually, he'd need a way to earn some money. He'd already submitted a few applications, but he wasn't hopeful. Maybe he would have no choice but to ask around in the local community. The only issue was maintaining his glamour. Although, if he could find something part-time, where he could wear his hair down, he might be able to manage.

Thus a week quickly passed. He was alone, but mostly he kept busy enough never to notice he was lonely. The only time such thoughts struck him was after dinner, when he sat in front of the television, not watching whatever mindless program happened to be playing. Then, his mind would drift as he fingered the ring that dangled against his chest. He'd considered disposing of it during the move, but he'd been unable to bring himself to act. Instead, he'd found some cord, threaded it through the ring, and fastened the makeshift necklace around his neck. There it remained.

He liked to pretend it was a cautionary reminder—a talisman of sorts. In reality, he knew it was more a maudlin memento of a time best forgotten. So what? Maybe one day he'd remove it, shove it in the back of a drawer, and never think of it again. But he wasn't ready for that just yet. His mixed bloodline made it difficult to determine his expected longevity. However, for all he knew, he might live forever. At the very least, he had centuries ahead of him. There was no rush. He'd already switched county and moved house. One step at a time.

As he sat in one of these contemplative trances, his phone rang. He answered without looking at the screen. There was only one person it could be.

"Started the evening debaucheries yet?"

Raoul chuckled. "Why? Feeling left out?"

"No." It was no lie. He wasn't ready to go *there* again yet either.

Raoul made a choking sound. "Urgh! You got me! Right in the pride!"

"Come off it. We both know you're thicker-skinned than that. Besides, if you're feeling needy, there're plenty of people who'd be more than willing to stroke your vanity."

"Among other things." Holden could hear the smirk in Raoul's voice. "So, how's life in the sticks?"

"Quiet."

"Dead."

"Peaceful."

"Dull."

They shared a laugh. Then Raoul continued.

"Actually, I was surprised you didn't ring last night."

"Why would I? Fates! I didn't miss your birthday, did I?" With all the drama of the last few months, Holden realised he didn't even know what day it was anymore.

"No. It's only November, so unless you've invented time travel since you left..." Raoul paused. "Are you telling me you haven't heard?"

The tonal shift in the conversation wasn't lost on Holden, and he experienced a flicker of unease. "What happened? Is it Va—Blackwood?"

"Not exactly, but, well, there's been another murder."

"He escaped?"

"Hell, no. No one gets out of the dungeons unless the Council brandishes the key. However, it seems he has a fan. Someone killed a witch in St. Pancras. I don't know how you've missed it. It's been all over every supernatural news channel for nearly twenty-four hours."

"I've not been on there."

Since the move, Holden had restricted his online activities to safe, human-run sites, fearing what he might read about Blackwood, and himself, were he to visit any of the secret community web pages. Human news channels still mentioned Blackwood, of course, but only in passing. He was apparently on an extended overseas humanitarian aid trip. No doubt, after a suitable period of time had elapsed, they'd report him as killed abroad in a tragic accident, to account for his disappearance from public view.

"It was sloppy work by all accounts," Raoul explained, "with none of Blackwood's finesse and forethought. So much so, the human reporters and the human police got there before the Fellowship. Your father and his cronies are spewing. They couldn't even view the scene, let alone control it."

Holden relaxed. "So, you're saying it's just a bizarre coincidence?"

Raoul hummed. "I don't believe in those. More likely someone decided to take advantage of the Blackwood debacle to settle a personal vendetta, thinking to hide behind someone else's pattern."

"Is Owens on it?"

"I believe so."

Holden considered. Technically, it was nothing to do with him anymore. Nevertheless, he wondered if he should ring her, to see if she needed anything.

"It's not your concern, Hol." Raoul knew him too well at times. "If I'd realised you knew nothing of it, I never would have brought it up. Return to whatever it is you're doing in the back of beyond, my friend, and forget I said anything. Doubtless the Fellowship, or even the human police, will nab the guy in the next few days anyway."

They exchanged a few banalities, and then Raoul rang off. Holden immediately turned on his tablet.

He went straight to the Fellowship's official site and checked the details released. The killing had occurred during the last full moon. Perhaps Raoul was right and this *was* merely opportunistic. Yet, what if there was more to it? If Blackwood failed to complete the sacrifices at the correct time, the demon wouldn't manifest. He knew that much. But what would happen if someone else continued the work?

Holden shook his head and closed the screen. He was leaping to conclusions. This was one of the reasons he'd left the city. Had he still been on hand, he'd have been hammering on Owens's door by now and would look like a total nutcase. Copycat killers sprang up from time to time. It wasn't unheard of. Besides, Raoul had declared the murderer to be 'sloppy', and that suggested a hasty act, rather than a planned ritual. It was an unfortunate reminder which had set him on edge. But that's all there was to it. They'd catch the culprit soon enough, and in the meantime, he'd waste no more time and emotion thinking about it.

Chapter Nineteen

DESPITE HIS GOOD intentions, Holden wasn't able to put the murder completely from his mind. Once or twice during the first week, he checked the sites for updates. No announcement came of any capture, but as the days passed, the media lost interest, and gradually it ceased to occupy Holden's thoughts too. He had other things to contemplate: he'd found a job.

It wasn't much, and it was only temporary, but it was a start. The extra money was welcome, as was the activity, which helped distract his mind by keeping his body moving. From now until the end of January, he was a casual employee of a nearby supermarket. They needed additional pairs of hands during the festive season. It was shelf stocking, essentially, and most of the work took place either late at night or early in the morning, meaning he didn't have to maintain his glamour for too long or in front of too many people. Though the task was mindless, he found the work rather soothing. Boxes went up and boxes came down. No one stared or jeered. Aside from a few greetings at the start of each shift, and goodbyes at the end, he was practically invisible.

It was five a.m. one day in early December when his phone vibrated. He set aside the carton of sultanas he was in the middle of unpacking, tugged the mobile free from his back pocket, and accepted the call with a flick of his thumb.

"I'm at work, Raoul. Can I call you back tonight?"

"Holden?"

Holden nearly dropped the phone. "Captain?" He glanced around. No one was in sight, and everything seemed normal, but he had to have nodded off.

"How've you been?" The question—as mundane as they came—convinced him he was awake.

"All right." He hesitated. "You?"

"Same old." Owens drew an audible breath. "Listen, Holden. Can you come in?"

"In? You know I moved, right?"

"I know. You said you were at work?"

"Yeah. I finish in an hour."

"Can you drive down after that?"

The 'yes' was on the tip of his tongue, so used was he to immediate acquiescence to any request from above. But then he paused. Owens wasn't his boss anymore. He didn't owe the Fellowship anything. He was out. He was clear of that world, with its social hierarchies and snobberies. And he intended to keep it that way.

"Sorry, but it's been a long night, and that's no short distance to cover on zero sleep."

"Don't you even want to know why?"

She sounded weary and on edge, and the first chink appeared in Holden's hastily fashioned mental armour. A thought occurred to him.

"Is it Blackwood? Is he okay?"

"What?" A note of exasperation crept into her voice. "This has nothing to do with Valerius fucking Blackwood. There's been another murder."

"I heard about St. Pancras. Did you get the guy?"

"No, not St. Pancras. That was last month. I'm talking about last night."

Holden's stomach dropped so fast he had to catch the shelf's edge to stop him from falling. "Same MO?"

"Yes."

He did the math. There'd been another full moon last night—the last of the year. That was disquieting, to be sure. Unless their copycat had more than one axe to grind, or there was more than one copycat, it looked as if last month's murder had not been coincidental or opportunistic. Was this new perp following Blackwood's pattern, or had he simply taken Blackwood as his inspiration and started the process from scratch? Did it matter? It wasn't his case anymore. He wasn't even on the Fellowship's payroll. They'd kicked him out.

"Why call me?" One reason came to mind. "Fuck! I'm not a suspect again, am I? My supervisor will confirm that I've been here all night." He glanced at the cameras overhead. "There's security footage."

"Calm down. No one's suggesting this was you."

"Well, that makes a change." He knew he was being snarky, but he couldn't help it. "Usually everything's my fault somehow."

"Holden, I'm asking you to come in because... Well, the truth is, we need your help. Just take a look at the scene and tell us what you think."

"What? You can't be serious. Captain, I failed to spot a serial killer when he was right in front of me, when he—" He decided it would be better not to go there and changed tactic. "What can *I* do that the others can't? It's not like my track record's been stellar."

"Blackwood fooled us all. But prior to that, you uncovered a lot of useful intel, seeing things we'd missed. This isn't coming solely from me. It was the Council who instructed me to call you."

"The Council?"

Holden's brain turned to mush. Why would the Council request his return? They were all pure-blood snobs. He couldn't see why they'd want a halfen's help...unless they considered him to be a last resort, which meant things were even more dire than the picture Owens was painting. A rebellious part of him wanted to tell them to get stuffed. He'd found some semblance of peace here. Why should he return to the city? However, at the same time, he felt a degree of responsibility he couldn't shake. Then there was the fact a request from the Council was tantamount to an order, and if he refused, it would be within their power to make life difficult for him, even all the way out here.

He sighed. "As it happens, I have the next two days rostered off. I can come down when I finish this shift, but I've gotta be back by Wednesday night."

"Thank you, Holden. I do realise this must be...difficult." There was an awkward pause. Then Owens returned to her usual brisk and efficient self. "I'll text you the address. Come straight there. The team will be done by the time you arrive, but I'll have them hold the scene for you."

IT TOOK NINE cans of energy drink to get Holden to London. By the time he'd made it home, got changed, and departed, he caught all the rush-hour traffic heading into the city. Sitting immobile in queues for minutes at a time wasn't helping him keep tired eyes open. Hence the multiple caffeine shots. They did the trick—maybe too well. He was buzzing when he parked close to the address Owens had provided. Or maybe it was an adrenaline rush.

He knocked, surprised at the lack of activity around the building, thinking he'd made an error. However, he knew he was in the right place when Owens answered the door.

"Where is everybody?" He stepped inside and glanced around. The interior of the house was as deserted as the street.

"I sent them back to the office temporarily. I thought you'd prefer to take a look without being subject to scrutiny yourself."

It was only as the wave of relief swept through him that Holden acknowledged how on edge he'd been. "Thanks, Captain."

Owens suddenly lurched forward and enveloped him in a hug. She seemed as taken aback by the action as he was, however, for he had barely moved to return the embrace before she pulled away and focused on a point to the left of his head.

"I'm glad to see you looking well. Country air must agree with you. Come on. Let's get this over with."

Holden followed Owens down the hallway and up the stairs. The scene that greeted him in the bedroom was both familiar yet foreign. He saw at once what Raoul had meant when he'd called last month's attack 'sloppy'. That descriptor was apt for this scene too. Blood had sprayed everywhere, and the wound in the victim's chest was jagged and messy.

"We already did the blood work," Owens said, "but no luck on an ID. She saw the guy, but he wore a balaclava."

"He doesn't have a steady hand, whoever he is. Or else he doesn't care."

Something else occurred to him. "These are more like the Ripper murders—the added sense of aggression and pleasure in his task, the lack of precision. If we didn't already have a killer for those, I would think this was our man."

"We don't."

"But...Blackwood?"

"Never confessed to the human deaths. I've seen the interview transcripts. He denied knowledge of them the one time the question was put to him. No one bothered to mention it again. Those deaths weren't even raised during the trial."

"You think he was telling the truth?"

Owens shrugged. "You were closer to him than I was." She quickly glanced away. "But I don't see why he'd freely admit to the others and yet refute those, unless he really had nothing to do with them."

"I agree."

There was a pause. Holden knew they were both thinking about just how close he'd been to Blackwood, if only briefly. It wasn't a subject upon which he wished to linger, so he returned his attention to the crime scene, focusing on what other clues the room had to offer.

He advanced and studied the bed upon which the victim lay. There, again, things were different yet the same. The sigil was in place. However, the mark was not as well hidden as the others had been, nor was it as deftly executed. The chips in the wood were as uneven as the cuts in the victim's flesh. He leaned in to study the carving.

"It's a new one." He swallowed. "It could just be a coincidence."

"You don't believe that any more than I do."

"No. I don't."

Any hope he'd retained that these killings were mere coincidences had fled when he saw the mark. He remembered it as another from the page in Blackwood's book. Someone was continuing the original summoning. Or trying to, anyway. Holden didn't know enough about the ritual to be sure whether or not that would work. Could another hand complete the sequence? It wasn't something there'd been any call to investigate before.

"There was one at the November murder too?"

Owens nodded. "Although, what we know about that murder is all second-hand intel, obtained from Scotland Yard, and they had no idea what they were dealing with when they processed the scene."

Holden stared down at the blood-splattered mark. "That means only two more murders to complete the summoning." He turned back to Owens. "I need to take another look at that spell."

BACK AT THE office, Holden found his desk exactly as he'd left it. There'd been plenty of head turning and gaping at his arrival, but so far no one, save Owens, had addressed a single word to him, and that suited him fine.

The minutes and hours ticked by as he pored over the scans. There had to be something here they could use. However, despite staring at the writing and illustrations until he went cross-eyed, nothing new jumped out at him. If he'd failed to solve the mystery before, how did they expect him to do so now? The crime scene photos were likewise void of anything inspiring or revelatory, and his caffeine buzz had long since worn off, leaving him with a pounding headache. He didn't notice the others had packed up and gone home until Owens appeared at his side, a handbag slung over her shoulder and her coat buttoned.

"Do you have someplace to sleep tonight?" she asked, glancing at the wall clock. "Sorry. I should have thought to book you in somewhere."

Holden followed the line of her gaze. How was it that late already? "Yeah," he lied. "A friend of mine offered to put me up." He hadn't called to tell Raoul he was in town yet, but he could do so in a minute. He didn't think Raoul would turn him away.

"Get some sleep," Owens advised. "We'll talk again in the morning."

She departed, and Holden slumped in his chair. He pinched the bridge of his nose and squeezed his eyes shut. When he tried to reopen them, he found it a struggle. A five-minute doze couldn't hurt. Then he'd ring Raoul and call it a night.

As he drifted, a thought occurred to him. It was a potential solution to their problem, a way to progress the case, and by far the best idea he'd come up with so far. The trouble was, he doubted the Council was going to like it.

Chapter Twenty

FIVE MINUTES TURNED into nine hours. Holden only woke when Owens arrived the next morning. She raised an eyebrow but said nothing, and he ventured no explanation, launching instead into an outline of his plan, before he chickened out. At the conclusion of his rapid speech, she looked at him as if he'd grown an extra head and plague sores covered both visages. Nevertheless, he stood his ground and awaited her response.

"Fucking hell, Holden! The Council will never agree to this."

"I was thinking we didn't need to involve them just yet. You have access yourself, don't you?" He couldn't see that she wouldn't, in her position.

"Holden, charges were nearly laid against you last time. If you do this, it'll look like you..." She grimaced.

"Like I what? The Council called me back here because they're desperate. We both know that, so there's no need for pretence. Given how worried they are, I can't understand why someone hasn't thought of this already. Surely it should have been their first choice, before contacting me. Any one of you could have gone down there."

"It's not the Council's policy to engage with committed felons."

"Fates! Spare me the company line, Captain. *You* called *me* here. Tell me you have a better lead since last night, and I'll drop this one. However, this is the only suggestion I can come up with. If you won't entertain it, there's little point in me sticking around any longer."

Owens hesitated, and Holden knew why. He was putting her in a difficult position. Nonetheless, she had to see they were out of options. They either tried this, or they had to accept there would be two more murders. The Council members would agree with him. Of that he was certain. Assuming they could manage to peer over the top of their egos long enough to view it objectively.

"I can get you in," Owens finally said. "One visit. If nothing useful comes of it, I'm not sticking my neck out again."

"Got it." Holden suppressed the grin that threatened; it hardly seemed appropriate. Instead, he tried hard for sombre seriousness. "When can we go?"

"We'd better do it right away, before I come to my senses and realise what utter lunacy this is."

OWENS'S PASS GOT them into the only lift that descended below the legal floors—a tiny, ancient cage that rattled and creaked and juddered—but either the dungeons were deeper than Holden had imagined or time had slowed to a crawl, because the trip down seemed interminable. Was this death-trap-waiting-to-happen ever going to halt?

"Stop fidgeting!" Owens whisper-snapped. "They're never going to let us in if you don't quit acting so fucking suspicious and guilty. Or else, they'll let you in, but you'll never get out again."

"Sorry." Holden linked his hands behind his back and repressed the urge to rock backwards and forwards. He'd been pondering something all the way down, and now seemed as good a time as any to voice it, especially if they'd face scrutiny upon arrival. "Listen. I think I should go in alone."

"Uh-uh. No fucking way."

"Come on, Captain. It makes sense. With you there, it's all formal and intimidating."

Owens snorted. "He's not someone easily intimidated. You know that." She sobered and subjected Holden to a pitying look. "Holden, if you've developed some romantic notion of him in his absence, it's all the more imperative I accompany you."

"I know who and what he is, Captain. I'm not an idiot. I'm just saying, if it's a one-on-one chat, he's more likely to relax. I know *I'd* be more inclined to talk if it were just me and a friend, rather than half the department crowding around."

"I may be big-boned, but I'm hardly the equivalent of half the department. And you are not going in there as his friend. I thought I made that clear."

Holden sighed. "Yes, yes. But you see what I'm getting at, don't you?"

There was a long pause. Then it was Owens's turn to expel a deep breath. It had a tone of defeat that Holden greatly appreciated.

"Very well. You've got to keep it strictly professional though. I don't want to find myself accused of abusing my position to arrange a fucking lover's tryst."

"Captain!"

The protest was heartfelt, but at the same time, Holden couldn't deny that he thrilled at the thought of seeing Blackwood, in a way that had nothing to do with solving the case. He'd never expected to lay eyes on him again, and it was a heady feeling to think that, in a few short moments, he would be doing just that.

Although he'd pooh-poohed Owens's objections, she was right in one respect: he did need to keep in mind why he was there. He couldn't allow any lingering emotions to interfere with his questioning. These new murders didn't absolve Blackwood of the older ones. He remained a killer. That was something Holden couldn't afford to forget.

The lift finally shuddered to a gut-wrenching halt, and Owens straightened her jacket. "Follow my lead and say nothing unless you have to."

Holden fell into step behind Owens, who led the way. In violent contrast to the archaic lift, the corridor they traversed looked almost futuristic. CCTV cameras recorded their every move along the steel-clad tunnel, and when they reached the door at the end, Owens looked up into the closest of them. From the way she maintained the position, keeping her expression neutral, Holden assumed some kind of facial recognition scan was taking place. A moment later, a panel opened beside the door, revealing a fingerprint scanner. Owens placed her hand upon it, the LED flashed from red to green, and at last, the door thundered open.

The hallway beyond was steel-walled like the last. It looked long, and the path sloped downward. Softly flickering halogens provided the only light, lending the confined walkway a ghostly feel. A sudden and severe drop in temperature reinforced that impression, and Holden saw Owens tug up her collar against the chill. Eventually, they reached another door, which swung open at their approach. The sight that met Holden's eyes as he crossed the threshold was like nothing he'd imagined.

When anyone spoke of the dungeons, the term Medieval frequently arose. However, up till now, Holden had assumed that to be solely an affectation, meant to inspire trepidation. As it turned out, it was the stone-cold truth—stone and cold being appropriate terms.

Rather than the state-of-the-art facility Holden had expected, given the walkway by which they'd reached them, the dungeons did, indeed, appear to be Medieval in origin—a little slice of history concealed beneath the modern city streets. The few electric lights overhead, and the computer system at the guard's desk, seemed to be the only grudging concessions to technology. There was certainly no hint of central heating. The guard was well rugged up against the cold, cocooned in a heavy wool-lined coat and matching hat. Holden wondered what the guy had done wrong in the past to land this gig. It didn't seem the sort of assignment designed to entice legions of eager volunteers. But what did he know? Maybe it offered an excellent pension plan.

Owens was already talking. In his fascination with his surroundings, Holden had missed the start of the conversation. He rectified that now, focusing all his attention on the exchange.

"...essay investigating the workings of the modern criminal mind."

The guard—a witch, and a boulder of a man—peered at Holden. "He looks familiar. Has he been here before?"

"The Council recently awarded him a prestigious scholarship. You probably saw his picture in a newsletter."

Holden now understood it had been more than a turn of phrase when Owens said she was sticking her neck out for him. Apparently, getting him in required outright lies.

He felt a twinge of guilt, accompanied by an attack of nerves. Owens had always been decent toward him. He didn't want to get her in trouble. Then again, this was no pretence. He really did believe it was their best shot at stopping the summoning. End results would surely outweigh a few initial falsehoods. Wouldn't they?

"All right." The guard gave Owens a curt nod, and then addressed Holden. "Thirty minutes tops. He's not really authorised to receive visitors." He turned back to Owens. "Consider this a special favour. You'll owe me one."

Owens offered a sweet smile and a coquettish flutter of her lashes. To Holden, it looked put-on, and a blatant attempt to distract and disarm with her feminine wiles, but apparently the guard didn't notice, or didn't care, because he gave a perceptible leer.

"Thanks, Ike." Owens affected an uncharacteristic simper. "I won't forget it."

Ike turned back to Holden. "The cells are fully warded against anyone except Council members. Even a hint of magic will result in a complete lockdown. So, if you want to get out again, don't go pulling any party tricks."

"No, sir."

The deference apparently flattered Ike's ego, because he cracked a brief but noticeable smile, revealing a row of nicotine-stained teeth. "Play by the rules and you've got nothing to worry about. Now, head on through. Third cell on the left."

Ike reached under the desk, and a door immediately appeared to Holden's right. It was a highly efficient concealing spell. He'd not even sensed the magic disguising the entrance. He glanced at Owens, who nodded him on. She attempted a smile. He guessed she'd intended it as a form of encouragement; however, it ended up looking more like a grimace. That did nothing to steady Holden's nerves, but he forced himself to move toward the doorway. Once he crossed the threshold, the heavy wooden door closed behind him and disappeared from view, sealing him in.

There was only a single, dull bulb illuminating the entire corridor, offering scarcely enough light to see where he was stepping, even with his enhanced vision. He could have improved the visibility with magic, but he'd not forgotten Ike's warning. He had no intention of ruining this mission before it had even begun, or being trapped in here on lockdown. His eyes would soon adjust. Until then, he'd have to make do as best he could. He wondered vaguely if a generator was out. Surely they didn't keep it this dark all the time?

At first, he couldn't perceive any doorways, but at last he came across the first cell. The room was misshapen, dug out haphazardly like a man-made cave. Bars ran vertically across the opening, with a door near the centre. Holden approached and peered through the bars, but if there was anyone within, he couldn't see them, and no one called out to him.

He stepped back and hurried on, passing the next cell without pause. When he reached the third set of bars, he ground to a halt. He waited a moment, listening. Somewhere nearby, an underground train roared along its tracks. Then another, heading in a different direction. Behind him, he heard the steady drip of water. Was anyone even in this place apart from him? He glanced back the way he'd come. Trapping him down here would be a great way to get rid of him. But, no. Owens would never go along with something like that. He was being paranoid. Finally, as the last rumble from the Tube faded, eliminating the worst of the white noise, he heard a heartbeat. Someone else *was* here.

Holden forced his feet forward—one step, then two. He was now within touching distance of the bars, but again he hesitated, wondering what to say. Given the circumstances, the standard "Hi. How are you?" wasn't going to cut it. How did you greet an ex-lover now imprisoned for multiple murders? They definitely hadn't covered that one in any of his childhood etiquette classes—a major omission in the curriculum.

"I know you're out there. All that stomping and heaving breathing is hardly subtle. What do you want, Ike?"

The voice was rasping—as brittle as dry leaves crushed underfoot—yet Holden recognised it. "Val?"

A heartbeat passed. Then another.

Holden was about to try again when Blackwood suddenly spoke.

"Is this some new torment meant to quail me? If so, you're wasting your time. I'll not fall for your tricks, Ike. Not again." The sense of emptiness in Blackwood's tone made Holden shiver.

"Um. No. It's not a trick, and it's not Ike. It's me. It's Holden," he added, a little desperately, after receiving no response. Had he been so unmemorable that Blackwood had forgotten him in just a few weeks?

"Holden?" There was movement. Holden could make out shifts in the shadows between the bars. "Did they arrest you?"

"No. I'm just here to talk." Holden swallowed his sudden and inexplicable fear and took a step closer.

"Ah. Well, that's something, I suppose. After the trial, I was concerned they wouldn't let you be."

Blackwood approached, and between his proximity and the adjustment of Holden's vision, Holden could see him reasonably clear, if not exactly well. And maybe it was a good thing the light was so dim, because Blackwood had undergone a shocking change. He was pale, and definitely thinner than the last time Holden had seen him. However, that might simply have been an illusion caused by his current attire. The pyjama-like grey ensemble was a far cry from the elegant, well-cut suits of the past. It hung off him like a sack. His hair was as uncombed and wild as it had been on the stand, but longer now, as was his scraggly beard. The bruise on his cheek had disappeared, but a new one graced his temple. When he shuffled up to the bars, Holden noticed that he was barefoot.

"Aren't you freezing?" Holden was feeling a little chilled, and he wore multiple layers and possessed a modicum of a vampire's imperviousness to the cold.

Blackwood shrugged stiffly. "You get used to it."

Holden seriously doubted that, but he wasn't going to argue the point now. He wanted Blackwood talkative, not vexed. "I wanted to ask you some questions."

"You want to know why I did it." Blackwood leaned heavily against the bars. "I'm surprised the Council agreed to let you down here. They were careful to ensure that nothing about the summoning or my motives came out during the trial."

Holden tensed. "What do you mean?" He shifted forward and almost reached out to brush Blackwood's hand, until he thought better of it and crossed his arms instead, removing the temptation. "Are you suggesting it was about more than keeping the truth from the public to avoid panic?"

"They don't know you're down here, do they?" Blackwood straightened, suddenly alert. "By the powers, Holden. You're playing with fire. If they find out they'll—"

"There's been two more murders." So much for the slow approach. He'd intended to lead into the topic with more subtlety, but the words had come out of their own accord.

Blackwood tightened his grip on the bars, visibly agitated. "Tell me everything."

Holden paused before responding. How much could—and should—he reveal? That was a crucial point he'd neglected to raise with Owens before they came down here. Surely he had to be able to say something. Otherwise, how did they expect Blackwood to help? Besides, what harm could there be in telling him? He was shut away. What was he going to do with the information?

He met Blackwood's gaze. "The first was in early November."

Chapter Twenty-One

BLACKWOOD LISTENED AS Holden related what little he knew of the November murder, and what he'd seen of the last attack. Aside from pursing his lips and grimacing a few times, he offered no response to what Holden was saying, and when Holden finished his narrative, an uncomfortable silence reigned.

"What do you want from me?" Blackwood finally asked. He sounded weary, defeated. "I can't tell you who's behind these killings, because, I swear, I don't know. I was certain all this would end once I'd turned myself in."

"But you must know *something*. This was your ritual. You set it in motion."

"The Council doesn't want the truth to come out. That much was obvious during my trial. They suppressed and obfuscated."

"But they're the ones who called me back to help catch the killer, so whatever other motives they may have had, they can't want the summoning to succeed."

"Back? Back from where?"

A tidal wave of guilt washed over Holden, though he wasn't sure why. Perhaps he was loath to have Blackwood think that he'd run away, that, as usual, he'd taken the coward's way out. "I-I left London after..." The words caught in his throat, but his meaning was clear.

"Oh." Blackwood frowned. "Who knows you're down here?"

"Only Owens. Well, and that Ike guy, since he let us in."

"Don't trust Ike. Owens…I don't know." He cast a beseeching look through the bars. "Holden, do something for me. Consider it a last request, if you wish. Tell them you're at a loss. Admit defeat, and get out while you can."

Holden shook his head. "I can't. I have to see this through now."

That hadn't been part of his plan. He'd told Owens that he'd take a look at the scene and offer his thoughts—no more. Yet, he'd changed his mind. Whether it was seeing the crime scene or seeing Blackwood, he couldn't say, but he knew he'd be calling the supermarket when he got out of here, to tell them he couldn't return to work on Wednesday.

Blackwood sighed. "Very well. I'll do what I can to help. As little as you may believe it, I don't want the ritual to succeed."

"I do believe you."

Somehow, he did. There was something in Blackwood's expression, and in the tone of his voice, that made Holden accept every word as true. He knew he was probably being naive, and Blackwood could easily be manipulating him again. However, he couldn't help his credulity. After a lifetime as a silent observer, Holden considered himself well versed in reading people, and Blackwood seemed sincere. He glanced down at Blackwood's bare feet again; they had to be like ice blocks. Then he focused on the fresh bruise that marred Blackwood's forehead. The latter made him recall that Blackwood had assumed he was Ike when he'd first entered.

"Why can't I trust Ike?"

"Was he pleasant? Did he smile?"

"Briefly."

"He's a Janus. He's different unobserved. I've yet to ascertain if that's his nature or if he's acting under instruction. Either way, I advise steering clear of him."

Holden clenched his fists. "I'll tell Owens what's going on. She'll raise it with the Council."

"To what purpose?" Blackwood didn't pretend to misunderstand, which only confirmed Holden's suspicions about his ill treatment. "All that will do is alert them to the fact you were here without authorization. Besides, I'm a convicted criminal. I doubt they'll care, and neither should you. Forget about me, Holden. There are more important things afoot."

Holden knew Blackwood was right. That didn't make it any easier to stomach, but he'd promised Owens that he'd keep this meeting professional, and Blackwood's living conditions were not the reason he was here.

"Okay. Tell me how to stop the summoning. There's got to be something we can do to, I don't know, block it, nullify it."

"There is no counterspell, no quick fix. The only way is to prevent whoever's continuing the ritual from seeing it through to completion. Get to him before the next full moon. If that night passes without an offering being made, the ritual is over."

"But how am I supposed to find him? You say you don't know who it is, and I haven't a clue where to start."

"The problem is you don't know what's really happening. You never did. You see, demons are not what we've always been told. They're—"

Blackwood cried out and staggered back. The bars to his cell were glowing, as if burning from within. A bright light pulsed down the corridor, so blinding that Holden, too, retreated, shielding his eyes. Nonetheless, he recognised the illumination for what it was. Someone was opening a portal.

When the light faded and Holden uncovered his gaze, he immediately dropped into a deep bow. "Father."

Cadeyrn stormed toward him. He grabbed Holden by the collar and jerked him upright. "You dare to address me as such when you heap further disgrace upon me? You will come before the Council. Perhaps now they'll realise they should have listened when I counselled against your recall."

"Wait! Give me a moment, Father. I need to—"

"Silence!"

Cadeyrn dragged Holden with him down the corridor, toward the exit, which shimmered into view at their approach. Meanwhile, Blackwood charged back to the bars and stretched an arm through them, reaching out.

"Holden! Holden, you need to know—"

Cadeyrn waved his free hand, and the bars gave another heated pulse. Blackwood emitted a second pained scream and then fell silent, disappearing back into the shadows.

Ire replaced shock and fear, and Holden jerked free of his father's hold. However, it was too late to race back to Blackwood. They'd already reached the door, and Ike was there to meet them. He was smiling again, but this time it was a different kind of smile—one that promised danger and pain—and Holden saw what Blackwood had meant in his assessment of the man. Ike's hand replaced Cadeyrn's on Holden's shoulder, and Holden could tell there would be no reprieve. Whether he liked it or not, he was off to see the Council.

THE COUNCIL'S CHAMBERS were on the top floor of the Fellowship building. Wards kept the room a portal dead zone, which was part of the reason why they'd had to take the long way up, via the lifts. Though Holden expected the extended journey was also an attempt to make him sweat. Cadeyrn hadn't spoken since his outburst in the dungeons, and Holden had nothing to say to him. No, that was incorrect. He actually had a great deal he'd like to say to the Minister for Justice, but now did not seem a good time to push his luck—not when he was already in trouble.

Holden knew most of the current twenty-seven Council members by sight. However, he'd met only a couple of them, and never formally like this. A summons before the Council was rarely an auspicious occasion. It was probably something of a miracle he'd avoided it until now.

When they entered, eight councillors sat in a semicircle on a raised platform, one empty seat making up the nine members required to form a quorum. Their backs were perfectly straight and their expressions solemn. It made Holden wonder if they monitored the hallway via live feed, so they could school their features and postures before the doors opened, thereby creating the right impression: equal parts authority and condemnation.

His father guided him to stand before the assembly, then took his place among them. When Holden glanced down, he noticed the floorboards directly beneath his feet were worn, lacking the shine seen elsewhere in the room. How many had stood here prior to him, eyes downcast, shuffling their feet, rubbing away the polish bit by bit?

"Holden Fay."

Holden looked up and met the speaker's gaze. It was Ursus Lanstrom, the witch who held the position everyone believed would eventually go to Blackwood. Or, at least, that *had* been the assumption. It seemed unlikely now. Holden didn't suppose Lanstrom had any complaints regarding Blackwood's downfall. It had rid him of a competitor.

"Do you know why you're here?" Lanstrom continued.

"I'm sure you're going to tell me." It was borderline cheeky—more than borderline, judging by his father's stormy expression—but Holden suddenly found he didn't care.

Lanstrom ignored the backtalk for the time being and proceeded. "Breaking into the dungeons is a serious offence."

"I didn't break in. The guard admitted me." It seemed a distinction worth noting.

"But you had no authorization from the Council, so it amounts to the same thing," Lanstrom grumbled. He reminded Holden of one of his former tutors. That fellow had often huffed in a similar manner, usually when Holden had failed, yet again, to master even the simplest of the magical arts. "An example must be made, so you will spend one week in a cell. Captain Owens, for her part in this, will stay there for a month, and she'll lose her badge."

"That's unfair. This was my plan. I persuaded her to take me down there."

"The sentences have been passed. A guard waits outside to escort you back downstairs."

Holden sagged. He never should have returned to London. He'd been happy in the cottage—mostly. If only he'd stayed there. Perhaps he ought to accept this punishment and count himself lucky it wasn't more severe. It was only one short week. After that, he could go home and return to obscurity. But what of Owens? What of Blackwood? What of those who'd died and the two deaths still to come?

Inspiration struck. Those two future murders were the ones they'd called him back here to prevent. This punishment was a farce. They wanted him cowed. That's what this was really about. They wanted him to go meekly to his cell so that, upon his release, they could wield power over him with the threat of further incarceration. He needed to believe in himself, as Blackwood had once told him. He had to stop acting like the old, downtrodden Holden Fay and start reacting more like... Well, more like Blackwood. Were Valerius Blackwood standing in his place right now, he'd not bow under pressure. He would play them at their own game and dissemble.

Holden straightened. Rather than turning to leave, he forced himself to look up and meet each Council member's eyes, one after the other. "I'm not going to any cell, and neither is Owens. If you lock us away, who will stop the summoning?"

Two Council members exchanged uneasy glances, and Holden knew he was on the right track.

"Unless you want it to succeed," he continued. "I know you kept the truth out of the courtroom."

His father scowled. "Whatever you *think* you know, whatever lies Blackwood has spun, it makes no difference."

"Really?" Holden shrugged, feigning a nonchalance he was far from feeling. "I'll leave you to it, then. Good luck."

As he started to turn, his vampiric hearing caught the catch in the throat of one of the witches seated to his right. Bingo!

"Wait." This came from Lanstrom. "Assuming we forget this matter and let you go free, what will you do?"

"I'll do my best to catch this new killer before he completes the ritual." Holden spread his arms. "Look. I couldn't care two figs what secrets the Council keeps from the masses. All I've ever wanted is to do my job and be left in peace. And currently, my job is to help the Investigations Team catch the bad guys."

"You really believe you can find the person responsible?" Stephan Ivans, a witch from Belgravia, looked incredulous.

Holden gave a firm nod. "If I have the information and resources I need."

It was a bold statement, and he had nothing with which to back it up. However, he couldn't afford to show weakness now. He had to exude confidence if he wanted to leave this chamber a free man and have any chance of catching the killer.

"This is nonsense," Cadeyrn spluttered. "What do you expect this fool to accomplish that others can't?"

Nice to know his father supported him. Not that Holden had anticipated a better response. Still, the continued uncertainty within the room meant it was time to play his final card.

He assumed his best poker face. "*You* called *me* back to town. You wouldn't have done so unless you believed I could solve this. If you doubt that now, I'll happily return to the Cotswolds and not give the case, or your little cabal, another thought. It's all the same to me."

Cadeyrn glared in response, but another member spoke up.

"What would you require? You mentioned resources."

Holden turned to the woman—a fae—and smiled. "I'd like a few guarantees, in writing, for a start."

Lanstrom bristled. "You dare to make demands of the Council?"

Holden's will nearly crumbled at Lanstrom's domineering tone, but he thought of Blackwood and held firm. "I do if you want my help. Naturally, they will be dependent on whether or not I succeed in stopping the killer. If I fail, you won't have to fulfil them. I think that's fair. Don't you?"

Murmurs broke out among the Council members, until Lanstrom loudly cleared his throat and restored order.

He met Holden's gaze. "And what is it you want?"

Chapter Twenty-Two

THE COUNCIL HAD requested time to take Holden's demands under consideration. Nevertheless, when he returned at the appointed time the next evening, they capitulated. Of course, it wasn't all kittens and rainbows. If he failed to deliver on his promise to stop the summoning, he would be facing jail time, as would Owens. When he'd called last night to share the news, she'd reacted to his gambit with mixed feelings, but she had still promised him her full support, along with whatever resources he required, and he couldn't ask for more than that. Now, there was only one thing left to do before he threw himself back into the investigation in earnest.

Ike looked far from pleased when he admitted Holden to the dungeons. However, clearly the Council had been true to its word and someone had informed him of the situation, because he asked no questions, waving Holden through with a surly grimace and tossing him the key as he passed.

Though the cells remained dreary and frozen, on this second visit, Holden thought they had lost some of their menace. Whether that came from increased familiarity or the fact he now wielded the key, he couldn't say. But he experienced no sense of dread as he made his way, unhesitatingly, down to the third cell.

"Blackwood?" He paused, then tried again with a more tentative "Val?"

"Holden." Blackwood emerged from the shadows. He stepped close to the bars but didn't touch them. "How is this possible?" His expression darkened. "Are they locking you in?"

"No. Look!" Holden brandished the key. "As I told you before, I need your help." He slid the key into the lock and turned it. The mechanism emitted a heavy *click-clunk*, and the door opened. It seemed flimsy security, now that he stopped to think about it. Then again, he supposed the cell door was merely perfunctory. The wards, coupled with the high-tech systems in the outer corridors, were the real locks.

Rather than rush eagerly through the open doorway, Blackwood took a step back. "What is this?"

"You're free. Temporarily, anyway. Until we get this guy. I made a deal with the Council. I would suggest you hurry though. We don't want them changing their minds while you dilly-dally." Holden tried to keep his tone light, but in truth, his emotions were churning. This was a huge risk; he accepted that. He only hoped he wasn't mistaken in Blackwood. If he was, this wouldn't end well.

Still Blackwood hesitated. "What kind of deal?"

"I'll explain everything, but I'd rather do it someplace warmer."

Blackwood shuffled forward. He scanned the hallway, as if expecting a trap. Holden could hardly blame him, especially when he saw the fresh bruising around Blackwood's eye and the burns on his palms. Cadeyrn and Ike had a lot to answer for—the whole Council did. This wasn't the Middle Ages. You couldn't torture prisoners with impunity. At least, you shouldn't be able to. It was a point he intended to press home when the chance arose. However, that would have to wait. He had a case to solve first, and Blackwood was safe under his supervision until then.

"Here." Holden held out the forest-green, hooded cloak he'd brought with him, purchased hastily from a fancy-dress shop on the way over—part of a Robin Hood get-up. "The Council has arranged a portal to your house, but until we get to an unwarded space, the fewer people who see you the better. Your release is not being made public knowledge."

Blackwood nodded and pulled on the garment. With the hood masking his face from casual view, the only real oddity was Blackwood's grimy, bare feet, but they would have to roll with that. Perhaps anyone they encountered would take him for a wandering mystic. One still encountered them on occasion. Although, it was considered something of a cliché these days.

As it happened, the precautions proved unnecessary. They met no one on their journey to the Council chambers. Every corridor stood empty, and that was unusual. Holden guessed the Council must have orchestrated it that way. He could picture them issuing a building-wide edict that no one could leave their rooms until further notice. None would disobey.

Although nine Council members had been present prior to Holden's descent into the dungeons, upon his return, only his father remained, standing outside the open chamber doors.

Cadeyrn scowled as they approached. "Don't think I'm going to save you from this folly when it backfires. You made this bed an—"

"And I shall lie it in. Yes, I know the saying." Holden steeled himself. "All I ask from you is a portal to the Blackwood mansion, as the Council promised."

Knowing he had the Council's backing, at least for the present, lent Holden strength. However this drama ended, he promised himself one thing: his days of desperately seeking his father's approbation were over. Cadeyrn was never going to be proud of him, no matter what he did or didn't do, and finally he'd realised it didn't matter. He would not allow his father's opinions to define him. Not anymore.

Cadeyrn's anger glimmered behind his eyes. Nevertheless, he said nothing and conjured the portal. Holden waited until he could clearly see Blackwood's library through the brightness, not entirely trusting that his father wouldn't send them to Siberia, or back to the dungeons, out of spite. Only when he recognised the scene did he grasp Blackwood's arm and step into the swirling mists.

HOLDEN ABANDONED THE latest of his failed attempts to read the book lying open before him and glanced again at the clock. Only three minutes had elapsed since last he'd looked. Was the timepiece running slow? Surely it had to be later than that. Regardless, three minutes was plenty of time for Blackwood to have escaped through a window, giving him the slip. He didn't *think* Blackwood would run. However, he couldn't be certain his feelings weren't screwing with his judgment. It wouldn't be the first time that had happened where Blackwood was concerned. He was still debating whether to go upstairs and check on him when the library door opened and the object of his contemplations entered.

Blackwood's hair was damp from the shower and stuck to his forehead. He hadn't attempted to trim the locks, despite how much they'd grown during his period of captivity, but he had shaved off his scruffy prison beard, once more revealing his sharp cheekbones and the subtle cleft in his chin. His suit hung a little loose, highlighting his weight loss, but even so, donning it seemed to have done wonders for him mentally, because his bearing had improved, returning to him a portion of his former aura of authority. The only thing marring the image was the bruising on his face, which was worse than Holden had initially thought in the dim dungeon lighting and with the beard in the way.

As he crossed the room, Blackwood adjusted his tie. "Apologies for keeping you waiting. The hot water felt like such a luxury after the cold bucket washes of past weeks I lost track of time." Although he tried to mask it, when he straightened his fingers, Holden caught his pained flinch.

"Let me see those."

There was a pause, during which Holden thought he might face a refusal, but then, without a word, Blackwood extended his arms, palms facing up.

Holden gingerly assessed the burns, trying not to put too much pressure on the wounds. They were bad, and it was obvious no one had treated them. He added that to his list of complaints when the time came to return Blackwood to his cell.

"There are no wards to block your magic here. Can't you heal them? There must be a spell in one of these books that could help. A potion, perhaps? I'm happy to help mix it."

Blackwood withdrew from Holden's touch. "I'm hungry and exhausted. I don't have the strength to channel energy and cast at present. It's no matter. I'll attend to them in due course. I can bear the pain awhile longer."

"Maybe I can do it. I'm not great at the healing arts, I've gotta say. But I could try." In truth, he wasn't great at any of the magical arts, but healing a burn seemed straightforward. It was only surface damage. It wasn't like mending broken bones or ruptured organs. "It's better than nothing," he added, with an accompanying shrug.

Blackwood glanced away. "I wouldn't ask that of you."

Seeing Blackwood so abnormally subdued was almost physically painful, and Holden had had enough of it.

"You didn't ask. I offered. Now, are we going to dance around social niceties all day, or are you going to let me do this so we can get on with more important things?"

Without waiting for an answer, he grasped Blackwood's hands again. Blackwood shuddered at the contact, but Holden ignored that and closed his eyes, hoping any momentary discomfort Blackwood experienced from the pressure would be worth it. He felt his way to the cells that made up Blackwood's skin and pushed energy into them, willing them to repair. Exhaustion followed swiftly, as it so often did when he performed magic. It forced him to stop sooner than he would have liked, and when he released Blackwood's hands, they still looked red.

"Damn. I'm sorry. I really thought that would work."

Blackwood flexed his fingers, and his lips curved into the ghost of a smile. "It did. The worst of the pain is gone. There is only a dull ache now, and that and the redness will fade in time." He met Holden's gaze. "Thank you, Holden."

They were close. Too close. Holden wasn't sure which of them instigated it—perhaps it had been a mutual draw—but the next thing he knew, they were kissing.

Blackwood's lips were as warm and inviting as he remembered, and he groaned into them. He pulled Blackwood to him, pawing at his jacket before finally finding purchase and hanging on. Images of their night together flooded his mind. Unfortunately, other pictures soon followed: snapshots from the murder scene Blackwood had left before coming to him.

Holden repulsed Blackwood with a shove, and Blackwood stumbled, coming to a halt against the bookshelf. His eyes, when they sought and found Holden's, were dark with desire, and Holden nearly reached for him again. However, he came to his senses in time.

"We can't do that again. That's not why we're here. It's not why *you're* here."

"Holden, I—"

"No. Let me finish." Holden swallowed heavily. His jeans were uncomfortably tight, his arousal acute, but he couldn't let that distract him. "We have a murderer to catch, and if you aren't going to help, you can go back to your cell." As much as he hated that idea, he accepted it as just and necessary. He mustn't forget his own future was on the line, as was Owens's. "I won't let you trick me a second time," he added, trying to steel his heart...and de-harden other body parts.

"It was never a trick." Blackwood held Holden's gaze, his expression pleading. "Whatever else I may have done, nothing that happened between us was a lie."

"*May* have done?"

"An expression, not a caveat." Blackwood straightened his back but bowed his head. "I committed terrible atrocities, and I accept full responsibility for my actions."

Holden sank to rest on the edge of the desk. He felt so weary. It was as if all the stresses of the last few months were catching up with him at once. "That's what I've been unable to understand. You killed all those people, and we were nowhere near you. You'd have gotten away with it, finished your ritual, yet you chose to give yourself up. Why?"

"Honestly? Because I realised I could."

"That makes no sense."

"Do you remember the day we met?"

"It's hard to forget."

"I didn't insult you because your parentage repelled me. I panicked, plain and simple, and a haughty manner was my ploy to deflect attention. The way you looked at me... There was something so earnest and penetrating in your gaze. You seemed to bore into my very soul, and I feared you would discern the truth, see behind my façade."

"Okay. But why ask me to come to your house that night if you wanted to prevent me from discovering your secrets? Seems counterproductive."

"Because, once I'd calmed, I came to understand you were my one chance. If I drew you close, if I pointed you in the right direction, you would discover my guilt and stop me."

"Wait a minute." He had to have misheard. Blackwood couldn't be saying what he thought he was saying. "You're implying you *wanted* me to catch you."

"Yes!" Blackwood began pacing. "I waited and waited, but I'd been wrong. You didn't see me in the way I'd expected. I'm to blame. If I'd kept things strictly professional, you'd have gotten there, I'm sure. However, I let my growing feelings for you sway me, and it distracted us both. In the end, I had to take matters into my own hands." He halted and turned to Holden. "Though it was still thanks to you. That night, as I held yet another innocent heart in my hands while an invisible force consumed it, I kept seeing your face. I imagined the way you'd look at me if you knew the truth, and that thought—the thought of you, of how much you meant to me—finally gave me the strength I needed to break free."

"Hold on." Holden's head spun as he tried to process this unexpected twist. "Are you trying to tell me you never wanted to kill anyone? That you wanted to stop from the start?"

"Precisely."

The glimmer of hope that warmed him was strong, but Holden did his best to hold it at a distance. Wasn't this too good to be true? All along, he'd struggled to believe Blackwood capable of cold-blooded murder simply to gain power. Nonetheless, Blackwood had probably guessed that and was now telling Holden what he knew he wanted to hear.

"Why should I believe you? It still doesn't account for why you started the summoning to begin with, if you didn't want to do it."

"That I can explain by finishing what I tried to tell you in the dungeons."

Holden straightened. "About the demons?"

"Yes." Blackwood indicated behind Holden with a flick of his chin. "Look over there and tell me what you see."

Still wary, Holden briefly twisted in the direction Blackwood had indicated, determined not to completely turn his back on him. "The painting?"

Blackwood nodded. "You know who it is?"

"Of course. It's Aetius Blackwood—your father. But what does that have to do with demons?"

"Everything."

Chapter Twenty-Three

"DEMONS ARE DEAD witches?"

It was the second time they'd been over this point, but it was so alarming Holden believed it warranted reflection and certainty. Such an idea never would have occurred to him, not even in his wildest fantasies. In all his schooling, demons had been treated as a separate species, something 'other'. That was accepted as indisputable fact, as absolute truth. Or, at least, it had been.

"Only those not laid to rest correctly," Blackwood said, answering the question with no hint of impatience. "When a witch dies, any residual magic within them must be returned to the earth. I was always told it was part of a purification ritual from a bygone age, maintained solely for the sake of tradition, but apparently it does have a purpose. Should any magical power linger in the body too long after the time of passing, it clings to the witch's soul, condemning it to an incorporeal eternity—with us and yet unseen—what humans would think of as ghosts. Only those with the strongest will can make themselves heard and contact the living."

"Say I go along with that..." Holden weighed his words, considering where that left them in terms of the investigation. "I still don't see how that could have happened to your father. He was always big on ritual. I remember that much from his public appearances. Wouldn't he have ensured he was put to rest the right way? And wouldn't you have noticed if something wasn't done correctly?"

"Maybe, if I'd been here. I was overseas at the time. My father had sent me to Australia in his stead, to foster links with several of the major covens there. The funeral took place before I could organise a return flight." Blackwood closed his eyes and rubbed the back of his neck, the gesture heavy and drained. "I confess, I was surprised it was such a hurried, small-scale ceremony, but when I spoke on the phone to our family lawyers, they insisted such had been my father's wish, according to his will. Once I returned home, I barely spared the matter a passing thought. It was over. He was already entombed, and I was immediately overwhelmed with work. I had my new position as head of the coven, and there were numerous financial matters, pertaining to the estate, to settle."

"I remember now. His funeral wasn't even filmed for Fellowship-wide broadcast." Thinking about it, Holden *did* recollect his surprise that Aetius Blackwood's passing hadn't been a grander, more public affair, considering the eminent position he'd held in both supernatural and human communities. He recalled discussing it with Raoul. The conversation stuck in his mind because Raoul had gone on to comment that Holden's father would expect far more pomp and ceremony were *he* to pop his clogs.

"The first time he called to me, I thought I was dreaming," Blackwood continued, his gaze fixed on the carpet. "During the fifth encounter, I began to fear I was going insane. By that point, he'd gained strength—in will, if nothing else. What he asked of me was no longer a desperate plea but a fierce command."

"Your father told you to kill people?"

"Yes."

"For power?"

"No. At least, not for myself. He wanted me to bring him back to this plane, to help him manifest, as he put it."

Holden frowned. "And you didn't think it was wrong?"

"Of course, I thought it was wrong!" Blackwood resumed his frantic pacing. "When I learned what it would entail, I refused. I resisted for as long as I could, but he gave me not a moment's peace. He railed at me, calling upon the bonds of family and the honour of our name. Even then, I stood firm. However, it became too much to bear.

"He haunted me every minute of every day, his voice a constant cacophony of chatter in my head. He even found the means to infiltrate my dreams, denying me repose, waking me with nightmares. I couldn't sleep. I could barely eat. I had to cancel engagements. There was no way I could go out in public. I'd have appeared irrational, even mad."

"This was in May, wasn't it?"

Blackwood nodded.

"You were supposed to present one of the coven award ceremonies, but when I tuned in to watch the broadcast, they said you were ill—a summer chill."

Blackwood barked a harsh laugh. "I was ill. Not with a cold but with hunger, exhaustion. I was haunted, in all senses of the word. He told me that was the price of filial disobedience. However, he proceeded to make me a promise. If I did as he required, if, for a few short months, I obeyed him without question, he would never call on me again after his return. He would release me, and I would be free to live my life as I saw fit, without constraints." He met Holden's eyes. "You, of all people, should understand my dreadful predicament. Suppose it was your father. Suppose he pushed you to the limit of endurance and then made such an offer. Would you have continued to disobey? Could you have maintained your resolution, your moral fortitude?"

Holden shuddered. He wanted to protest that he'd never do evil, no matter who was asking and what the circumstance, but even in his head, the words didn't ring true. Yesterday had been the first time ever he'd stood up to his father, and he'd had the benefit of surprise. Cadeyrn had not expected rebellion from the son he'd quelled into a constant state of submission, so Holden's actions caught him off guard. Had Cadeyrn been better prepared, had he made a counterattack, Holden couldn't state with any degree of certainty his will wouldn't have crumbled. Nevertheless, that was an entirely different situation.

"Maybe not, but your father wasn't like mine. You had a good relationship. I can imagine he was stern at times, sure, but he cared about you, was proud of you."

"He was a monster!"

The words hung in the air, heavy in the already-claustrophobic atmosphere, and Blackwood slumped over one of the high-backed armchairs. The position obscured his face, but Holden could see his torso shudder with each ragged breath. He wondered if he should say something, do something. However, before he could decide on a suitable course, Blackwood spoke.

"Nothing was ever good enough for him." His voice was low but steady, though he didn't alter his position or look at Holden. "Lessons began as soon as I could walk and talk. Whether in magic or mundane studies, he expected nothing but top marks. Even when I did well, there was room for improvement, and punishment followed swiftly if I erred from his proscribed course or failed to meet his exacting standards. I had to be the best witch, in all disciplines. I had to know law, medicine, politics, business. I had to excel in all the social graces—the perfect conversationalist, the most elegant dance partner. The pressure was nigh on unbearable. To this day, I'm amazed I didn't crack. But it did make me adept at creating masks—a public face that hid the private trauma. A smile, when inside I was screaming.

"Naturally, my being gay rather ruined his carefully laid plans. I refrained from telling him until I was thirty-six, keeping my preferences so secret not even my closest associates guessed the truth. By then, his attempts to orchestrate a suitable marriage for me had hit fever pitch. Like a Victorian patriarch, he started lining up eligible daughters from important local families, all but parading them outside my front door every morning. Coming clean was the only way to end it, and I did so in a public broadcast."

"I saw it." Holden didn't think he'd ever forget the moment that had cemented his admiration for Blackwood. "I thought it was brave. I really respected you that day."

Blackwood grimaced. "It wasn't bravery; it was guile. He'd trained me too well. I knew the only way to guarantee he couldn't manipulate me into an unwanted relationship was to ensure everyone knew the truth about my sexuality. Then it was undeniable, and inviolable. He didn't speak to me in private for over a year after that. No one would have guessed though. In public, he played the role of doting father as brilliantly as always."

"I'm sorry," Holden whispered when Blackwood fell silent. "I had no idea."

"How could you? No one had any inkling of the truth, save for the servants, and they knew they'd lose their positions if they dared to breathe a word of it."

Blackwood straightened and smoothed his jacket. By the time he was done, no outward sign of his impassioned outburst remained. His expression betrayed nothing of his feelings; his face had become a stone mask.

Holden's curiosity and empathy prompted him to probe further, but common sense persuaded him against it. The moment had passed, and there were more pressing concerns at present than their mutually horrific upbringings. Although, perhaps it explained why he'd been drawn so strongly to Blackwood right from the start, and Blackwood to him. Below the surface differences, they were two of a kind.

"So, what exactly does your father want? What does 'manifesting' mean?"

The question reanimated Blackwood. He nodded and wagged a finger, before striding to the nearest bookcase. "That is the question." He scanned the titles, then pulled out a few volumes and carried them to the desk. "He never said much to me on the subject—aside from what I needed to know to play my bloody part—and I spent hours poring over these books, looking for answers, only to draw a blank."

"So, we have no way of knowing his true intentions?"

"Not necessarily. We will review them once more, together, in case there's something I missed. In addition, there is one avenue I've yet to explore. It came to me while I was in my cell. Witches are often buried with their personal talismans. Those without direct descendants also take their spell books to the grave. No one passed me my father's grimoire when I returned, nor did I locate it anywhere in the house when I conducted a brief search before all this began. Ergo, it seems reasonable to suspect it's buried with him. Perhaps, once found, it will contain the answers we seek."

"Are you serious? You're suggesting we dig up your dead father?" Holden pictured them creeping through a graveyard at night, shovels in hand, like Resurrectionists of old. What if someone saw them? This was London. There were always people about, no matter the hour. Besides, he was squeamish about decomposition. Could he bear to open a coffin and see the rotting flesh within? And why was Blackwood suddenly smiling in that amused way? It seemed totally inappropriate.

"You look as if you're about to throw up. Don't worry. There'll be no clawing through the sod. My family owns a crypt beneath the chapel a few streets away. Although we have the elaborate ceremonies at St Paul's, all Blackwoods are eventually cremated and their ashes placed there. One panel hides a compartment in which we store family heirlooms." He glanced down at his hand. "Nonetheless, some breaking and entering will be required, since I lost my key."

"Key?"

"My signet ring. It opened the entrance to the crypt and the hidden compartment within. I only noticed it was missing after my arrest. I don't know what happened to it."

"I do."

Despite the confession, it took a few seconds, and Blackwood's raised eyebrow, for Holden to summon the willpower to withdraw the cord from beneath his shirt.

He'd grown accustomed to the feel of the metal band against his chest. So much so, its removal left a gaping hole, a cold absence. He held it up so Blackwood could see. "You left it at my house. I found it on the floor after…" He couldn't bring himself to finish.

Blackwood's gaze left the ring and settled on Holden's face. "Now I recall—it tickled. And you kept it with you all this time?"

"I should have handed it in. But I couldn't. I guess that's lucky, since we need it." He fingered the ring, running his thumb over the crest one last time. "It's yours though. Here." He started to loop the cord over his head.

"No." Blackwood stepped forward and stilled Holden's hands. He eased the cord from Holden's grasp and returned it to its former place, tucking the ring back beneath Holden's shirt and pressing his palm over it. "You keep hold of it. It's safer with you and…" He swallowed. "Well, I hope that leaving it in your care will help prove to you my repentance, and my desire to help end this bloodshed. I will never lie to you again, Holden, and I will never betray you. This I swear."

It was Holden's turn to gulp. Not trusting his voice, he nodded. The warmth of Blackwood's hand, which he felt even through his two layers of clothing, was more than he could handle, so he took a deliberate step back.

Blackwood made no attempt to prolong the contact. When Holden moved away, he returned his hand to his side, his expression blank. "I suggest we wait until evening to visit the chapel. The fewer people who see us there the better, even if we are making an unforced entry."

"Sure. That makes sense. I should let Owens know what we're doing though. We need to keep her up to speed."

At first, Holden thought Blackwood was going to object, but eventually he acquiesced with a subtle wave of his hand.

"As you think best."

A strange tension rose between them that made Holden uneasy. If they were going to work together on this, he needed to dispel it. But how to do so in a manner that wouldn't degenerate into the kind of intimacy they had to avoid?

His stomach chose that moment to growl loudly. Food would be welcome, and it might also provide a way to restore some sense of normality to a situation that was anything but normal, if only until they went grave robbing.

"I don't know about you," he said, with forced cheerfulness, "but I could eat a horse."

Blackwood's hesitant smile did somewhat ease the heavy atmosphere. "After weeks of slop, I do believe I could devour three."

"Unfortunately, I'm not sure the consumption of horse flesh will go down well with the animal rights activists. How about we order a pizza instead? Or maybe nine."

Chapter Twenty-Four

THE AFTERNOON AND early evening passed swiftly, and with greater ease than Holden had anticipated, given the earlier awkwardness. In the end, they'd devoured three family-size pizzas between them. Blackwood had consumed two of those almost singlehanded, eating with a ravenous speed that left Holden wondering what, and how little, the Council had provided him during his stay in the dungeons.

After that, they'd hit the books. Blackwood said he'd already scoured every relevant page, but Holden initially held out hope that a fresh pair of eyes might help. Sadly, that expectation proved to be in vain.

Blackwood was correct: the books offered nothing enlightening, at least in relation to their present situation. The sole focus of the tomes was summoning demons to harness their power. Not a single text even posited a theory on the true nature of demons, or what those demons would get out of any deal made with the witch who summoned them.

Holden set the last of the books back on the shelf and then stretched. He cringed at the audible click in his spine, which had twisted after too long spent bent over the desk. "Is it time for our expedition? I could do with walking out a few kinks."

Blackwood glanced at the carriage clock on the mantelpiece. "Yes. All should be quiet there now. Let me get my coat."

Holden waited in the entrance hall, and after a few moments, Blackwood appeared at the top of the staircase dressed in a full-length, charcoal-coloured woollen coat, a pale-grey scarf hanging loose around his neck. He epitomised fashionable elegance, and this time, even the bruises couldn't mar the effect.

Upon reaching the ground floor, he cast an assessing glance over Holden's attire. "Won't you be cold? You can borrow something of mine."

"Thanks, but I don't feel the cold much." It wasn't an outright lie. The cold affected him far less than it would a mortal, but he did still notice it. However, wrapping himself in one of Blackwood's garments, upon which Blackwood's scent no doubt lingered, was not a distraction Holden needed. He'd take the cold. At least that would keep him alert.

It was a journey of barely five minutes on foot to reach the chapel. No lights shone through the stained-glass windows, and there was only a handful of passing cars. A caw from a nearby tree drew Holden's attention. The crow seated on one of the bare branches watched him for a moment, before taking to the skies, leaving them entirely unobserved as they entered the chapel grounds.

Blackwood led the way to the rear of the building. He halted before a heavy wooden door set deep into the stonework and turned to Holden expectantly. It took a second for the meaning of this pause to sink in.

"Oh. Sorry." Holden pawed at his sweater and T-shirt, dragging down on the rounded necklines of both to retrieve the cord, and the ring that hung from it.

"Just press the crest against the lock."

Blackwood stepped aside to give him room, and Holden surveyed the door. The lock looked old, and in need of an antique key to work its mechanism. The idea that a ring could open it might have seemed laughable to some, but powerful magical ability ran in the Blackwood veins, so Holden didn't doubt this alternate method would work.

Unwilling to remove the cord from around his neck—which would have felt tantamount to relinquishing his claim on it—Holden bent at the waist and stretched the ring toward the low-set lock. He felt the immediate puff of magic. He saw the shimmer in the air. And then the bolt slid back.

Holden straightened and turned to Blackwood. "Doesn't seem very secure if anyone with the ring can open it."

"You would be right were that the only factor. However, the spell is far more complex than a simple opening charm. Only those of my bloodline, or those freely gifted the ring by someone in my bloodline, can wield it in this manner. Had I not expressly told you to keep possession of the ring, it would not have worked."

Holden stared at Blackwood. "Blood magic. That's serious stuff, even for a powerful coven leader. I thought witches shunned anything blood-related."

"In general, yes. But that is a modern sensibility, and these rings have been in my family for several generations. Over time, tastes change and moral compasses shift. Blood magic and elemental witchcraft used to go hand in hand, but a few centuries ago, blood magic became stigmatised, linked with ideas of evil. It's no different from the way the tide of popular opinion turned against shifters. Many witches of the past were passionate about transmogrification—we have their diaries to prove it. Nowadays, those who transform for pleasure are treated like outcasts." He flashed a brief smile Holden's way. "But we didn't come here so I could bore you with a coven history lesson." He nodded toward the door. "Shall we?"

Inside, all was dark. Holden's eyes started to adjust. However, once they'd closed the door behind them, Blackwood murmured, "Accende," and a tightly packed ball of flame appeared in his palm, illuminating the path.

"Nice trick."

Blackwood gave a wry smile. "Fire has always been my best element. Nevertheless, my magic is still depleted, so I don't know how long I can maintain it. I suggest we hurry to the crypt. There's electric lighting once we get there."

They made their way down a sloping corridor that led to a flight of steps. By the time they reached the bottom, Blackwood's fire spell had begun to fade, but Holden spotted the light switch and flicked on the overhead bulb before the magic expired.

The crypt was a single square room. It was far smaller than Holden had imagined, given the grandeur of the family that owned it. Then again, urns didn't take up that much space, and looking around, it appeared the vault could house a few more generations of Blackwoods before it reached capacity.

Blackwood crossed to the far wall and tapped one of the unclaimed tiles. "Here."

When Holden pressed the ring against the marble, the panel swung open, revealing a collection of scrolls, ancient tomes, and boxes. Blackwood reached inside and withdrew each item in turn. Some of the gems within the caskets looked expensive, but Blackwood tossed them around as if they meant nothing, growing visibly more agitated as the final items gave way to a gaping black hole. He flung everything back inside and slammed the tile shut.

"I don't understand it. I was certain it would be here."

Holden glanced around, seeking any other hiding places. His gaze moved over the inscriptions on the plaques that marked the occupied recesses. When he reached Aetius Blackwood's memorial, a thought occurred to him.

"Will the ring open all the tiles?"

"Yes. But there's nothing behind the others but ash."

"Are you sure?"

Blackwood's head shot up. "You truly think it could be there?"

"Only one way to find out."

Holden approached Aetius's tile and pressed the ring against it. The panel opened with a sigh, and he and Blackwood edged forward to peer inside. Blackwood's close presence at his back, coupled with the warm breath that buffeted his ear, was both welcome and unwanted, but Holden tried to ignore the sensations and concentrated on the view before him.

All he could see was the urn, and he could sense Blackwood's tension. Nevertheless, he reached in and lifted out the ashes, determined to be thorough. Setting the container carefully at his feet, he stretched his arm into the darkness. His fingers met with stone and dirt. Experiencing his own surge of disappointment, he was about to withdraw his hand when he brushed against something far at the back, almost out of reach. He clawed at the solid object, dragging it forward by the tips of his fingers until he could get a firm grasp on it. When he drew it forth and studied it under the light, he saw that he held a worn leather-bound notebook.

"That's it!" Blackwood plucked the volume from Holden's hands and flicked through the handwritten pages. "Holden, you're a genius."

"I don't know about that."

"Yes! I'd have given up. But you—"

A loud creak from somewhere above made them both freeze. They listened, but no further sound came, except the whisper of the wind and the distant hum of traffic.

Holden gave a laugh which came out sounding more nervous than he'd intended. "We'll be jumping at shadows next."

Blackwood didn't crack a smile. "It was probably just the building shifting. Nonetheless, we should get back to the mansion. We can study the book properly there."

They replaced the urn and closed the tile. Then Blackwood slipped the grimoire inside his coat, and they quit the room, Holden leading the way.

Returning to the surface was easier than the descent, and they proceeded without light, taking their time on the stairs, before picking up the pace as they followed the path back to the main door.

Outside, the night sky seemed bright after the darkness of the tunnel, and they paused a moment while their eyes adjusted. Holden's vision returned to normal first, and he turned to secure the door behind them. He gave the handle a shake for good measure and then slipped the ring back into place beneath his clothing.

Blackwood caught Holden's gaze. "Right. I think we should—"

Holden never got to hear what Blackwood was going to suggest, because in that instant, something flew at them from the shadows. It struck Blackwood on the shoulder, spinning him and knocking him to the ground. By the time Holden pivoted in the direction of the attack, it was already too late.

Chapter Twenty-Five

THE NEXT BLAST clipped Holden's arm. His partial turn had saved him from a harder blow to the back, but even so, the impact was strong enough to knock him off balance. He stumbled against the door. The chapel's stone wall offered a modicum of cover, so he rested there for a heartbeat, to get his breath back and assess the situation.

Blackwood was on the ground a few feet away, already pushing up onto his knees. Before he could get any farther, though, another burst of energy slammed into the back of his head, sending him facedown into the grass once more.

A figure in a hoodie dashed toward Blackwood's prone form, and Holden reacted, charging forward with a burst of vampiric speed to intercept. He tackled their attacker, and the two tumbled. They vied for supremacy, one atop the other. Holden managed to knock back the man's hood, but it did him little good. The fellow was wearing a masking spell. His face was an unrecognizable blur. It did confirm their assailant was a witch, regardless of any scent markers. A fae would have used a glamour to project a different face, rather than obliterating all features.

Holden became the defender again in their struggle, and a punch connected with his jaw. It stung, but he shook it off. The time had come for something decisive. In the next breath, he gathered his strength and thrust his adversary up and off him, buying himself a few seconds to regroup.

During this brief moment of respite, Holden risked a glance to check on Blackwood. To his horror, he saw another figure bending over him—a second attacker. Instinctively, he spun in that direction, intending to launch a rescue. But in doing so, he nearly let his own assailant gain the upper hand.

His senses heightened by the adrenaline coursing through him, he heard the telltale crackle of magic in the air and swayed back just in time as a ball of energy zoomed past his head. Combat magic was another skill he'd never fully mastered. However, accuracy was less important at present than gaining time. He needed to distract his opponent so he could get to Blackwood.

Holden dragged energy from the earth and catapulted it toward his attacker. His aim was way off, his ball of light poorly formed, but it still forced his assailant to leap to the left. He already had another projectile ready, and he spun on his heel, casting it in the opposite direction. The second man was back on his feet and easily sidestepped the blast, but he didn't hang around after that. He sprinted along the side of the chapel, heading for the street, and his accomplice raced to join him. Holden briefly considered pursuit, but he swiftly abandoned the idea and flew to Blackwood's side instead. He skidded to his knees beside him, scanning for any obvious signs of injury.

Blackwood was on his back now. When Holden gently shook his shoulder and called his name, his eyes shot open. He emitted a groan that turned into a racking cough, and Holden supported him as he struggled to sit up.

"Are you okay, Val?"

After further dry-retching, the fit passed, and Blackwood was able to speak. "What happened?" He rubbed the back of his head and winced. "I feel like I was hit by a truck."

"A magical blast, actually. Two people attacked us, and they weren't holding back any punches. One was definitely a witch, so I guess the other was too. They're gone now."

"Are you hurt?"

"I'm fine. It's you I'm worried about."

"My head's spinning, but I'll be all right in a moment. They must have spotted us and recognised me. I don't imagine I'm particularly popular among the covens after everything I've done—and deservedly so. I'm sorry you got caught in the crossfire." He held out his hand. "Help me up, would you?"

Holden rose, and then tugged Blackwood to his feet. Blackwood swayed violently. Holden had to grab his elbow to steady him.

"Perhaps you should sit down again."

"I'll be fine. I'm a little dizzy, is all. Besides, we ought to get out of sight in case those two spread word of my presence here." He tugged free of Holden's grasp and attempted to brush down his grass-stained, bedraggled clothing. As he pressed his hands over the front of his coat, he froze. "Oh no."

Holden could guess what had happened. While Blackwood checked every pocket, he searched the ground where Blackwood had fallen. When they were done, they both stood empty-handed. Aetius Blackwood's grimoire was gone.

"Those fools. They don't know what they've done."

"Unless they do." Holden grimaced as he considered the possibility. "What if this wasn't a random attack because someone saw you? What if they were after the book all along? If the person who's taken over the summoning knew there was information in that book that could stop them, wouldn't they try to obtain it?"

"If you're correct, they've succeeded." Blackwood's expression was unreadable, but Holden thought he detected a note of censure in his voice.

"I'm sorry. I tried to get to you, but I wasn't fast enough."

"I don't blame *you*, Holden. I blame myself. I was too cavalier. I didn't even bother to conceal my face. Whoever took over the summoning naturally has a vested interest. They won't risk forfeiting whatever my father promised them. Breathing the free air again, being with you, has clouded my judgment. Only cunning and clear thinking will defeat my father. That book was our best hope, and now it's gone."

Although he knew Blackwood hadn't intended a slight, Holden flinched at the suggestion he was impairing Blackwood's judgment, that he was a distraction. Would it be better if they didn't work together, given their history? Was doing so a hindrance rather than a help? Yet, the Council would hardly allow Blackwood to remain free if he went off on his own crusade, unsupervised. Nor could Holden hope to stop the summoning without Blackwood's guidance. It seemed, therefore, that there was no choice but to continue their collaboration. Nonetheless, Blackwood was right: they needed to be smart and careful. The loss of the book was a blow, but surely it wasn't yet checkmate.

"Our best hope, maybe, but I can't believe it was our only one." Holden reached out and tentatively brushed Blackwood's sleeve in a gesture of solidarity. He really wanted to pull Blackwood to him and hold him tight, but this was all he would allow himself. "It never occurred to *me* that we would meet opposition either, and it should have done. This isn't all on you, Val. It was *our* naiveté, *our* mistake. But we'll find another way."

"You sound so certain."

He wasn't—far from it—but he was glad it didn't come across that way. "I won't rest until we stop this."

"Neither will I." Blackwood squared his shoulders, shaking off his despondency.

"So, what next? Do we risk returning to your place?"

"Eventually we must. We'll need my books and equipment. However, regardless of whether this was a coincidental encounter or a planned attack, it seems likely the mansion will be watched from now on, and I would prefer it if we entered undetected. That's possible, but first I will need to pick up a few supplies."

He took a determined step forward, only to sway once more. This time when Holden steadied him, he didn't shake him off. Nor did he protest when Holden slipped his arm around his shoulder, taking his weight, propping him up.

"You're in no fit state to do anything at present. You need to rest first. We could go to the office. Owens would conceal us there."

"No. It's too risky. Assuming our attackers were after the book, they may not choose to broadcast my release from the dungeons. Striding into the Fellowship building will only advertise that fact unnecessarily. Plus, if anyone wanted to come after me again, it's likely one of the first places they'd look. We need somewhere safe but unexpected." He glanced down at Holden, his gaze worryingly unfocused. "Where are you staying?"

"I spent the last two nights at the office. I could book a hotel room."

"No. It was a bad idea in any case. They saw you with me. Chances are any hotel room booked in your name would also be on their watch list, and I'm not up to magically creating a fake ID at present."

An idea came to Holden, but he wasn't sure either of the parties involved was going to like it. "There is one place...but you won't approve."

"Is it safe?"

"Yes."

"Untraceable to you?"

Holden considered. "Not entirely, but neither is it obvious."

"Then it will do." Blackwood tried to walk again and stumbled. "I don't suppose you could portal us there?"

"I can't." Holden lowered his gaze, flushing. "I've never managed to create a workable portal over any real distance. They fizzle out before I can get from A to B." He paused and looked up again. "There is another option though. If you don't mind sacrificing a little dignity."

Chapter Twenty-Six

KEEPING TO THE quieter side streets as much as possible, Holden sped across town. He moved quicker than a human, but not at full speed. There was the extra load to account for, and he didn't want to burn out before they reached their destination. If anyone spotted them, hopefully they'd take them for two chaps horsing around during a night out on the town. However, at their current velocity, they'd most likely be an indistinct blur, in any case.

Blackwood was a solid, warm weight upon his back. Holden tightened his grip on Blackwood's thighs, doing his best to ignore the closeness, thankful that their flight and current predicament partially tore his traitorous mind from other thoughts. At least Blackwood had had the foresight to centre his own hold more on Holden's shoulders than around his neck, ensuring that Holden could still breathe easily. He had expected objections to this mode of transportation, but Blackwood, usually so dignified, hadn't baulked. Holden hoped that didn't signify that Blackwood's head injury was worse than he'd assumed.

Luckily, they didn't have far to travel, and when they reached the house, lights burned within. He set Blackwood down and was disturbed to find him still a little unsteady on his feet. However, Blackwood once again waved away his concern, so he turned instead to the door and rang the bell.

When Raoul appeared in the doorway, clad only in a pair of silky black boxers, he beamed to see Holden, but his smile faltered as his gaze flicked to Blackwood. "What the hell, Hol!"

"Can we come in? Please, Raoul."

Holden glanced behind him. He checked the street in both directions, relieved to find the pavement clear. This furtive action seemed to alert Raoul to the seriousness of the situation, too, because he stood aside and beckoned them forward.

"Go into the kitchen and keep out of sight." He kept his voice low. "I have company, but I'll get rid of him."

Holden guided Blackwood to the far corner of the kitchen, while Raoul disappeared upstairs. He discerned muffled voices, followed by petulant stomping. As the footsteps drew closer and the stairs creaked, he ducked behind the kitchen counter, dragging Blackwood down with him. A moment later, he heard the front door open and close, and only a single set of footsteps returned. He rose, but Blackwood remained seated on the floor, resting his forehead on his knees.

Raoul, now more decorously attired in a dressing gown, strode toward them. "Now, you'd better spill. Please don't tell me I'm embroiled in a prison break. I'm willing to do a lot for you, Hol, but that's stretching the bonds of friendship a little too far."

"It's nothing like that. I promise. The Council released him to help us catch this new killer. He and I were pursuing an important source of information when we came under attack. Val took a solid blow to the head. We couldn't return to his place, in case someone's watching the house. I didn't know where to go except here."

"Hmm." Raoul rounded the counter and studied Blackwood. "By the blood, he does look rather the worse for wear."

"I'm worried he's concussed. He's speaking fine, but his balance is way off."

"Did he black out?"

"I don't know. Maybe briefly."

"I am here, you know." Blackwood raised his head. It looked as if the action took supreme effort. "I was badly dazed, but I'll be—"

"Fine. I know. You keep saying that." Holden hadn't intended to snap, but his concern was only growing now the immediate danger had passed. "Stop being so pig-headed and let us help."

Raoul knelt beside Blackwood. "Do you know who I am?"

"Raoul Dubois." Blackwood managed a grimace, so clearly he did remember him.

"What's the date?"

"The sixth of December."

"And what's your name?"

Blackwood's expression was a blend of contempt and exasperation. "Seriously?"

Raoul smirked, then rose. "I don't think it's serious. With a little rest, he'll probably be back to normal in a few hours. I'm no doctor, though, so I would recommend he take some blood."

"You think that will help?"

"It can't hurt, and if there are any internal injuries we can't see, it will help him heal. A few drops will suffice." He shook back his sleeve, bit into his wrist, and held out his arm toward Blackwood. "Here. Drink this."

Blackwood gave a vehement shake of his head and then had to steady himself against the cupboard. "No... thank you."

"You're really going to be like that? Honestly, Blackwood, you witches are so high and mighty. Everyone knows vampire blood is fine in small doses. There's no risk of catching the virus unless you've already sustained huge blood loss. It's scientifically proven. You should know that, as well read as you are. Now, fucking drink, before I change my mind and make you sit it out."

Holden crouched beside Blackwood. "Please do it, Val. I'm... Well, I'm worried about you."

"It's unnecessary."

"What if it's from me? My blood won't be as strong as Raoul's, but it will still help."

Blackwood looked deep into Holden's eyes for a moment, squinting as he tried to focus. "Okay. From you."

Raoul gave a dramatic sigh. "Witches! Oh well, waste not want not." He lapped his tongue over the puncture marks in his wrist, which had already started to close. "I'll be in the lounge. Come find me when you're done. I'm going to need more of an explanation than 'the Council let him out' if you expect me to let him spend the night under my roof."

Once Raoul was out of sight, Holden returned his attention to Blackwood. He shoved up his sleeve and willed his fangs to descend. He'd never bitten into his own flesh before—he'd never had cause—and it was a strange sensation, as was the taste of his blood as it trickled over his tongue. The fact it came without attached memories was also a novelty. He licked the remnants from his lips and extended his arm.

Blackwood still looked unconvinced, so Holden shifted closer. "I promise it will help. Just a few small sips. You don't need much. The virus will heal you, your immune system will fight off the virus, and it will be over before you know it."

After a moment, Blackwood nodded, and Holden held his wrist to Blackwood's lips. The first lap of Blackwood's tongue over the wound was so tentative it tickled, but Holden resisted the urge to squirm. He didn't want to put Blackwood off. The next pull was stronger, and this time Holden repressed a sigh at the pleasurable pressure. The third tug caused a distinct stirring in his groin, so it was likely a good thing Blackwood then pulled away.

"I saw things." His eyes had regained focus, and they met Holden's with an expression of wonder. "Is it always like that?"

"It is for vampires. I didn't realise it worked that way for mortals too." Holden moistened his lips, suddenly uneasy. When he'd offered the blood, it hadn't occurred to him it might betray anything. "So...what did you see?"

"Nothing worth mentioning." Blackwood glanced away. "And I do feel better." He sucked in a deep breath, then clambered to his feet. Holden hurried to follow suit, ready to lend his arm. But this time it wasn't necessary, as Blackwood displayed no further signs of giddiness. He studied Holden, an ironic twist to his lips. "Raoul Dubois? You really thought *he* was our best option?"

"He was the *only* option. I knew you wouldn't like it, but if it's any consolation, neither does he. He's hardly your number one fan."

"No, no. You're right. Do many people know how... close the two of you are?"

"Some of his crowd do, and obviously those at the trial know he visited me that night, but I doubt our friendship is common knowledge outside those circles. It's not like I ever had many people to tell."

"Then we should be secure here for the night."

"He wants an explanation."

"Of course he does. I would, too, under the circumstances. For better or worse, he is currently our host, so I guess we shouldn't keep him waiting."

Holden started to turn, but Blackwood caught his arm.

"Thank you, Holden."

"It was Raoul's idea. I'm just glad it worked."

"Not for the blood. Well, for that too. I meant in general. I've done terrible things, things I would have believed utterly unforgiveable, yet you're still here."

Holden shuffled, unable to meet Blackwood's eyes, fearful of what he'd see in them, and how that would affect him. "It's my job. We need to work together to stop the summoning."

It was true, but it was far from the whole truth. At present, however, it was the only thing that made sense to him. The rest of his feelings were in turmoil, changing from minute to minute until he no longer knew what he believed, what he needed. For instance, he was currently caught in the throes of a strong desire to grab fistfuls of Blackwood's ruined coat and pull him in for a kiss. Yet, at the same time, their proximity was too much, and he longed to establish a greater distance between them. One thought prompted that Blackwood meant more to him than anyone in the world. The next whispered of spilled blood, stolen hearts, and sinister magic.

Blackwood took a step back, saving Holden from his dilemma. "Shall we join Mr Dubois? We still have a few hours until dawn, but there are things we must arrange with him before he retires."

They spent the remaining time until sunrise filling Raoul in on the events of the last few days. Holden had assumed that Blackwood would be reluctant to reveal too much to someone he disliked, but apparently practicality trumped loathing, because although he spoke succinctly, he omitted nothing during the moments when he contributed to the narrative. Well, almost nothing. Neither of them mentioned the kiss in Blackwood's library. Holden had no compunction about taking Raoul into their confidence. Raoul had never betrayed him, in all their years as friends.

It was only as they approached the end of their tale, when he called on Blackwood for his opinion about something and received no response, that Holden noticed Blackwood had nodded off. He paused midsentence to study him. He'd never seen him asleep before. With the care lines of the day rubbed away, he exuded an aura of innocence that threatened to steal Holden's breath. His gaze zeroed in on Blackwood's slightly parted lips, and he moistened his own.

"It seems my warnings to be careful around Blackwood were in vain."

Holden jerked to face Raoul. He'd been caught out, and that made him defensive. "He's done wrong, terrible wrong, but he's not a monster."

"Maybe not, but your feelings for him are a weakness. Lust is all well and good—you'll never hear me say otherwise—but—"

"It's not lust. I love him." The truth of it only now hit him. In saying the words aloud, he could no longer deny the depth of his feelings.

"Does *he* know that?"

"No. At least, I've never said so."

"Keep it that way." Raoul glanced at Blackwood. "At the end of all this, he returns to the dungeons. Yes?"

Holden limited his answer to a nod. Blackwood's reincarceration in that hell hole, with that sadistic guard, was not something upon which he wanted to dwell.

"All the more reason not to start something that's never going to end well. What if he decides to make a run for it? If he knows how much you care for him, he may try to manipulate you into helping him."

The discussion was making Holden uncomfortable, not least because it touched on many of his own concerns. Now wasn't the time to face them, however, so he evaded the matter with a change of topic.

"He saw something in the blood earlier." It was a subject he'd been meaning to raise anyway. He told himself that made it a legitimate digression, not a spineless act of avoidance.

Raoul straightened. "Really?"

"He said so," Holden confirmed, thankful Raoul had let the other issue slide. "Is that usual?"

"Not among mortals. Then again, witches, with their magical potential, may well be different. Since they shun our blood on principle, I doubt there are many, if any, recorded cases to compare." Raoul glanced at the window, and then at the clock. "Dawn approaches, my friend, and I need to get to my safe room. Will you be all right here?"

"Yes. What time does your cleaner come?"

"At ten. Pass her the list of things you need and she'll see to it. You don't have to worry about her. She's nothing if not discreet."

"Thank you, Raoul."

"I'll say this, Hol. I never suspected that friendship with you would be such a challenge." Raoul bemoaned his fate with a heart-rending sigh. However, the smile that followed belied his words. "At least it's not dull. There's nothing worse than that."

Holden leaned in and pressed a chaste kiss to Raoul's lips. "Goodnight."

"Don't leave the house until I wake. I'll see you at dusk."

Chapter Twenty-Seven

RAOUL'S CLEANER—A lady who seemed more like someone's grandmother than a domestic—looked askance at Holden when he presented her with their shopping list. Nevertheless, she was clearly savvier than her appearance suggested, since she slipped the note into her apron pocket without enquiring from whence she was to procure such unusual items.

Three hours later, she returned bearing a nondescript plastic bag. When Holden tried to tip her, she acted offended, so he slid the money back into his wallet and repeated his thanks instead. At this, she gave a curt nod and then departed.

Holden had let Blackwood sleep through the morning and into the afternoon. Neither the earlier rumble of the vacuum cleaner nor Holden's telephone conversation with Owens had disturbed him, so he must have sorely needed the rest. Owens had been far from thrilled at last night's turn of events, but Holden had reassured her with promises of Raoul's absolute silence. There was nothing new to report regarding her end of the investigation. Therefore, it seemed it truly was up to him and Blackwood if they were going to solve the mystery in time, and that meant seeking a new way forward now the grimoire was lost to them.

He glanced at Blackwood's sleeping form. He was reluctant to wake him, but it wouldn't be too much longer before Raoul rose, given how early the sun set at this time of year, and he wanted to speak with Blackwood prior to that, to check they now had everything they needed to get back into the mansion.

"Blackwood?"

The call did nothing—Blackwood didn't so much as stir—so Holden moved closer. He settled carefully on the edge of the sofa on which Blackwood lay, agonizingly conscious of the way his pulse peaked at their proximity. He willed it steady. Then he gently shook Blackwood's shoulder.

"Val?"

Blackwood shot upright so suddenly that Holden, startled, slipped off the sofa and landed on his arse with a solid *thump.*

"Ow!"

Blackwood looked around wildly, but then his gaze settled on Holden, and he calmed. "Apologies. For a moment, I'd forgotten where I was." He held out his hand and helped Holden back onto the chair.

"How are you feeling?"

"Better. Good, in fact. I can't remember the last time I had such a restful sleep."

Blackwood *did* look better. The dark circles under his eyes were gone, his bruises had faded to almost nothing, and he was no longer as pale as he'd been yesterday. It could have been thanks to the rest, or it could have been due to the vampire blood he'd ingested. Holden guessed it was a combination of both. Either way, he no longer appeared quite so broken as he had when they'd first quit the dungeons.

"What time is it?"

"Nearly four."

"In the afternoon? You shouldn't have let me sleep so long."

"You needed it. Besides, there was nothing much to do here all day."

Blackwood nodded his agreement. "The ingredients?"

"See for yourself."

Holden gestured to the bag on the coffee table, and Blackwood rummaged through it, making various hums and clucks of approval as he checked each item.

"Good. This should do it."

"And what is 'it' exactly? You never said."

"There's a wine cellar beneath my house, with a hidden passageway between it and Hyde Park. And I do mean hidden. My forebears believed it too dangerous to leave the Hyde Park doorway accessible from the outside. My great-great-grandfather wanted to seal it completely, but my great-grandfather persuaded him to mask it instead. Those of Blackwood blood know its location, but it hasn't been used in many years and will, therefore, require a potion to reawaken its latent magic—a jumpstart of sorts."

"Seriously? A hidden tunnel? That's pretty cloak-and-dagger!"

Blackwood cracked a sardonic smile. "My family is nothing if not paranoid. My grandfather was the worst, truth be told. He used to see plots everywhere. He even kept a journal of them—a new conspiracy for every day. It's actually quite amusing reading."

"And the people who attacked us won't know of this tunnel?"

"No. It's always been a closely guarded secret, limited to immediate family members. Not even old James has a clue about it, and he's served the Blackwoods since he was a lad."

Holden had all but forgotten Blackwood's former team of servants. "Where *are* your staff now? There was no one around when we arrived by portal."

"Retired or in new employ, or so I hope. Following sentencing, the Fellowship froze my assets. According to law, it was, therefore, their responsibility to assist anyone in my service to find new positions. We're extremely lucky the Council hasn't stripped my house yet. There's plenty there they'd dearly love to get their hands on. We have my lawyer to thank for the delay. He's keeping them tied up in legal red tape, with talk of locating an heir for that part of the estate. That man is worth every penny of his exorbitant retainer. It will take them many months to unravel the matter, so we're in no danger of eviction for the time being. Even if they felt inclined to do a spot of pilfering prior to a legal resolution, they'd never get inside. I put up those wards myself. There's no one in the city capable of breaking them."

The remaining hour and a half until Raoul joined them proved awkward. After exhausting all talk of their immediate plans, a silence fell. It was not one of those comfortable, companionable silences Holden had enjoyed with Blackwood in the past. Rather, it was a pregnant pause, the air heavy with things unsaid.

Holden's conversation with Raoul the previous night played over and over in his mind. He knew in his gut Raoul was right. He had a few weeks at most before Blackwood returned to the dungeons, and this time there would be no excuse for a further reprieve. He'd resigned himself to it the first time—at least, he'd thought he had—but somehow doing so a second time was harder. He couldn't let himself care. That was the only way to get through it. There could be no more random kissing, no confession of his feelings. He needed to shut off his heart until this was over. If he could.

It was a relief when Raoul entered the room, breaking the worst of the tension, and they spent a few minutes going over with him the details he'd missed. He expressed no surprise at the existence of a secret tunnel, which made Holden wonder if London wasn't peppered with them. Raoul had, after all, inhabited the city far longer than he had, having fled France for England during the height of the Terror in early 1794. Holden *was* shocked, however, when Raoul showed himself determined to accompany them to Hyde Park.

"You surely don't expect me to let you wander off alone when you've already been attacked once since your return?"

"I won't be alone. I'll be with Blackwood."

Raoul ignored this. "You seem determined to get yourself into scraps, so I want to be there to prevent another."

Holden glanced at Blackwood, who was watching Raoul thoughtfully.

"I see no reason why Mr Dubois must stay behind. If you trust him, so do I."

Raoul's left eyebrow twitched—an action Holden recognised as one of suppressed surprise. "Then it's settled."

"But—"

"No buts, Hol. It looks like it's time for a field trip."

THEY DECIDED TO wait until eleven p.m. before departing, and the earlier part of the evening passed uneventfully. Once a Chinese takeaway order had arrived for Holden and Blackwood, Raoul went out to feed, and after that, he and Holden chatted happily about films. They didn't exclude Blackwood; however, he mostly sat fiddling with his ingredients, mixing them in one of Raoul's numerous cocktail shakers, before pouring the finished concoction into an empty whisky bottle. Then he disappeared into the bathroom in search of peace and quiet while he channelled the energy he'd need for the spell.

When the hour struck, they made their way to Hyde Park. Holden assumed the hidden doorway would be only just inside the grounds, as close as possible to the house. Instead, Blackwood strode farther in. He only stopped upon reaching the circular memorial known as the Reformers' Tree.

"The tree itself was still here at the time my ancestors built the passageway," Blackwood explained. "Its loss was a shame, as it did provide more cover for entering and exiting the door than we have now." He gave the whisky bottle a good shake and studied the sloshing contents. "I think we're ready."

Holden glanced around. The park wouldn't shut for another forty-five minutes. Nevertheless, at this time of night, few wandered its paths, and he was relieved to confirm there was no one currently in sight. "Okay. Let's do this."

"Stand well back. I've never used this before, and I'm not sure how volatile the reaction will be."

Holden and Raoul obeyed, and Blackwood unscrewed the cap on the bottle. He walked the circumference of the circle, drizzling the liquid and muttering in Latin as he went. When he halted, the bottle empty, Holden was disappointed. Nothing had happened.

He almost proposed they'd gotten one of the ingredients wrong, or that this wasn't the correct spot, but he held his tongue when he noticed that Blackwood didn't appear disconcerted. As it turned out, the age-old adage of patience is a virtue proved apt.

A few seconds later, a golden light burst up around the circle. In some ways, it had the look of a portal about it, except for the fact Holden couldn't make out their destination within its rays.

"Would you like to do the honours?" Blackwood asked Holden, gesturing toward the circle.

Raoul moved in front of him. "Holden's not setting foot anywhere near that thing unless you go first, Blackwood."

He and Blackwood stared at each other for a heartbeat, but then Blackwood acquiesced with a tilt of his head. "As you wish."

Without further ado, he stepped into the circle of light and disappeared.

Holden tapped Raoul on the shoulder. "Can I go now, mighty bodyguard?"

Raoul frowned. "I'm only trying to keep you safe."

"I know." Holden slipped his arm through Raoul's. "Together?"

Raoul nodded his agreement, and as one, they entered the circle.

Chapter Twenty-Eight

ONCE THE BRIGHT light subsided, only darkness remained. Holden jumped when something brushed his chest, but then he recognised the press of fingers—the press of *those* fingers.

"Did you both make it through?" Blackwood's voice echoed, hanging in the air for several seconds after he'd finished speaking.

"Yes." Holden gave Raoul's arm a quick squeeze and then released it.

"Then I think it's time for a little light."

Blackwood used the same trick he'd employed in the church, creating a ball of glowing energy in his palm, and now Holden could see they stood in a long tunnel. Its ceilings were high enough for them to walk without stooping, but it was only sufficiently wide for them to travel comfortably single file. He glanced up. The ceiling showed no sign of an entrance, and to his back was a solid wall of packed dirt. He couldn't pinpoint the exact location of their entry. Though he did wonder about the circle of light somewhere above them.

"Are we sure no one can follow?"

"I only held the passageway open long enough for the two of you to pass through. Don't worry, Holden. I know how to work a spell, and how to watch my back."

Raoul snorted, and Holden elbowed him in the ribs.

Blackwood's lips quirked. "Shall we, gentlemen?"

The walk, which they conducted in silence, save for their echoing footfall, seemed long, even though, in real terms, it was only the matter of a few blocks. Finally, Holden detected a shift in the air, and a moment later, they arrived at what was to be the first and only bend. Around the corner, a doorway came into view. When they reached it, Blackwood placed his free hand against the wood, muttered a few Latin phrases, and pushed.

Nothing happened.

Blackwood tried again. This time, the door shifted, but not by much. Using his shoulder, he made a third attempt. There was a little more movement, but still the gap was too tight to grant access.

"Oh, move out of the way."

Raoul edged past Holden and then brushed Blackwood aside. He placed both palms against the wooden panels and gave a solid shove. The door flew back without further resistance. However, it emitted a protesting screech of grinding metal.

"I would prefer if you didn't take it off its hinges," Blackwood muttered.

"Well, I had to do something, or we'd still have been here come the new year."

Holden sighed, thinking he'd better nip this in the bud before things escalated. "Not that I'm not deeply impressed by the display of testosterone on both sides, but could we save it for later?"

Raoul laughed. "I guess there really is no need to compare dick size, Blackwood. After all, Holden can tell us who wins. Shall we ask him?"

Blackwood looked ready to punch Raoul, and on this occasion, Holden wasn't sure he could blame him. However, after a lengthy glare, Blackwood simply shook his head, barrelled past Raoul, and crossed the threshold, disappearing into the room beyond.

"What are you doing?" Holden demanded of Raoul in a fierce whisper too low for human ears. "We need to work together. You're antagonizing him on purpose."

"I don't trust him." Raoul, too, kept his voice hushed. "He's a killer, no matter where he tries to place the blame."

"We've been through this before. You've taken lives too."

"Not for more than a century, aside from during legitimate warfare. That's completely different, anyway. For one thing, times past had their own sets of rules. Secondly, when you're first turned, it's unfortunately all too easy to become lost in the bloodlust. Failing to stop in time due to inexperience is a far cry from premeditated murder." He gripped Holden's shoulder. "Look, Hol. I just don't want him getting any ideas that he can wheedle his way back in. I'm looking out for you."

"He and I already discussed that. We're keeping this strictly professional, so there's no need for interference."

"I only have your best interests at heart."

Holden swallowed down the lump that had formed in his throat. He knew Raoul meant well, but the last thing he needed right now was to linger over any thoughts not directly linked to solving the case. His personal dilemmas belonged on the back burner...for as long as possible. "I know. But keep it civil. Okay?"

"Are you two coming or not?" The dull echo enhanced the note of exasperation in Blackwood's voice.

"Coming!"

Holden headed through the doorway. He tried to imagine a world in which Blackwood and Raoul were friends. Unfortunately, he found that even his bountiful imagination was unequal to the task.

The room into which they stepped was spacious but shadowed. Blackwood had turned on the light, but the single bare bulb illuminated only the spot directly below it, leaving the rest gloomy. Wine racks full of dusty bottles lined one long wall, and several huge oak barrels lay upon supports to one side. Holden could smell the alcohol as it permeated the wood, that delicious scent mingling with another. He sniffed again. The second scent was vaguely unpleasant, but he couldn't quite place it, and his attention soon moved to the rows of stacked cardboard boxes that stood in front of the wall opposite the wine racks. Their exteriors were plain, their contents unclear.

"Cans, mostly." Blackwood appeared at his elbow and gestured toward the cartons. "There's enough food down here to feed a small family for about three years, give or take. My father liked to be prepared. Anyone would have thought he expected a zombie apocalypse, even though that type of necromantic practice ended worldwide over a century ago."

He moved past Holden and shut the tunnel door. Not that it was as easy as that. It took him two attempts and several heavy grunts, but Holden guessed that Blackwood had something to prove after his earlier failure of strength, so he didn't offer to help. At least Raoul kept out of it this time. He kept *his* attention fixed on the wine racks until the door sealed and vanished from view.

"I'll give you this much, Blackwood: your family has exquisite taste in wine."

"Bring a bottle upstairs with you, if you like. Given the choice, I'd rather see it go down your throat than end up gracing the table during one of the Council's soirées."

Raoul didn't need to be told twice; he snagged not one bottle but two.

In the library, Blackwood produced three glasses, and Raoul poured them each a drink. He and Holden settled into the room's two armchairs, while Blackwood perched elegantly on the edge of his desk.

"So, what's the next move?" Holden leaned forward, nursing his glass between his hands. He glanced across at Blackwood. "Is there anything else you can tell us about the ritual? Anything we can use to locate this guy?"

"Nothing comes to mind. For the most part, I received my instructions and acted upon them. I know little other than what I was told to do, and what is in the books you and I have already studied cover to cover." He shook his head. "I'd hoped to find out more from the grimoire."

"How did you pick your victims?"

"Raoul!" Holden's jaw dropped. What was Raoul thinking? Witch-vampire natural animosity, coupled with Raoul's desire to protect him, was one thing, but this was taking his dislike too far. It was macabre and provoking.

"No one went into that line of questioning during the trial," Raoul continued, ignoring Holden's protest. "Did you choose them in advance? Did you stalk them first, learning their routines? I can't imagine it was a spur-of-the-moment decision each full moon."

"Stop it!" Holden leaped up, nearly spilling the contents of his glass. "Stop it right now, Raoul."

Blackwood briefly glanced at Holden, his expression blank, before returning his attention to Raoul. "No, it wasn't random. I chose loners—people who were unlikely to be missed immediately. Why?"

Raoul set down his glass and shifted forward in his seat. "It seems to me books are pointless at this stage in the game. Without this spell book—assuming even that wasn't another dead end—your only option is to wait until the next full moon and catch the killer when he strikes again."

"We can't sit here twiddling our thumbs for weeks." Holden gulped down the rest of his wine and sank back into the armchair. "And what does that have to do with Blackwood's choices?"

"Everything, if you want to get to the next victim before the killer does."

Blackwood straightened, alert. "I believe I see your meaning."

"If this new guy is getting instructions from your father, as you were, chances are he'll be after similar targets, so if we identify anyone *you* would have chosen—"

"We can watch over them and catch him when he makes his move!"

Blackwood and Raoul grinned at each other. The sudden spark of amity and agreement was so disconcerting Holden had to blink several times to stop his brain seizing up.

"You think that would work?"

Raoul turned to Holden, his smile fading. "I think it's the only option you have. Whether it will work depends on timing, and if we're correct in the assumption that Blackwood's replacement will follow his former patterns." He addressed his next comment to Blackwood. "The Whitechapel and Mayfair covens remain. Yes? Which of those would you have struck first?"

"Whitechapel. My father said our own coven had to be last."

"And had you already selected someone?"

"No. Whitechapel was always going to be the hardest. They keep more to themselves than the other central London covens. The only members I know well are the high-ranking representatives who attend all the intercoven functions, and none of them would have been suitable. I'd anticipated having to trawl through the coven records, then spend a day or two trailing any potentials."

"Can you still do so?"

"Yes. If the Investigations Team can get me access to the files. The coven will have revoked my old login. Tracking them could prove difficult though. In light of last night's attack, I think it unwise for me to leave this place until the full moon."

"Owens could get the others to do the leg work, once we've narrowed it down," Holden suggested. "They've pretty much exhausted their own leads and ideas." He paused. "Do you really mean to stay here for weeks? What about me?"

"For your own safety, you should probably stay here too." Blackwood glanced at Raoul. "I realise you won't like that, Dubois, but there are strong wards around this building. No one will get near him in here."

Raoul grimaced, but he gave a curt nod. "Very well. But I expect regular contact."

"Of course."

Holden whipped out his phone. "Then let's get to work."

Chapter Twenty-Nine

THE WEEKS THAT followed were some of the most difficult Holden had ever known. To begin with, they were hectic. The Whitechapel-Shoreditch coven, though one of the city's least elite, proved to be the most populous. Hundreds of witches filled its ranks, and he and Blackwood had to sort through them one at a time. Owens granted Holden access to the files via the secure server, and he and Blackwood sat side by side staring at Blackwood's laptop screen for hours each day, reviewing the information.

The treaty all parties had signed at the time of the Fellowship's formation in 1536 stated that every witch living within the boundaries of the agreement had to register when they came of age at sixteen. They then had to update their details on a yearly basis. The files included all the usual demographic information, along with notes on their magical abilities. It wasn't a literal witch hunt, however. All vampires and fae registered too. Although, their files tended to be slimmer, since little changed with them except the mundane information such as addresses.

Vampires all had essentially the same skill set once the virus had taken hold—improved speed and strength, and heightened senses—and in all cases those abilities increased incrementally with age. Meanwhile, the fae were born with a certain level of power, and that was the end of it. Fae magic was purely inherent, their connection to elemental energy ceaseless from birth until death, whereas a witch constantly had to channel power for use in their spells. Therefore, only with witches was there room for major change, as they could expand and improve their skills through constant study.

Holden and Blackwood had to review the file of each Whitechapel witch. Those who lived in a family group or held an important position they could discount immediately. They needed to find those likely to be spending their nights alone, and those whose absence wouldn't be noted immediately. Although, Blackwood had hesitated over the second point. Upon his father's suggestion, he had disguised the exact time of his killings, ensuring the bodies weren't found the same night. However, that hadn't been the case with the last two victims. Either his successor didn't care, or else he lacked Blackwood's skill in sealing the room and covering his tracks. Holden knew Blackwood was hoping for the latter, since he would then have the upper hand—at least magically—if a fight erupted when they caught the guy.

By the twenty-second of December, through a mix of file study and social media stalking, they had narrowed the list down to six names. That morning, Holden called Owens and relayed the information. She'd agreed to have the team trail the first five people on the list, come the night of the full moon. He and Blackwood would handle the sixth. Nothing was certain, but short of taking every Whitechapel witch into protective custody—a logistical nightmare even if the coven leader agreed—it was the best they could do.

Those two weeks of constant screen work had been tough. However, the agony of the last few days had been far worse. Their task complete, and with nothing further to do until the full moon, Holden had found it harder and harder to control his errant thoughts. Aside from his nightly check-ins with Raoul and the occasional call to Owens, he had spent three weeks in close proximity to Blackwood, with no other company. Their search had provided a distraction, but now that was gone, he lay awake in the guest room every night, the thought that Blackwood was just across the hall providing both reassurance and constant torment. He wondered if Blackwood felt the same way every time *he* retired alone, but he had more sense than to ask him.

Holden spent most of his daylight hours in the library, consuming everything from classic fiction to legal treatises, immersing himself in Blackwood's vast collection until he went cross-eyed. Blackwood employed the bulk of his time in his workshop, tinkering with his spells and potions. But on occasion he wandered into the library, draped his jacket over the back of the chair, and took a seat opposite Holden, his long legs stretched out and a book lying open in his lap. At those times, Holden's ability to concentrate dropped one hundred fold. Instead of moving from one line to the next in his text, his gaze strayed to Blackwood. Now and then, he thought he caught Blackwood looking at him, too, but neither of them ever mentioned it.

When they dined together, they talked mostly of books. Blackwood ate heartily at every meal, and Holden noted he had put back the weight he'd lost during his stay in the dungeons. That had gladdened him at first, until he remembered it would only be temporary. He couldn't afford to get used to Blackwood's presence, to the way the two of them together felt so right. It wouldn't last. And that reminder turned a potential dream into a nightmare.

One evening, as Holden rose to collect the plates at the end of their meal, Blackwood cleared his throat.

"You know we missed Christmas?"

"Did we?" Holden checked the date on his phone and saw it was true. He shrugged. "I never celebrated it anyway. Did you?"

"Not in a religious way—naturally, the solstice means more to my family—but we did exchange gifts, and, well..." Blackwood reached into his inner jacket pocket. "I made this for you."

He held out his fist, and Holden reached forward. What Blackwood dropped into his palm was a delicate gold chain.

"I thought you might prefer it to the cord. Don't let its weight fool you. I spelled it never to break."

Holden risked meeting Blackwood's eyes. "It's beautiful. Only...don't you want your ring back once this is over?"

"No. You keep it. Or destroy it, if you prefer. I want no reminder of my family legacy when I'm back in the dungeons. Ike would probably relieve me of it, in any case, and then take great delight in telling me how much he'd made auctioning it off to some morbid collector. I'd much rather leave it with you."

"But I have nothing to give you in return."

"You gave me your trust, Holden, at a time when you had every reason to doubt me. That is a far greater gift than a simple chain."

Holden's throat had constricted—not that he knew what he would have said had he been able to speak. Wordlessly, he tugged the cord loose and removed the ring. Then he threaded the golden chain through the band. When he tried to fasten it around his neck, however, he struggled to coordinate between clasp and link.

"Let me."

Blackwood stepped behind Holden and eased the chain from his grasp. The brush of Blackwood's fingertips against his neck made Holden shiver.

"There."

Blackwood released the chain, but he didn't move away. Instead, he slid his hands to Holden's shoulders. Then he swept aside Holden's hair and pressed a kiss to the side of his throat.

Holden shuddered, and a moan tore from his lips. Blackwood wrapped his arms around him, hugging him close, and Holden could feel the hard line of Blackwood's erection against his back. He ground against him, wanting more. He whimpered when, instead of continuing, Blackwood abruptly released him and retreated several paces.

"I'm sorry. I know what we promised, but it's been difficult these last few days, and for a moment there… Please accept my apologies." Blackwood swallowed visibly. "I think it best that I retire."

Surely he wasn't leaving? Holden knew he should let him go. However, he found he couldn't. Screw broken hearts and doubts! If all went to plan, in a few short days, he'd never see Blackwood again. Why did they have to waste what little time they had?

Holden surged forward and grabbed Blackwood's arm, spinning him back towards him. They collided in a desperate tangle of limbs, pulling each other closer as hands and lips roamed. Never had Holden experienced such overwhelming need. Although the rational part of his brain acknowledged it wasn't true, part of him was convinced he would die if he didn't immediately feel Blackwood's naked skin against his own.

He must have drifted in and out of conscious thought, as he had no idea how they made it to Blackwood's bedroom. They were just suddenly there. Like magic, his mind supplied, and he might have giggled if Blackwood hadn't been hungrily plundering his mouth at the time.

The stripping of clothing was as much of a blur as their journey between rooms. However, he was fully aware the moment Blackwood breached him. In that instant, he felt everything: the delicious stretch, the flush that permeated his skin, and the bruising press of Blackwood's fingers. Blackwood's eyes bore into his with a look of smouldering ecstasy that stole his breath. It was different from Raoul's desire, which centred on the physical. This was an all-consuming melding of souls. It was like he'd leaped off a cliff and was free-falling, only he wasn't afraid, because Blackwood was right there with him.

They moved in perfect unison, and Holden went from fearing he'd come too soon to thinking he'd never find release, that the pleasurable agony of hovering on the brink of orgasm would continue into infinity. Meanwhile, Blackwood thrust into him over and over, deeper and harder, until he was seeing stars.

"Val! Fates!"

He came in a flash of blinding white light. A moment later, he was vaguely aware of the sound of his own name on Blackwood's lips. His ears were ringing, and the voice seemed distant. However, there was no mistaking the pulse of Blackwood's cock deep inside him.

Utterly spent, they collapsed in each other's embrace.

"Val, I love you."

Already sinking into blissful oblivion, Holden couldn't tell if the words were only in his head or if he'd spoken them aloud.

Chapter Thirty

ONE YEAR TICKED into another, and the dawning of the second of January, night of the full moon, saw a return of the nerves Holden had banished for the past few days, lost in Blackwood's embrace. They had pinned all their hopes on tonight, and naturally, Holden wished to stop the killer and save a life. However, in his heart of hearts, he was torn, for success this evening would also signal Blackwood's return to the dark horror of the dungeons.

Throughout the morning, the atmosphere in the mansion was tense. Neither spoke what was truly on their minds, sticking to dull details of their plan, but in Blackwood's eyes, Holden saw a despair that mirrored his own.

At midday, they left via the front door. Appearing in a flash of light in the middle of Hyde Park during the peak lunch period had seemed ill-advised, and they hoped that, by now, any surveillance on the house would have ceased. They'd been careful to show no lights in the windows during the nights—Blackwood had a spell for everything it seemed—so there was no reason anyone would have suspected they dwelt within.

Holden had communicated with Owens earlier in the day. The Investigations Team was all set to commence operations at three. In teams of two, they would trail the potential victims. It would be discreet, but they'd stick with them until dawn. At the slightest sign of anything untoward happening, trained operatives would move in. He and Blackwood were collecting their target sooner. Her routine was less rigid than that of the others, so they wanted to get on her trail in advance, to limit the chance they'd fail to locate her before dusk.

Anne-Marie Watts was a freelance graphic designer, constantly flitting from here to there. So much so that Holden wondered how she ever got any work done. Unless she was more of a night owl in that regard. She was a fairly low-level witch, having only attained full proficiency in symbol magic and spell crafting. She'd flunked potions and had never managed a full shape-shift. She did seem rather ditzy, based on what Holden had ascertained from her social media profile. Therefore, he judged that her unimpressive test scores might be more the result of inattention, rather than lack of skill. Either way, she seemed sweet and kind, and she certainly didn't deserve to meet a grisly end tonight.

They had a note of the three places where they might find her, and as luck would have it, they spotted her in the first: a coffee shop near Petticoat Lane. An enormous mug of hot chocolate and a plated muffin sat before her, both as yet untouched. Meanwhile, she was doodling in a journal, apparently oblivious to the world at large. Since she looked set to stay there for a while, Holden and Blackwood found a free table of their own nearby, and Blackwood went to the counter to place an order.

Holden tried to keep half an eye on Anne-Marie, but mostly he watched Blackwood as he progressed down the queue. No one aside from Holden cast a second glance Blackwood's way, but then, he no longer looked like himself. One of the things Blackwood had been tinkering with in his workshop over the last few days was a spell whose effect was similar to that of a fae glamour. For as a long as the charm was active, anyone looking at him would see what he wanted them to see. It was advanced magic. Only a handful of the city's witches could have pulled it off. Blackwood had estimated he would get eight or nine hours out of it. By then it would be dark, and, with luck, Anne-Marie would be safely settled at home for the night, since she didn't seem to be the pubbing-clubbing type.

For now, Blackwood had given himself bleached-blond hair and blue eyes, and he'd shrunken his torso. The effect was pleasing but not excessively showy, and certainly not so attractive as to draw more than a passing appraisal. Holden didn't hate the look, but he much preferred Blackwood as himself. It felt a little surreal to see the man whose bed he'd left mere hours before, and yet not see him at the same time.

Blackwood returned to their table and slid a brimming mug, its contents topped with delicious whipped cream, across to Holden. "Drink up quick."

"What's the rush?"

"Our young lady is making short work of that muffin. I don't think she'll be here much longer."

A surreptitious glance to the left confirmed Blackwood's assessment. Journal set aside, Anne-Marie was attacking both cake and drink with gusto. Holden cursed his earlier inattention—or rather, his distracted attention.

Blackwood was already sipping his drink, so Holden did likewise. Thankfully, this was one of those places that served its beverages at ready-to-drink temperatures. Nonetheless, he had only just finished gulping down the hot chocolate when Anne-Marie rose. They waited until she was out the door and then followed.

For the next few hours, they trailed her in and out of shops and up and down streets. Holden's feet were tired, despite the fact he was wearing comfy trainers. How she could manage such a marathon in high heels was beyond his comprehension.

It was gone seven when she finally made her way home, but once inside, she showed no sign of emerging again, and Blackwood and Holden split up to watch the two entrances. Blackwood took the back, since there was less traffic there, meaning less risk of someone recognizing him when his spell wore off. Meanwhile, Holden stayed out front.

Anne-Marie's home was in a small side street near Rope Walk Gardens. It was a quiet area, and Holden was able to perch on a low brick wall, in a spot where some shrubbery hid him from view of all but those who passed directly in front of him. Despite his natural resistance to the cold, and the thick woollen coat Blackwood had loaned him, he noticed a distinct chill in the air. The weather report had warned of snow, but Holden took that to mean a light frost. Everyone knew it only snowed in south-east England on days when it *wasn't* predicted, when local councils *weren't* prepared. The best way to ward off snow, as far as he could tell, was to salt the streets in anticipation of it.

After he'd been there an hour or so, his earpiece crackled, and he heard Blackwood's voice. "Still clear this end. You?"

"No change."

The communications tech came from Owens. The paired teams could use them to talk to each other, and she could monitor all feeds, so she would know at once where to send backup. It was a good system, but also a frustrating one. These might be Holden's last few hours with Blackwood, and here they were, freezing their balls off in separate streets, unable even to talk properly with Owens listening in. Holden hoped the Council wouldn't sweep Blackwood back to jail the second they had the other guy in custody. He hoped they'd at least allow him a moment to say goodbye.

Lost in thought, Holden nearly missed the flash of shadow that darted across the street toward Anne-Marie's door. At the last moment, he caught it out the corner of his eye, and he leaped to his feet, fumbling at his earpiece.

"Something's moving here. Give me a second to confirm."

He peered at the figure. There were three apartments in the building; this could be another tenant. However, it was taking the guy a long time to open the door—surely longer than someone finding their key. Then he sensed a spark of magic in the air as the door finally swung open.

"Fates! It's him. Val?"

"Coming around to you now."

"Holden. Blackwood. A team is on its way. They'll be with you in two minutes. Wait for them before you go in." There was a nervous edge to Owens's voice. Her concern was touching, yet the idea of standing here doing nothing while Anne-Marie was in danger didn't sit well with Holden.

Blackwood, his true appearance restored, came racing around the corner, and they met by the front door.

Holden pulled out his earpiece and shoved it into his back pocket. "Does two minutes seem too long a wait to you?"

Blackwood tossed his own earpiece into the bushes. "Let's go."

The door still stood ajar, so they crept inside. Anne-Marie's rooms were on the upper floor, and the stairs were right in front of them. Holden's initial inclination was to charge up, but Blackwood held him back and signalled for him to be quiet. Blackwood was right: they didn't want to spook the guy. They needed to catch him red-handed. Just, Holden hoped, not literally.

They ascended slowly, with Blackwood leading. At the slightest creak, they paused and listened. When no reaction greeted their approach, Holden began to doubt his own senses. If not for the open front door, he might have assumed he'd imagined the shadowy figure.

Suddenly, there was a crash above them, followed by a muffled scream. Blackwood bolted forward, all caution forgotten. Holden was hot on his heels, and three seconds later, they charged through the open door into Anne-Marie's apartment.

Chapter Thirty-One

BLACKWOOD PULLED UP so abruptly that Holden nearly smashed into him.

"No! It can't be!"

The tone in which Blackwood uttered the words—one of mingled vehemence and shock—made Holden uneasy. He peered around Blackwood's shoulder, trying to see what was going on. When he managed to get a glimpse into the room, he understood Blackwood's reaction.

Far from heading for pastures new or a relaxing retirement, the Blackwood's butler, Arthur James, had embarked on a murder spree, and now he had Anne-Marie Watts pinned against his chest. She was struggling valiantly, but he held firm with a strength that had to be magically induced, given his advanced years. In his free hand, he brandished a blade. At their abrupt entrance, he'd swung the weapon toward them, but as Blackwood edged forward, he swivelled it and pressed the tip over Anne-Marie's heart.

"Not another step."

Blackwood halted. "James." He raised his hands in a gesture of peace. "Arthur," he began again in a softer, soothing tone. "Don't do this. It's not too late to stop."

"Like you did, *sir*?" James's voice dripped sarcasm. "I told him from the start you weren't right for this, that you were weak and would never see it through. I showed him my willingness to act in your stead. Here, in Whitechapel,

I proved to him my ability to do so. Nonetheless, he insisted it had to be you, saying that, as his son, you knew the importance of family obligation. At least I was here to pick up the pieces when you failed. *I've* never been disloyal."

"This is blind fealty, nothing more. And for what? Think of the consequences."

"To whom? I'm an old man. I may as well do one final service for my master before I shuffle off this mortal coil."

"What does Aetius want?" Holden asked, sensing an opening. "What does he get out of this?" He took half a step forward, but froze when James pressed down harder on the blade, and Anne-Marie whimpered.

"You have no business here, halfen filth. Keep out of matters that don't concern you." James spat in Holden's direction, then turned back to Blackwood. "Your father is disgusted that you are fornicating with the likes of him."

Blackwood gave a derisive bark of laughter. "You don't know what's going on here any more than I did, do you? For all your talk, you're merely another of my father's pawns—a mindless puppet."

"I know everything!" James shrieked. "He didn't trust you, but I've served him nearly all my life. I'm the only one in whom he always confided."

While Blackwood kept James distracted with talk, Holden quietly assessed the situation. The issue was the blade. If they could get James to drop it, freeing Anne-Marie from any immediate threat, between the two of them, they should be able to take him down, despite the possible strength spell in play. Holden wanted that knife gone before their backup arrived, lest the sudden influx of opponents prompted James to do something rash. Speaking of which, shouldn't those guys be here by now?

He began to wish he'd not been so foolhardy as to remove his earpiece.

"What is my father's grand plan then?" Blackwood asked. "If you know it, tell me."

"You think I'd share it with a nancy like you—a coward brought to his knees by a little blood? You're unworthy to hold the Blackwood name. I don't see why my master wants—" James broke off and tilted his head, as if listening to something...or someone. "Yes, sir. I understand."

Without warning, James thrust Anne-Marie to the left. She screamed in surprise, but the sound was instantly lost as a portal opened and closed around her, whisking her away. Meanwhile, James launched himself at Blackwood, landing a blow to the chin. Seconds later, a ball of energy cast from his other hand, at close range, sent Blackwood stumbling back. He readied another blast, but Holden moved faster, knocking his arm upward so the energy bounced off the ceiling instead.

Holden and James grappled.

After a few moments of frantic wrestling, Holden knew for certain that magic lent James strength. True, Holden's abilities didn't hold a candle to those of a pure-blood vampire, but they should have been sufficient to subdue a septuagenarian. Instead, he and James were equally matched, and neither proved willing to release their current hold on the other to attempt a decisive blow and break the stalemate.

Thankfully, Blackwood had recovered. He charged toward them, readying a blast of his own, and at his nod, Holden jerked free of James's grasp and leaped to the side. The energy struck James clean on the chest, throwing him back into the wall. The impact made a resounding *thump*. A normal human might well have been knocked out, or at least dazed, but clearly there were other forces at work here. Instead of slumping, James shifted. His clothes dropped to the floor, and he flew at Holden in a flurry of feathers, emitting a piercing caw.

Holden raised his arms to protect his face as the crow's razor-sharp talons slashed through two layers of clothing and scratched his skin. From somewhere to his right, Blackwood loosed a war cry. A moment later there was a loud *smack*, and Holden lowered his arms to find Blackwood wielding a standard lamp like a staff. Its hideous orange shade wobbled from the vibrations, and its cord, still plugged into a nearby socket, was pulled taut. James, no longer in bird form, lay in a crumpled heap on the other side of the room.

Blackwood dropped the lamp. "Are you okay?" He ran his fingers through Holden's hair and over his face, checking for damage.

"I'm fine," Holden said, before belying the statement with a wince as Blackwood's assessment moved to his arms. "They're superficial cuts. They'll heal fast."

"Would blood help?" Blackwood thrust out his arm and yanked back his sleeves. "Here."

The veins in Blackwood's wrist pulsed with life. Holden's gums ached, fangs threatening to descend. He wanted that blood. He wanted to taste Blackwood in a way even more intimate than all those in which they'd indulged during the past few days, and this might be the only chance he had. In other circumstances, he would have accepted, as little as he actually needed it. But his thoughts strayed to James. This wasn't the time. In any case, he wanted Blackwood to be sure, not to offer because he thought he had to pay a debt or return a favour.

"No." He was surprised to see that Blackwood looked hurt by the refusal. "It's not urgent. I'll be fine without it. Right now, we have bigger fish to fry."

Blackwood turned to glance at James, who hadn't moved. "Where is that damned backup, anyhow? They should have been here by now."

"I'll call Owens." Holden reached into his pocket for his phone.

"I never suspected it could be James. If I'd thought it possible, even for a moment, I would have said. Please believe me."

"I do." There was no doubt in Holden's mind on that score. Any lingering concerns he'd had upon freeing Blackwood from the dungeons had long since vanished. He trusted Blackwood with his life, let others think what they would.

"The speed in which he shifted suggests it's a familiar process. He kept those tendencies well concealed too. At least from me. Though, if my father protected his secret, that does go some way toward explaining James's absolute devotion to him. If he's been shifting regularly for years, I also wouldn't like to comment as to his mental state."

Holden raised his eyes, still hovering his finger over the screen, ready to dial. "You know, I saw a crow outside your chapel shortly before we were attacked there. He must have watched us go in, called his partner, and then waited for us to come out. He wasn't working alone, either then or now. Nor is this solely the labour of witches. One of the fae opened that portal, Val." He started as another thought came to mind. "Fates! Anne-Marie! We've no idea where she is. James's accomplice could have killed her already."

"Maybe not." Blackwood moved behind Holden and bent to retrieve something from the floor. As he straightened, he waved James's dagger. "They'll have a hard time completing the sacrifice without this. It took me a full day to consecrate the blade I used. Whoever took her won't have time to prepare another before dawn."

"Unless they have a second one ready."

Blackwood grimaced. "You're right."

There was a moment of heavy silence. Then Holden spurred himself into action. Recriminations and analysis of their failure could wait. Perhaps there was still something they could do to rectify the situation.

"We have James. Let's get Owens here. Maybe she'll persuade him to tell us where to find Anne-Marie."

"I don't doubt your captain's will, but James can be stubborn at the best of times, and he seems to think he has nothing to lose." Blackwood sighed. "However, it's worth a try. I don't see any other way forward."

Holden dialled, and Owens picked up on the first ring.

"Holden, what's going on?"

"Where's the backup?"

"We had a—"

A blast knocked the phone from Holden's hand. As it fell, it caught the corner of the coffee table and the screen smashed. Holden whirled to find James back on his feet. Either he'd been faking his faint or whatever spell he'd cast packed quite the restorative punch, because he looked none the worse for wear following his altercation with the furnishings.

This time, though, Blackwood was ready for him. They exchanged blow for blow, taking turns to block each other's attacks, before launching their own. The balls of energy flew so thick and fast even Holden had trouble keeping track of them. He wanted to step in to help, but he couldn't see how to do so without getting in Blackwood's way. One deflected blast headed straight for him, and he ducked to let it fly over his head.

"Holden!"

Blackwood had glanced toward Holden out of concern, but it was a costly lapse in concentration. James's next blast clipped him on the shoulder, and another smashed into his back, propelling him over the sofa in an inelegant somersault. As he landed, a portal opened behind him.

James dashed across the room, barrelling past Holden, eyes fixed on the portal. Holden tried to grab him, but he dodged at the last moment, zigzagging toward his goal. Holden assumed he'd leap over Blackwood and complete his escape, robbing them of any chance to save Anne-Marie. What actually happened was far worse.

Rather than avoiding Blackwood, James skidded to a halt beside him, fisted his coat, and dragged him toward the swirling mists.

"No! Val!"

Holden surged forward at the same moment their long-awaited backup poured into the room. Misreading the situation entirely, one of the team fired a paralyser not at James but at him. The spell hit him just as his fingertips brushed Blackwood's outstretched hand. Suddenly unable to move, he could do nothing but stare into Blackwood's frantic eyes until, a second later, he and James were gone.

Chapter Thirty-Two

BY THE TIME Holden emerged from questioning, his eyes were tired and his nerves frazzled. Not to mention the fact his limbs still felt stiff and cumbersome from the paralyzing spell. For hours, since they'd unfrozen him, he'd sat with a potent truth spell shining directly into his face, going over the events of the evening time and time again, until he feared he was stuck in some never-ending loop. Finally, the witch administering this so-called debriefing ended the session and told him he was free to go.

Once out of that torture chamber, he headed straight for the office, desperate for an update on the situation. Considering what had gone down at Anne-Marie's house, he'd expected a flurry of activity. Instead, he found the place abandoned, every desk empty. It appeared the mass exodus had occurred on the spur of the moment, however, since folders lay open in some workspaces and several of the computer screens remained aglow. Had they all gone looking for James? That wasn't standard procedure, but this was hardly a normal situation, even by supernatural standards. Thankfully, a light still shone in Owens's office, and the closed door suggested that wasn't through neglect.

When he knocked and entered, he found Owens at her desk. She was staring straight ahead at the wall and didn't stir until Holden sank into the seat directly in front of her.

She blinked, then looked away. "Holden, you should go home."

"Home? What are you on about? I'm going to help. I'll sleep once we find them."

"We won't *be* finding them, with or without you. The case is closed, at least as far as we're concerned."

"What?" An icy chill swept through Holden, rendering him as immobile as Owens had been when he walked in. "Who's taken over? Who's going to rescue Val?"

Owens frowned. "Rescue him? Holden, he betrayed us. He betrayed *you*. It's clear he and Arthur James have been working together from the start."

"That's nonsense. Who told you that?"

"The testimony from the special ops team. They saw him leave with James."

Holden slammed his fist on the table. "No! James knocked him down and dragged him through that portal against his will. I'd have had a chance at saving him if those morons hadn't shot their spell at me instead of James."

Owens sat rigid. "The report says differently."

"Then they're all lying bastards!" Holden leaped to his feet. He wouldn't stay here and listen to this. The Fellowship had wasted enough time already with all those pointless rounds of questioning. He'd find Blackwood on his own, whatever it took.

"Wait!" Owens drummed her fingers on the desk. "I believe you. After everything that's happened in the past few hours, something just doesn't fucking add up."

"Why did the backup arrive so late?"

"The plan was to portal them straight to you, but we found all three members of the assault team knocked out, and there was no sign of the fae tasked with their transportation. We had to scramble more people and get them there by road."

"Who was in charge of the portal?"

Owens hesitated. "Draper. He'd offered."

Holden swore. "Where is he now? I hope they're grilling his arse."

"No one knows. He's still missing."

If Draper was in on it with James, he'd likely been feeding him information all along. But how had they come to know each other? It wasn't as if they had anything in common. Although, Draper did have a history with those demon texts. Perhaps that was the connection.

"Who's in charge now?"

"The Council will handle the matter personally. Last I heard... Well, I understand your father has issued orders to kill both James and Blackwood on sight."

"Can't you call them off? I spent hours telling that stupid witch what happened—under a truth spell, no less. My testimony proves Blackwood wasn't in cahoots with James. Why are they ignoring my account?"

"Maybe because it doesn't suit them to believe you? Look, Holden, my fucking hands are tied. I no longer have jurisdiction, and when I spoke to the Council's representative earlier, he made it perfectly clear that I should let it go and keep my head down for a while. Otherwise, he threatened to have me up on charges of incompetence, or even abetting."

"Abetting? You? That's ludicrous."

"After the incident in the dungeons, they would say I have a track record of it. There's something fishy going on—I thought so before, and now I'm fucking certain of it—but I can't risk antagonizing them. I have to think of my family."

"I know." Holden rubbed at his temples. A dull throbbing had started during his questioning—interrogation, he amended—and it was only getting worse.

"Take my advice, Holden, and get the hell out of here. You're lucky they let you walk and didn't try to call you a collaborator too."

"I'm not going to leave Val. He needs me. No one else is out to help him."

"Even if you're right and he's not with James willingly, any friendship that sprang up between you isn't—"

"I'm not bloody leaving him!"

Holden stormed out. He heard Owens call after him, but he ignored her. He understood her position. That didn't mean he had to act likewise. He'd never be able to live with himself if he rolled over and played dead to save his own skin.

No one prevented him from exiting the building. Although, he did catch the wary looks that passed between the two guards on duty when he marched through the foyer. He kept going until he reached Raoul's place. By now, it wasn't long until dawn, but he rang the bell and hoped for the best. Raoul grumbled at first, but when he got a good look at Holden, he dragged him inside. There was no time for anything more than the briefest of explanations before the rising sun forced Raoul to retire. However, Raoul's instructions for him not to go anywhere alone were unnecessary. Despite his determination not to rest until he'd found Blackwood, exhaustion overcame Holden almost as soon as his head hit the sofa cushion, and he fell into a fitful sleep.

ON THE DAY following the full moon, news broke of the discovery of a body. In a Whitehall street, an early morning walker had found the remains of a young graphic designer named in the press coverage as Anne-Marie Watts. That story came over the human TV channels, and Holden caught wind of it upon waking late in the afternoon. The reporter had linked this death to the one in St Pancras. However, the police spokesman had stressed that, although the mode of death was similar, they'd found nothing to connect the two victims.

News of a second death came on the third morning after that dreadful night, via a phone call from Owens. She informed him that Fellowship members had pulled Draper's corpse from the Thames. The official cause of death was iron poisoning. Someone had poured a litre of molten metal down his throat. She'd called because she thought he'd want to know. However, when he attempted to question her further, she grew nervous and found an excuse to hang up, unable, or unwilling, to say more. Holden tried to find it in his heart to mourn Draper, but it was a struggle. Nevertheless, Draper's death remained a mystery. Had James decided to rid himself of a troublesome accomplice? That would make sense in one respect, but surely it was always useful to have the ready services of a portal-making fae?

Raoul had been uncharacteristically subdued since Holden's arrival on his doorstep. Upon waking the next evening, he'd listened to Holden's tale almost without comment, but Holden had caught a number of uneasy glances cast his way. Even more so on the second night, when Raoul had arisen to find him hard at work.

In truth, since that initial, unintended sleep, he'd barely ceased his activity, taking breaks only when Raoul forced him to do so. He'd reviewed everything at least three times. Most of his original paperwork was no longer in his possession, being either shut up in Blackwood's house or requisitioned by the Council, but he'd scribbled down everything he could remember on scraps of paper, and these now littered Raoul's coffee table, and the floor surrounding it. No matter how many times, or in how many different ways, he looked at it, though, there was nothing to indicate where James could have gone, and the days were ticking by. The next full moon was on the thirty-first. That would be the night of the final sacrifice—their last chance to prevent the summoning.

Every day, Holden tuned into the human news, as well as keeping a constant eye on the secret supernatural online channels. He was trapped somewhere between hope and fear. Each new sunrise could bring news of Blackwood's death. Meanwhile, each sunset brought fresh hope that he was still alive. As long as no body appeared, Holden would cling to that supposition. It was all he had.

He glanced up as Raoul entered, newly awoken with the setting of the sun and still in all his undressed glory. Once, the sight of Raoul naked would have distracted Holden from anything. That was no longer the case. He forced a brief smile of greeting, then returned his attention to his papers.

Raoul moved aside some of the sheets and sat beside him. "Hol, how much longer are you going to keep this up?"

"As long as it takes."

"What do you expect to see today that wasn't there yesterday, or the day before?"

Holden paused his reading midsentence and forced his gaze up. "I'm not going to give up, Raoul. Val wouldn't give up on me."

"Are you certain of that?"

"Yes." He was. It wasn't simple hope or wishful thinking; he knew it to be true.

"Then let me help."

Holden set down the sheet. "I'm not asking you to get involved in this."

"I'm offering. Besides, it's a bit late for that sentiment, don't you think? I got involved when I took you and Blackwood in that night. I'm sure the Council won't look the least bit askance at that. And then there's the fact that I've let you sit here plotting for days."

"It's hardly plotting."

Raoul raised a hand for silence. "But mostly I'm involved because I'm your friend. I may not care much for Blackwood, but I do care about you, and I'll help if I can."

Tears threatened, but Holden blinked them away. On his own, he'd been able to delude himself into thinking he was doing something worthwhile, but faced with Raoul's willingness to assist, he was forced to admit the truth: he had nothing.

"For all I know he's already dead."

"Do you *feel* that he is?"

Holden fisted the ring that hung from the chain around his neck. Blackwood's scent lingered on the gold, and it brought him comfort. "No. Don't ask me how—I realise it must sound like romantic nonsense—but I think I'd know if he were gone."

Raoul scrunched up his nose. It was something he'd started doing every time Holden touched Blackwood's ring, as if it emitted some foul odour that turned his stomach. As always, Holden chose to ignore the gesture, rather than risk an argument.

"I don't think he's dead either," Raoul said at last.

Hope tugged at Holden's heartstrings. "You don't?"

"No. I've been pondering it since yesterday, but I wasn't sure whether it was a good idea to share my thoughts." He gave a wry smile. "I guess that's a moot point now, so…" He took a deep breath. "I think he's safe until the full moon."

"Why the— Oh!" Now that Raoul had voiced it, Holden saw that it was obvious. He had never considered it himself for one simple reason. "But surely Aetius wouldn't sacrifice his own son?"

"A son he manipulated into killing for him? A son who, to his thinking, has since betrayed him? Trust me when I say, he doesn't care about him all that much—certainly not as much as he cares for himself. I know Aetius Blackwood far better than you do, and I consider him perfectly capable of such a deed."

"Even so, the Mayfair-Belgravia coven isn't small. James has plenty of other options."

"Under different circumstances, I might agree with you, but the Fellowship now knows who's behind the newest murders. Arthur James is exposed, and that leaves Aetius vulnerable too. They could choose to follow their normal process and go after someone else, but why take such a chance when they already hold a suitable witch as their prisoner? If they use Blackwood, all they have to do is hole up somewhere and avoid detection until the end of the month. It limits their risk."

It made complete sense. Nevertheless… "But still, Raoul. Val is his only son. He'd be destroying his family bloodline."

"What would your father do, if it came down to you or him? Do you think Cadeyrn would hesitate, even for a second?"

Holden grimaced. "I get your point."

He knew first-hand how callous fathers could be toward their own flesh and blood. How awful would it be for Blackwood to die, knowing that it was at his father's behest? Except, that wasn't going to happen, because Holden was going to find them before it did. No matter what it took, he would save Blackwood and put a stop to this nightmare once and for all.

Chapter Thirty-Three

RAOUL WAS TRUE to his word. Not only did *he* help, he also roped in a group of his friends—those who had a bone to pick with the Fellowship for one reason or another and who, therefore, didn't mind a bit of rebellious action. They couldn't do much during the day. However, at night they roamed the streets, looking for any sign of Arthur James.

Holden set aside his paperwork in favour of field excursions too. Raoul had been wary of that idea at first, but Holden had pointed out that no one at the Fellowship had actually ordered him out of the city, or point-blank forbad him from seeking Blackwood on his own. Therefore, he was breaking no decrees, and they had no reason to pull him in. He half wondered if they *were* watching him though. Perhaps they hoped he would lead them to James and Blackwood. It was a vexing thought. He didn't want to find Blackwood only to lose him again. Nevertheless, that concern wasn't enough to make him stop looking. For all the good it was doing.

So far, neither he nor any of the vampires had caught so much as a glimpse of James, bnd the days were ticking by with what Holden judged to be obscene haste. He could scarcely bear the sight of a clock at present. Noticing this, Raoul had hidden all those in his house. It was a kind gesture, but a pointless one. Holden could still sense time trickling away from him...and from Blackwood.

He had let Blackwood down. That was how he viewed it as hours, and then weeks, slipped through his fingers. In desperation, he'd tried to call Owens two days ago, hoping she might have something she could share. She'd not answered her mobile, and when he'd called the office, Peters had informed him that she was on a sabbatical. Holden prayed that was all it was and she'd not gotten in trouble for sharing with him the news about Draper.

Yesterday, he'd gone to Blackwood's house. They'd not checked there before, thinking it far too obvious a hiding place, but the idea had niggled at Holden ever since. Perhaps the fact that it was too natural a choice meant James considered it safe, certain everyone would immediately discount it. Holden had intended to get inside and take a quick look, eager to discount it fully, if nothing else, but a Fellowship guard posted at the gate turned him away. His dejection must have been visible on his face, however, for the young witch had taken pity on him and explained that she and her colleagues had been watching the place twenty-four seven since the 'incident'. No one had gone in or out in all that time. The place was empty.

Holden had not told Raoul about that visit, unwilling to face what he knew would be blatant disapproval. Raoul would have considered revealing his continued interest in Blackwood to be the height of folly. Yet, no one from the Fellowship had come looking for him, so either the witch hadn't mentioned his appearance in Grosvenor Square or the Council didn't care.

By the thirtieth, Holden's slender hopes were pulled taut. One definitive blow would shatter them into a million pieces, and his heart along with them. He wasn't oblivious to Raoul's growing concern—he felt the constant stares like pinpricks of ice on the back of his skull—but at least his friend had seen fit to keep his mouth shut on the issue thus far. Holden was likewise aware that, if he didn't find a lead of some kind soon, in less than forty-eight hours, Blackwood would die. All his life he'd been a failure, and now he couldn't even save the one he loved. Blackwood's death would be on him, because he'd proven unequal to the task of rescuing him.

"You're not to blame, Hol."

Holden looked up to find Raoul leaning against the doorframe, watching him. Deep in thought, he'd not even noticed that the sun had set. As usual, Raoul could read him like an open book.

"I *am* to blame. I should have grabbed him quicker that night, or found some way to track him during these last few weeks."

"You tried."

"Trying isn't good enough."

"Hol, we can't cover every street and building in London, even with help. It's a needle-in-a-haystack scenario. The only way to help Blackwood now is if we can somehow narrow it down." Raoul swept into the room and crossed to the bar, where he poured two drinks. He handed one to Holden, then took a sip of the other, and Holden sensed a flash of hesitation before he finally spoke again.

"Listen. I've been thinking. Maybe we've been going about this the wrong way. Rather than all this frantic citywide searching, we need to try to think like James, to anticipate him. You know these crimes better than anyone, so tell me where James would go. Don't overthink it. Say the first thing that comes into your head."

"All the past attacks took place in the victims' homes. However, Blackwood's house is under constant guard. They're not letting anyone through. I tried." He ignored Raoul's frown, pressing on before any verbal admonishment followed. "Besides, the Blackwood mansion would be, perhaps, too obvious a choice if James is determined to finish the summoning without risk of interruption."

"Go on."

Holden took a deep swallow of his drink, letting the liquor warm his mouth and throat. He closed his eyes. As hard as it was, he tried to release his angst and still-whirling thoughts and follow his gut.

"This is the last one. Aetius Blackwood was heavily into ceremony and tradition, and Arthur James seems that way inclined too. They'll want somewhere special, somewhere meaningful." His eyes flew open, and he slammed down his glass, sloshing the amber liquid over the coffee table. "The family crypt. It's in the chapel near Blackwood's house. Fates! I'm such a fool. Aetius Blackwood's remains are there. It would have huge symbolic significance." It seemed so obvious; he couldn't believe he hadn't thought of it before.

He leaped up, but Raoul caught his arm.

"Not tonight."

"But if they're there..."

"That's still a big 'if'. Suppose James intends to use it but hasn't set things up yet? If he sees us snooping around, he might change his mind and pick a different venue. Then we'll be left with nothing to go on."

Holden saw the wisdom in Raoul's comments, but it was hard to hold back after such an epiphany. Of course, they wouldn't know if his instincts were correct until tomorrow night. Nonetheless, hope rekindled and expanded within his chest, making it easier to breathe.

"I'll go with you, when the time comes." Raoul studied his nails, but for once his nonchalance was a transparent feint, as Holden could see the tension in his shoulders.

"You don't have to. You've done enough."

"I know. But there's no way I'm letting you wander off alone with no idea what you'll be walking into. Besides," he added, giving a wide grin that bared his teeth, "it's been too long since I last had a truly epic fight, and taking a witch down a peg or two is always a pleasure."

AS THE SUN slowly sank below the horizon the following evening, Holden was a bundle of nerves and adrenaline. The wait for Raoul to rise seemed interminable, but at last he was up and they set off. It was raining, and Holden was grateful for that. The cool tickle of the droplets as they splashed his head and ran down his neck gave him something on which to concentrate, rather than worrying about what lay ahead.

When they reached the chapel, all was silent within. Holden worked the lock on the back door with Blackwood's ring, as he'd done before, and they stepped into the tunnel. They didn't want to risk a light, so Raoul took the lead, his eyes adjusting faster than Holden's to the gloom.

The closer they got to the crypt, the more disconcerted Holden became. As they descended the steps to the small room, he waited to glimpse a light coming from within, or at least to catch the murmur of voices and the swish of clothing. Yet, there was nothing but darkness and silence ahead. What if he'd been wrong? Raoul must have been thinking along the same lines, because he suddenly sped up, no longer trying to disguise their approach.

Holden *had* gotten it wrong; he knew it. Another mistake to add to a lifelong list of errors. Only this time it was Blackwood who would pay the price for his bungling. It was over. It was all over. Raoul confirmed this assessment a moment later when he turned on the overhead light and they found the place empty.

"No, no, no!"

Holden spun, and punched the nearest wall. His fist cracked one of the marble panels, unleashing a shower of white and grey dust. He slumped against the tiles and slid to the ground, utterly defeated. He wasn't there long, though, before Raoul forcefully yanked him back onto his feet.

"Pull yourself together, Hol. Something doesn't smell right here." He released Holden and stalked over to the tile Holden had busted open. "This one."

Holden looked more closely. "Fates! That's Aetius Blackwood's spot." He surged forward as Raoul knocked away the remaining shards of marble and reached inside. "It's where we found the grimoire, before James stole it from us."

Raoul plucked out the urn, and before Holden could stop him, he yanked off the lid and took a deep sniff of the contents. "As I thought—not human."

"What?" Holden snatched the ashes from him and smelled them for himself. Raoul was right: the only scent was wood. "I don't understand."

"I think you were spot on that they'd perform the last sacrifice near Aetius's remains, but those remains aren't here. So, where are they?"

Holden took another sniff and tried to concentrate only on what he could smell in the room. With the lid off, the fake ashes were the strongest scent, followed by Raoul's potent aftershave lotion, but below those was the note of burnt flesh from the other urns. It was a familiar odour. At first, he thought he must remember it from their last trip here, but then another memory stirred. He had smelled true ashes in another location, only the scent had been so incongruous there that he'd not made the connection.

He dropped the urn, which smashed on the flagstones. "We need to get to Blackwood's house!"

Chapter Thirty-Four

THEY RACED THROUGH the streets as fast as the foot traffic allowed. Although the distance was short, they were catching the end of the working-day pedestrian flow, and with so many observers, they couldn't risk drawing attention by moving at anything above a human-velocity speed walk. Finally, they were able to cut away from the crowds. However, they pulled up short when they reached Grosvenor Square.

The team guarding the Blackwood mansion had tripled since Holden's last visit, no doubt on account of it being the full moon. There was no way they were getting inside unnoticed, and Holden couldn't see the Fellowship's officers simply opening the door and waving them through. Then Holden spotted the young witch from his previous visit. She'd shown compassion before, so maybe he could persuade her to help him now.

"We'll have to tell them what's going on." He started forward, but Raoul immediately drew him back.

"They'll think you're nuts, and even if they do believe you, they'll only storm the place and take out everyone inside. You know the orders your father gave: kill on sight. There's no other choice. We need to go in the back way."

"I'm pretty sure they'll have guards posted there too."

"No, I mean the *back* way."

Holden stared. Apparently, Raoul was as close to losing it as he was. "That's impossible."

"We have everything we need to access the tunnel. Trust me."

"But—"

"Do you want to save your boyfriend or not? Now, come on!"

Raoul shot off at a velocity that trod a fine line between supernatural and humanly possible, and Holden put on a burst of speed to follow. There was heavy traffic when they reached Park Lane, but that worked to their advantage. With vehicles at a standstill, they could dash across the road between cars without worrying about crossings and lights. One driver pointlessly honked his horn at them, but Holden didn't even spare him a glance. Rage over jaywalking was currently the least of his concerns.

Once within the boundaries of the park, they slowed their pace a little, to avoid spooking any walkers, but kept moving as fast as they dared. When they reached the Reformers' Tree memorial, Holden tugged on Raoul's sleeve, drawing him to a stop.

"How exactly are you planning on getting in there? We need Blackwood for that. It's blood magic. Or have you forgotten?"

"I've not forgotten." He fixed Holden with a contemplative look. "I have to admit, Blackwood is smart, and he clearly cares for you more deeply than I'd supposed. Now, go stand on the stone."

"Raoul—"

"Just do it. You'll see. Wait!" He clasped Holden's hand. "I don't know if it will admit me too. Better that we try to go together. That's the only way it might work. Otherwise, I'm afraid you'll be on your own down there, my friend, and that's not something I wish to risk."

Holden still couldn't see how Raoul thought this was going to work. But they had run out of other options, and, apparently, desperate times called for ludicrous, impossible measures. He at least had to try—for Blackwood's sake.

As one, he and Raoul stepped onto the circular stone. The flash of light that immediately erupted around them was blinding. Holden gasped and shielded his eyes with his free arm. His stomach somersaulted as the ground disappeared beneath them, and then...

"How is this possible?"

Holden glanced around the tunnel. Even in the pitch-black, and with his eyes still smarting from the earlier glare, he recognised the place. Nevertheless, he blinked a few more times, waiting for his vision to adjust so he could confirm it.

"That gold chain Blackwood gave you is more than just bling." Raoul gave Holden's hand a reassuring squeeze. "But why not let him explain after we get him out of here?"

Holden nodded. Explanations could wait. For now, he'd be thankful for small miracles.

They crept along the passageway, stepping softly to avoid any echoes. This time, they had definitely arrived at the right place. Even before they reached the door to the cellar, Holden could hear Arthur James's voice. The modulations had the ring of a conversation, but with no other voice filling the gaps between speech, James had to be talking to Blackwood's father.

When they got to the door, they stopped behind it and listened. Holden's instincts told him to burst in, grab Blackwood, and get him out of there. Nonetheless, rational judgment reminded him that he needed to assess the situation before he made a move. He had to ensure Blackwood wouldn't get hurt. He trusted that, between him and Raoul, they would know when the right moment came.

"I understand, sir. I'm ready to begin as soon as you give the word," James said. Then his servile tone changed to one of arrogance and contempt as he added, "Not long now."

Holden tensed, pressing his ear closer to the door.

"Anything to say before we begin?" James prompted.

"If you're waiting for me to beg for my life, I'm afraid I must disappoint you. Perhaps I can drum up a little gallows humour, if you believe a speech of some kind is strictly necessary."

Holden's heart rate spiked. Blackwood was still alive. They weren't too late. He experienced a burst of pride at Blackwood's stoicism in the face of death. But then, he wouldn't have expected anything less. The ability to disguise his true feelings when on public display was perhaps the one lesson for which Valerius Blackwood owed his father a debt of gratitude.

Raoul brushed his arm. "When the time comes, I'll handle the door. You just get in there. I'll be right behind you." He spoke lower than a whisper, the words inaudible to the witches in the room beyond.

Holden nodded his assent and steeled himself. His heart was racing, but he willed himself to take deep, slow breaths. This wasn't over yet. They had to deal with James before he could be certain of Blackwood's safety.

Suddenly, the scent of strong magic permeated the air. Holden recognised its note at once: someone was opening a portal. Raoul's nostrils flared as he, too, picked up the aroma. Holden wasn't sure if this new development was good or bad for their mission. It meant an additional opponent—if not more—in the room beyond, but hopefully it would allow them to catch all involved in one fell swoop, rather than risk any of the conspirators slipping away. It also explained Draper's death. He'd not been working with James and outlived his usefulness. He'd simply been in the way. Holden almost found it in his heart to feel sorry for him.

The tang of magic in the air faded as the portal closed. Beyond the door, Blackwood sucked in an audible breath.

"You?" His voice wavered. Whoever had entered the cellar, their identity had shocked him enough to break his cool façade. "By the powers! I see now why my trial went the way it did. However, I can't understand what part you mean to play in this."

"At this stage, why not think of me as an interested observer?"

Raoul's hand coming down over his mouth muffled Holden's gasp. Nonetheless, some sound must have escaped, since the room beyond fell momentarily silent. He and Raoul stayed motionless, not even daring to breathe.

"Nothing to fear, James," Cadeyrn snapped a few seconds later. "My people are stationed above, covering all entrances. No one gets in without my authorization. You won't be disturbed."

"Then it's time," James announced.

"Au revoir, Mr Blackwood," Cadeyrn said, and Holden could hear the sneer.

"Only for a time," Blackwood replied, his tone even, his careful veneer back in place. "I'm sure we'll see each other again soon...in whatever hell might exist for the likes of us."

Cadeyrn laughed, and Raoul released Holden and gave the signal. Holden shuffled a couple of steps to the side, making room. Then Raoul pressed back against the wall and aimed a sharp kick at the door, putting his full strength into the blow.

The wood splintered inward, pieces flying in all directions, and Holden dove through the gap. He drew energy from the earth, already forming it into a ball as he came out of his forward roll. Regaining his feet, he launched the missile toward his father.

The blast went wide, but it brought Holden a glimmer of pleasure to witness Cadeyrn's stunned expression. He clearly hadn't anticipated seeing Holden here. Holden's satisfaction was short-lived, however. Cadeyrn swiftly recovered, and this time it was Holden's turn to dodge attack.

His father's aim was far better than his, his power greater, and a quick succession of blasts forced Holden to dive between the wine barrels for cover. Luckily, Raoul entered the fray at that point, tackling Cadeyrn from behind.

"I've got this," he yelled as he grappled with Cadeyrn upon the ground. "Get Blackwood."

Holden leaped out of his crouch and dashed across the room. Shock had apparently held Arthur James in its grasp for the first few seconds of the fight, but as Holden moved purposefully toward him, he sprang into action. A blade flashed through the air, and Holden skidded to a halt.

Blackwood was on his knees, hands bound with a length of chain from which Holden could detect a whiff of virulent magic. That explained why Blackwood had not managed to overcome his much weaker opponent. He couldn't access his powers. A blood-red symbol marked his forehead—the last of the demon sigils.

James stood behind him. He fisted Blackwood's hair and tugged his head back, exposing his throat. Then he pressed the gleaming edge of his knife against Blackwood's jugular.

Holden's eyes met Blackwood's, asking an unspoken question and receiving a silent answer. Blackwood was okay for the time being, so Holden was free to focus on James.

A sudden crash sounded somewhere behind him, followed by the pants and blows of fierce combat. Holden tensed, but he resisted the urge to look over his shoulder. Raoul knew how to take care of himself. His task was here.

"It's over, James. But it's not too late to make this right." Holden tried to sound certain, convincing. "Let him go, and I'm sure the Council will show clemency." He actually thought the exact opposite, but that hardly seemed an argument likely to bring about surrender.

"Nothing's over." James glared, defiant. "You're the one who's too late."

The words were strong, but Holden noticed something. James's hand shook as he attempted to hold the blade steady. Whatever spell he'd used to enhance his physical prowess during the last full moon, he'd not repeated it tonight, no doubt deeming it unnecessary when he was so well hidden, his intended victim already captured and subdued. Although still possessed of a witch's powers, James was once again subject to the bodily frailties of his age, and that meant he was no match for Holden in a show of brute force.

"I'll take you down before you can get to his heart."

"His heart?" The distinctly sinister ring in James's chuckle froze Holden's blood. "Who said anything about his heart?"

Holden watched in horror as James flexed his arm. The eventual completion of the motion was obvious. He was going to cut Blackwood's throat. Holden had overplayed his hand. Rather than convincing James to surrender, his words had spurred him on.

He summoned a burst of speed and launched himself at James. By the time they collided, Holden could already smell Blackwood's blood in the air. The thought of failure nearly paralyzed him, but he forced himself on. If he hadn't been fast enough to save Blackwood, he'd at least avenge him.

He grabbed James's arm and twisted it up and back. The snapping of bone, accompanied by a pained cry, gave him a moment of righteous joy. James reached for the fallen knife with his other hand, but Holden was quicker. James's palm came down upon the blade, rather than the hilt, and he loosed another howl as the steel sank into his flesh, splitting open the skin.

Holden flung the dagger under the wine racks, putting it out of play. Then he shoved James aside and fell to his knees beside Blackwood, pulling him into his arms. Blackwood's eyes were open and he was still breathing, but blood was pouring from the deep wound in his neck. James had not completed the slice, but the damage was done. Holden pressed his hand over the cut, trying not to dwell on the warm, strong pulse as Blackwood's life oozed between his fingers.

"I have to try to close this. Then I'll—"

Holden stilled. There was something behind him. The strength of the malevolent presence raised the hairs on the back of his neck. Blackwood's gaze had moved from Holden's face to a spot just over his shoulder. The fear in his eyes did nothing to quell Holden's own terror. Whatever this was, it was like nothing he'd ever encountered.

James cackled. Though nursing his broken arm, and bleeding profusely from his wounded palm, he staggered to his feet. "You see? You see? You're too late. My master will take that body, and he will be restored."

That's what the summoning was: a form of possession?

At his back, Holden could sense the dark force growing. Although he couldn't see it, he could feel its movement through the shift of magical energy in the air. It was rearing up, preparing to strike.

As it shot toward them, Holden tightened his grip on Blackwood and squeezed his eyes shut. He had only one chance to get this right. With everything left in him, he pictured the spot three meters to their right.

Chapter Thirty-Five

EVEN AS THE portal shimmered to life around him, Holden wasn't convinced his plan would work. He could barely manage to portal a few meters on his own. He'd never reached the level of proficiency required to take anyone with him. Clinging to Blackwood so hard his knuckles whitened and his muscles screamed in protest, he willed them across the room with every fibre of his being. Clearly that *thing* was all that remained of Aetius Blackwood, and there was no way Holden was letting him get anywhere near his son. Not while he still had breath in his body.

When the portal closed, Holden slumped over Blackwood. The effort had been too much for him. It took all his remaining strength just to keep pressure on Blackwood's wound. He could do no more.

A fearful shriek drew his gaze to the left. It was only then that he realised it had worked. He had moved both him and Blackwood across the room.

With his son no longer in his direct path, Aetius Blackwood's spirit slammed into Arthur James instead. The dark mist enveloped James, cutting off his cry, and as Holden watched in mingled terror and fascination, it seeped into him through the cut in his palm. Once the last trace of vapour had disappeared, James dropped to the ground.

Raoul skidded to Holden's side. There were traces of blood over his clothing, and several fast-fading bruises mottled his cheek and jaw, but his eyes were bright from the thrill of the fight. "Your father's gone. I tried to grab him, but he fled through a portal as soon as he saw the way things were heading. Blackwood?"

"He's lost a lot of blood. He needs help."

"Can't you close it?"

"I've done too much tonight. I haven't the strength." He glanced down at Blackwood. His eyes had closed, and his skin was pale and clammy. He was still breathing, but Holden could hear that his blood pressure was dangerously low, his heart labouring.

"There's one thing we can do."

Holden knew what Raoul meant—his own thoughts had already taken him there—yet he hesitated to act. "We don't have his consent."

"And you'll never get it. Listen to that pulse. He's too far gone. He won't wake again, Hol, and even if I race him there myself, I doubt we could get him to a hospital before his organs fail. We act now or he dies. You'll have to make the choice."

"Do it, then." He wouldn't stand by and watch Blackwood slip away after everything they'd been through. If Blackwood hated him for it, if it ruined things between them, he'd have to find a way to live with that.

Holden managed to drag himself off Blackwood. When he removed his red-stained hand from Blackwood's throat, blood still oozed from the wound, but it flowed at a slower pace now, the supply almost exhausted. Raoul took Holden's place at Blackwood's side. He bit into his wrist and pressed the wound to Blackwood's mouth.

There was no response.

Raoul gave a soft growl of impatience and tugged down on Blackwood's chin, opening his jaw. His blood trickled between the now-parted lips, and after a few tense seconds, Blackwood stirred. Holden heard the moment when he actively began sucking, and the relief that washed through him, coming on top of his general exhaustion, was nearly enough to knock him out.

"Fools! He's as good as dead already. That cut was only supposed to be a nick, but your interference pushed the blade deeper. It's you who killed him."

In the rush to help Blackwood, Holden had temporarily forgotten James. He turned and watched warily as James stumbled and clawed his way to his feet, swaying in a manner that made him seem inebriated. Although utterly spent, Holden stood to meet him, placing himself firmly between James and his friends. Blackwood would need a lot of blood; he had to keep James occupied until Raoul was done.

"It seems your plan failed, James."

"Arthur James is gone." Aetius Blackwood forced James's lips into a crooked smile. "True, you stopped me getting my hands on the body I've spent nearly forty years preparing, but the process itself worked perfectly. All I need do is repeat the ritual and move into someone younger. It's a shame Cadeyrn left before he could see the fruits of our long labour. But he always was mostly bluster. When the going gets tough, you find out who really has a backbone."

Keep him talking, thought Holden. Yes, that was all he could do at present. *Keep him talking. Keep him occupied.*

"I'm guessing my father was the second attacker outside the chapel, and the one who opened the portals for James at Anne-Marie's flat," Holden said, latching onto Aetius's train of thought. "But I still don't see how and why he got involved in this madness."

"Madness? This is not madness, boy. It's about living forever."

Mortality had long been a sore spot for witches, but that didn't answer his question.

"I can understand that, coming from you, but it doesn't account for my father's interest in your scheme."

"The fae may live for many centuries, but they are no more immortal than a witch. Vampires are the only ones who come close to living forever. Time never touches them, and they exist exempt from illness. Only sunlight and a severed spine pose any real threat, and a careful spell or two would remove those obstacles. Unfortunately, simply infecting ourselves with the virus was never an option. It turns out it doesn't blend well with magic. Those turned in the early trials we conducted tended to lose their former abilities. So, we had to seek other viable methods. Why do you suppose you're here? The idea of blending two skill sets genetically, through interbreeding, had promise. Although, it soon became clear you were far from the perfect vessel of Cadeyrn's dreams, so that project also fell out of favour."

"Cadeyrn wanted to take my body?" Bile rose in Holden's throat. Suddenly, a lot about his childhood made perfect sense. His father hadn't been cold in Holden's early years. Things had changed only once he'd proven himself both inept at magic and in possession of only a modicum of the vampire skill set. He'd always assumed Cadeyrn's reaction had been one of paternal disappointment—the shame of a high flyer having such incompetent progeny. In reality, it seemed it had had more to do with Holden having shown himself unfit for purpose. Since Cadeyrn couldn't return him and demand a refund, he'd settled for casting him off.

"That was the plan," Aetius said, confirming Holden's supposition. "He would have become the perfect hybrid of fae and vampire, with magical ability and immortality. However, you failed to fully master the powers of either species." He sneered. "To leap into you would have been a comedown, not an upgrade."

"And my mother? Did she—"

"Oh, she knew nothing about it. Cadeyrn can be charming when he wants to be. He lured her to bed with promises of love everlasting. It was rather fortunate she died when she did. It saved him having to find a way to rid himself of her later."

Holden felt queasy. In some ways, it was freeing finally to learn the truth, but at the same time, it was like a blow to the gut. One thing was certain: this ended tonight.

"You do realise I'm going to take this to the Council and expose what you and he have done? There won't be a second jump."

"You truly are as dense as your father claimed, aren't you? No one will be spilling any secrets, boy, because none of you will leave this room alive." Aetius stalked forward, his lips twisting into a malicious smirk and energy crackling from his fingertips.

Holden resisted the instinct urging him to step back. He was too exhausted to put up much of a fight. Nevertheless, he'd hold his ground for as long as he could, to buy Raoul and Blackwood time to escape.

"You're stuck with James's body now. He's an average witch at best."

"It's not ideal, I grant you, having to channel my power through these weaker veins, this sluggish frame restricting me. However, it is sufficient for my current purposes. From the looks of it, you can barely stand. It's not going to take more than a flick of my wrist to put you out of your misery." As he finished speaking, he shifted his stance, preparing to attack.

Given the circumstances, defence seemed the best option. Lacking the energy to launch a counteroffensive, Holden concentrated on deflecting Aetius's blasts. For every one he sidestepped or brushed aside, however, another hurtled toward him, and slowly but surely, Aetius forced him backward.

Where was Raoul? Had he managed to get Blackwood out? Holden couldn't risk turning to look. Nor could he afford to lose his focus by trying to smell or hear them. Aetius hadn't been wrong in his earlier assessment. It was taking everything Holden had just to stay upright. A moment later, it no longer mattered. He was too slow with his countermeasures, and one of the blasts tore through his meagre defences, knocking him to the ground.

Aetius chuckled. "I imagine many would consider this a public service. They'll thank me for ridding the world of a filthy halfen." He raised his hand to strike the final blow, but then confusion creased his brow. Try as he might, he seemed unable to bring down his arm.

"Speak to him like that again and you won't live long enough to regret it."

Holden snapped his head around to see Blackwood back on his feet, Raoul standing resolutely at his side. Though still covered in blood, Blackwood's skin had lost its deathly pallor. The chains that had bound his magic lay broken at his feet, and his eyes blazed with barely restrained power. Holden glanced back at Aetius, gratified to see a spark of fear. Arthur James's limited abilities might have been enough for Aetius to take on Holden, but they were no match for the son he'd trained to perfection.

"Do it then!" Aetius snapped, his expression morphing from trepidation to snarling, mocking defiance. "You're already a murderer, Valerius. Your fingers drip with innocent blood. We both know you'll never escape the things you've done. You'll never wash clean those soiled hands. So, why not add patricide to your portfolio and cement your fall from grace?"

"I'm not going to kill you, Father. Not because I couldn't bring myself to do it, but because I don't trust you. Even if we did the consecration properly this time, I'd never be able to stand the thought that you might be out there somewhere, waiting to dupe some other unsuspecting witch into doing your bidding. Far better to keep you where you are until we can be sure your death will stick. But for now, I think it's time you got some rest."

"You wouldn't dare!"

Apparently, Blackwood did dare, because he reached out toward his father and murmured, "Dormi."

Aetius's knees buckled. By the time he hit the floor, his eyes had closed and he was already snoring.

Blackwood held out his hand to Holden and helped him up. His grip was warm and firm. Raoul's blood had restored him...but at what cost?

"I'm sorry, Val. I'm so sorry. There was no way to ask permission, and I couldn't lose you like that."

"I understand. And I'm grateful—to both of you." He flashed a brief, tight smile at Raoul, who nodded in acknowledgment.

"But the virus. You might turn."

"If I do, I'll deal with it."

"But—"

Before he could finish his next objection, Blackwood stopped his mouth with a kiss.

Holden sank against Blackwood, clawing at his clothing, desperate to keep him close. Fates, he'd longed for him these past few weeks. It was as if a piece of his soul had gone missing, only to return at last. He happily would have continued the kiss forever, but Raoul's loud and pointed cough finally forced them apart.

"Could the two of you leave off the making out until *after* we've dealt with this mess? I'd prefer to settle things before the sun rises. I don't want to be stuck in this cellar all day. The booze may be good, but the smell is now atrocious."

Holden stepped away from Blackwood and launched himself at Raoul, flinging his arms around him. "Thank you for saving him."

Raoul gave a half-amused, half-embarrassed huff. "Well, it seemed preferable to putting up with centuries of your moping." He glanced over Holden's head. "But seriously, Blackwood, what do you plan to do about your father?"

"It's not just him." Holden rubbed his temples. He was still groggy and flat, but he knew it would be a while yet before he could rest and recharge. "Cadeyrn was also involved. We can't let him get away with that."

"The Council will never believe us," Blackwood said with a shake of his head. "Why would they take the word of a convicted felon, a halfen, and a playboy vampire over that of a distinguished member of their ranks? And that's assuming more of them aren't in on it."

A passage of text from one of the old law books he'd read in Blackwood's library flittered through Holden's mind. "They'll have to believe us if we do this right." He whipped out his mobile. The screen had cracked during the fight—his second damaged phone in as many months—but luckily it was still working. "Leave this to me."

Chapter Thirty-Six

THREE HOURS LATER, the trio entered the Council chamber, along with the still-snoozing Aetius, whom Blackwood floated behind them. The full Council had gathered, all twenty-seven members dressed in formal regalia. Owens, always the miracle worker, had managed to do her part after Peters had finally relented and put Holden in touch with her. Holden briefly caught his father's eyes as he approached the stand. Cadeyrn didn't look the least bit ruffled. Clearly, he expected to get away with it. He was in for a surprise.

Neither Holden nor the others had changed their clothes or cleaned up before making the journey from Mayfair to the City, and Holden saw a few anxious glances cast at Blackwood's blood-soaked visage and attire, his appearance all the more alarming when contrasted with his obvious excess of energy. Holden's own strength was slowly returning, but he needed food and sleep to restore his powers fully, and both of those would have to wait. For now, he would make do with what he had. Besides, he didn't need to hear the whispered conversations occurring either side of him to get the gist of what was passing between the Council members. All present, save his father, were surprised and alarmed at the unexpected summons. Holden hoped that meant they were innocent of any complicity in the plot. If the full Council *had* known about the plan all along, everything they were about to say and do would be for nothing.

As they'd agreed outside, Holden took the lead when the time came to speak. "Distinguished Council"—a little buttering up at the start couldn't hurt—"we come here to hand over a dangerous criminal, and to report another."

"Isn't that Blackwood's butler?" one woman asked, looking aghast.

"It was until a few hours ago. This body now houses the spirit of Aetius Blackwood, brought forth during the supposed demon summoning which, as you all know, has claimed many innocent lives." His voice cracked toward the end, but the brush of Blackwood's fingers against his renewed his courage. "Demons are not separate beings. They are the souls of dead witches. Aetius Blackwood came back as such a spirit and forced his son to kill for him, before attempting to possess that son's body. But he and the late Arthur James weren't acting alone. Their accomplice sits in this chamber." He turned to face his father. "Doesn't he, Cadeyrn?"

Uproar broke out as the Council members alternated railing at Holden and at each other. With everyone speaking at once, it was impossible to hear anything until Cadeyrn called for quiet.

"Naturally," he said, his voice a gentle purr, "these accusations are unfounded. You only have to look at these three to see who the real culprits are. Their bloodstained clothes are testimony enough."

"I thought we might hit this snag." Holden cast a warm smile around the room. It was all bravado; inside, his pulse was racing. The vampires present would hear the drumming, but he couldn't help that. He pressed on, before anyone could interrupt. "That is why I request trial by blood."

A couple of the witches among the Council's ranks gasped. Then the Council member sitting directly opposite Holden cleared his throat. Holden dragged a name from the recesses of his memory—Féon, a fae nearly as old as his father.

"No one has requested trial by blood in over a century. It is an archaic practice long fallen out of use."

"True. But it's still written into Fellowship law. No one has ever called to have it removed."

"Very well." Féon glanced at the vampire seated beside him. "Would you do the honours, William?"

"You're not seriously going to allow this?" Cadeyrn had visibly paled, and a few mutterings across the room told Holden he was not the only one who'd noticed it.

"He is within his rights to request it."

The vampire councilman, William Beaufort, descended and approached. He nodded to Holden, who held out his arm. As Beaufort sipped from his wrist, Holden ran through his memories of the events of the last few months, omitting nothing. It was disconcerting to share so many deeply personal recollections with a stranger, but it was the only way to be certain their testimony would be believed. Truth spells were fine, but a skilled witch could potentially overcome one. Blood never lied.

Upon withdrawing his fangs and straightening, Beaufort looked at Holden in amazement. Then he turned to address his fellow Council members. "The halfen speaks the truth."

Holden's relief was palpable. Beaufort, at least, wasn't an accomplice, and that suggested that most, if not all, the other Council members were likewise in the dark. They would get a fair hearing. He reached back and caught

Blackwood's hand, giving it a brief squeeze, both to share the moment and to steady himself. Meanwhile, the room around them erupted.

Cadeyrn leaped to his feet, only to find himself detained by several of his neighbours. He cursed aloud and glared at Holden, but it was to no avail. He couldn't portal from the room, and two guards promptly rushed in and clapped him in magic-proof shackles. When they escorted him out, Blackwood also relinquished Aetius's floating form to their care.

Féon rose and addressed Holden. "I must ask that you and your companions say nothing of this incident outside these walls. The case will be classified as top secret. Therefore, speaking of it will constitute an act of treason against the Fellowship. Do you understand?" Without waiting for a response, he continued. "Aetius Blackwood and Cadeyrn will be dealt with appropriately, and I can promise you'll see neither of them again." His gaze flicked from Holden to Blackwood and back. "You and Mr Dubois are free to go once you have provided formal written statements to accompany your blood testimony. Since his assistance is no longer required in this matter, Mr Blackwood will return to the dungeons to resume his former sentence."

"No."

"No?" Féon looked confused, and a little wary. "What do you mean by that?"

Holden drew in a deep breath. Everything hinged on this. He needed to hold his nerve. "We'll keep the Council's dirty little secrets. We'll say nothing regarding the true nature of demons, or what these murders were actually about. I agree, it's safer that way. If word gets out, others may try the same thing, and none of us wants that.

We'll even keep shtum about the involvement of high-ranking officials in this plot, preserving the Council's pristine image. But I have a few requests of my own."

Féon huffed. "You mean demands."

"Semantics, Féon, my friend." Raoul offered a beaming smile that had the suggestion of a leer, and which made Holden wonder just how well the two knew each other. "Are we really going to argue the finer points of language at a time like this?"

The corner of Féon's mouth twitched, though Holden couldn't tell if he was repressing a glower or a smile. "Very well. What are these...requests?"

"We want your assurance that Aetius Blackwood will never be able to repeat what he did tonight."

"We will permanently bind his soul to that body, to those bones. When it dies, he dies within it, with no possibility of return. What else?"

"You will do the same with my father."

Féon hesitated a moment. He glanced around the semicircle, catching the eyes of several key members, all of whom nodded. Turning back to Holden, he elegantly tilted his own head. "Agreed."

"You'll also reinstate Captain Owens and expunge any black marks against her name. Everything she did was in an effort to catch the killer and save lives. She shouldn't be punished for trying to do her job."

"Very well. Is that all?"

So far so good, but the biggest request still remained.

"Just one more thing. You will offer Valerius Blackwood a formal pardon and release him at once."

"What?" Blackwood grasped Holden's arm. "We did not discuss this, Holden. And you cannot ask it. I have to pay for what I did."

"You have paid, if not in a conventional way. Besides, you were used. Your father shoulders most of the blame. As does mine, since he interfered in your trial, denying you the chance to fully explain your actions."

"If I may?" William Beaufort stepped forward again, and addressed the room at large. "In the blood, I saw Blackwood trying to stop his father. He almost died in the process." His gaze flicked to Blackwood's neck. "And he may yet turn for it." He waved away the murmur that broke out at this pronouncement. "He is not a hardened killer who will strike again if released, and I believe he has done sufficient penance to atone for his previous crimes."

"The Council must decide on this together," Féon declared. "All in favour of issuing Mr Blackwood a formal pardon, in light of services rendered, vote now."

A few Council members remained in place—Holden recognised them as his father's closest friends—but the majority raised their hands in support of the motion.

"The Council has spoken." Féon turned his attention to Blackwood. "You, too, are free to go once you've provided a formal testimony. We will issue the pardon in the morning. In it, we will attribute all the crimes to your father, who previously faked his own death and for whom you initially took the blame out of a misplaced sense of duty. But remember," he added, looking between the three of them, "if a single word of the truth gets out—"

"Don't fret, Féon," Raoul said with a wink, confirming Holden's earlier suspicions about the extent of their relationship. "We'll be as silent as the grave."

Epilogue

THREE WEEKS LATER

Holden snuggled against Blackwood, revelling in the way their bodies slotted so perfectly together—just like Blackwood had slipped effortlessly into life in the Cotswolds. Holden had assumed that Blackwood would wish to pick up where he'd left off, now he was once again a free man, and he had, therefore, been surprised when Blackwood had declared vehement opposition to the idea. Though happy not to be returning to the dungeons, the pardon hadn't sat well with Blackwood's conscience. The only way he'd been able to accept it was by leaving his old life behind. No more public spotlight. No more parties and lavish lifestyle. He'd packed up his treasured books and alchemical equipment, then sold house, cars, and most of his fancy clothes, donating the bulk of the proceeds to charity and keeping back only enough to live off for a while until he found work of some kind. They'd soon settled into a comfortable routine in Holden's cottage. Although, Holden still found it odd to see Blackwood in jeans and sweaters rather than snappy suits.

Blackwood's attire wasn't the only change. The vampiric virus had taken hold a few days after the events in the cellar. They'd first discovered it when Blackwood had sliced his finger while chopping apples, and the wound had instantly healed. Not long after that, he'd found it increasingly difficult to stomach food or endure sunlight, and as he'd made the switch from solids to liquid, Holden had called on Raoul, who'd spent several nights with them, guiding Blackwood through the transition and helping Holden daylight-proof the cottage.

In light of Aetius's comments, Blackwood had expected to lose all his abilities as a witch once he turned. However, though diminished, they didn't forsake him entirely. He could still draw on elemental energy to perform small tasks and simple incantations, and he didn't seem too distraught over the loss of his higher powers. So, here they were: a witch-vampire and a fae-vampire, shacked up in a cottage in a tiny village in the English countryside, doing their best to fly under the radar.

Stirring as the sun set, Blackwood wrapped his arms around Holden and pulled him tight against his chest. He pressed a kiss to the side of Holden's throat, his fingers straying to the gold chain from which his former ring still dangled.

"I'll never tire of waking to find you in my arms."

"Well, I'll never tire of being there." A question hung on the tip of Holden's tongue. It was one he'd wanted to ask for weeks, but from which he kept shying away, not wishing to remind Blackwood of that time unnecessarily. "Val?"

"Hmm?"

Perhaps it was the right moment. "Why did you make me this chain? You can't have known I'd need to be able to enter the cellar to rescue you."

"No. Of course not." He caressed the delicate gold links again. "I did it because I love you. I laced the melted gold with my blood so a part of me would always be with you, and so you would be able to open the secret door. Before they locked me up again, I'd planned to tell you to raid my library. You adored my books, and I would have preferred to see them in your hands, rather than relinquish them to the Council. I'm only glad it worked. I'd never tried a spell of that nature before. Had I failed, you wouldn't have made it down there, and my father would be marching around in this body by now, with no one any the wiser."

"He wouldn't have been able to do much on the run."

"Cadeyrn would have procured him a formal pardon in due course, on some pretence or another. Much as you did for me."

Blackwood's eyes darkened, as they always did when he dwelt on what he considered to be his escape from just punishment. Holden tried to think of something to distract him.

"When did you know you loved me?"

Blackwood's lips tugged into a smile, and some of the cloud lifted. "I believe I got the first inkling of it watching you eat those cakes when you came to lunch. You were trying so hard to look refined, sitting there in your ill-fitting suit, taking small bites, but I could tell you really wanted to devour the pastries whole. How I longed to lick the vestiges of cream from your lips. You've no idea how much self-restraint I had to employ.

"I knew you were attracted to me even then—you are the proverbial open book—however, I'd thought it mere lust. I didn't fully comprehend that your feelings were as deep as mine until you gave me your blood that day and I saw the truth of it."

"I think my feelings changed from attraction to something more the moment you stopped that dart from taking out my eye. Although, I tried hard to convince myself otherwise for a long time afterward. I was certain you'd break my heart if I let myself feel too much or dared to hope."

Blackwood chuckled, and it almost sounded like it had before. There was still an edge of restraint to everything he said and did, but as long as nothing reminded him of the bad times, he was starting to relax more, and to accept his freedom and this second chance at life. Holden's pulse fluttered at the thought that they would have centuries, if not forever, in which to explore the world, and each other. Nonetheless, a few worries still niggled at him.

"Don't you miss London, Val? Won't you grow bored with only me for company?"

"Not in the slightest. I never liked that hectic, artificial life. Not deep down. I would much rather be here. Alone with you. In your bed." He punctuated these words with a gentle nudge of his cock against Holden's back.

"Well," Holden said, his tone purposefully light and innocent, "what shall we do to pass the time this evening?" He paused briefly to rock back against Blackwood, eliciting a moan. "I suppose we'd better check the job ads. We both need to find gainful employment if we wish to stay in this state of rural bliss."

He tried to move away, but Blackwood tugged him back.

"Later. For the present, I'm setting myself the task of proving I haven't lost all my magic by making you see stars until you can think of nothing but me."

"How will you know if you've succeeded?"

Blackwood nuzzled Holden's neck, nipping lightly at the skin. "Your blood will tell me so."

Afterword and Extras

Dear Reader,

I hope you have enjoyed *Blood is Forever*. It has certainly been a labour of love for me ever since Holden and Val began knocking on my brain, and to that end, I have a few special 'extras' to share with you.

Twitter

Transmedia storytelling is something that has long interested me, so I decided to experiment with it a little in *Blood is Forever* by giving Holden his own Twitter account. He will be tweeting roughly once a week between January 2019 and February 2020, and certain tweets will tie in with events taking place on and around those dates in the novel. So do check out his comments to get some added insight into his thoughts and feelings.

https://twitter.com/HoldenFay2

Artwork

During the early drafting stages of the novel I was inspired to do some drawings. Naturally, I worked out the look of the nine sigils, but I also sketched how I imagined both Holden and Val, and designed the Blackwood coat of arms.

You can see these artworks (and learn more about the meaning behind the heraldic symbols I chose) by visiting my blog at the link below.

www.nickijmarkus.com/2019/03/blood-is-forever-extras.html

Thank you for stepping into Holden and Val's world with me.

Asta Idonea

About the Author

Asta Idonea (aka Nicki J Markus) was born in England but now lives in Adelaide, South Australia. She has loved both reading and writing from a young age and is also a keen linguist, having studied several foreign languages.

Asta launched her writing career in 2011 and divides her efforts not only between MM and mainstream works but also between traditional and indie publishing. Her works span the genres, from paranormal to historical and from contemporary to fantasy. It just depends what story and which characters spring into her mind!

As a day job, Asta works as a freelance editor and proofreader, and in her spare time she enjoys music, theatre, cinema, photography, and sketching. She also loves history, folklore and mythology, pen-palling, and travel, all of which have provided plenty of inspiration for her writing. She is never found too far from her much-loved library/music room.

Facebook: www.facebook.com/NickiJMarkus

Twitter: @NickiJMarkus

Website: www.nickijmarkus.com

Other books by this author

Souls for Sale

Beastly Businessmen and Guitar Gods

Old Acquaintance

Of Printers and Presents

"Full Marks" within *Teacher's Pet, Volume One*

Also Available from NineStar Press

Connect with NineStar Press

www.ninestarpress.com

www.facebook.com/ninestarpress

www.facebook.com/groups/NineStarNiche

www.twitter.com/ninestarpress

www.tumblr.com/blog/ninestarpress